LUCY CHRISTOPHER

PRAISE FOR STOLEN

From the Chicken House

From the stories we hear in childhood, to our fantasies
of freedom and fear, woods with their dark places
and sudden bursts of light mean a lot to us. Lucy
Christopher's brilliant and frightening imagination
takes an unexplained death, a complicated and
emotional set of teenage relationships, and one black
night in the woods to mix a sensual cocktail of terror
and suspicion. It's gripping, compulsive and totally
dangerous. I'm still scared. And, no, I didn't guess
the truth.

Barry Cunningham
Publisher

THE KILLING WOODS

LUCY CHRISTOPHER

2 Palmer Street, Frome, Somerset BA11 1DS

Text © Lucy Christopher 2013

First published in Great Britain in 2013
The Chicken House
2 Palmer Street
Frome, Somerset BA11 1DS
United Kingdom
www.doublecluck.com

Cover design and interior design by Steve Wells
Typeset by Dorchester Typesetting Group Ltd
Printed and bound in Great Britain by CPI Group (UK) Ltd, Croydon, CR0 4YY
The paper used in this Chicken House book is made from wood grown in sustainable forests.

1 3 5 7 9 10 8 6 4 2

British Library Cataloguing in Publication data available.

ISBN 978-1-906427-72-6

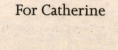

For Catherine

'I can see you
Through the branches and the leaves
So tenderly running
So far
So far
From me'.

— Quiet Marauder, Roda and the Bunker

BEFORE

1

Saturday Night. August.

Emily

Something was draped across Dad's outstretched arms. A deer? A fawn that was injured? It was sprawled and long-legged, something that had been caught in a poacher's trap maybe. A mistake. So this is where Dad had been all this time, in the woods and cutting this creature free. I breathed out slowly, squinted at the mist that hovered around Dad like a ghost. I took my hand from my bedroom window, leaving the memory of my skin on the glass. Then I raced down the stairs, through the hall and into the kitchen out back. Throwing open the door to the garden, I waited for him there.

It was ages since Dad had brought back something

3

injured, and he'd never brought back a deer, though I could remember helping him free a roe deer from a snare in the woods once. Back then his hands had moved quickly and gently, darting from the wire on the doe's leg and then to her neck for a pulse, stroking her constantly. This was something like that again. Saving another deer could be a good thing for Dad, something to take his mind off everything else, to help bring him out of his dark place.

I heard Dad's feet scuff on the cobbles in the lane, saw his movement. I tried to pick out the shape of the deer's body, but it was all wrong. The legs weren't long enough, neither was its neck. I took a step towards them. And that's when it made sense: the shape.

It wasn't a deer Dad was carrying. It was a girl.

Her neck was tilted back, her bare arms glowing in the moonlight. Her clothes were soaking. The garden gate creaked as Dad manoeuvred through, struggling. How long had he been carrying her? From where? I moved backwards into the kitchen. Dad had done things like this when he'd been a soldier who saved people, maybe he was being a hero again. Then I saw that this girl's skin was grey, blue around the lips like smudged lipstick. Her long hair was plastered across her face, dark from the rain. I saw her green short-sleeved shirt and the silver bangle on her arm. I wanted to sweep the wet hair from her face, but my hand was half-raised when I stopped myself. I recognised her. I *knew* this girl.

'What happened?' I said.

Dad didn't answer. His face was red and damp; he wheezed as he pushed past me. The girl's fingers trailed over my arm, and they were cold – dead cold – like a stone found in a cave. Dad laid her carefully on the kitchen table as if he were putting her to bed. He turned her head to the side and stretched out one of her arms so she was in the recovery position. He touched her neck gently, just like he'd touched the neck of the trapped roe deer so long ago. But this deer didn't move, didn't struggle or try to stop him.

Her name was Ashlee Parker.

I made myself bring my fingers to her wrist, waited long enough to be sure. I knew I should be panicking, should be calling an ambulance . . . but Ashlee Parker's eyes were staring at me, fixed in position, brown and big.

'She's got model's eyes,' Kirsty had said once. 'She's beautiful. It's no wonder Damon Hilary follows her everywhere.'

Damon Hilary. Something twisted inside me when I thought about him – of how he'd react to this.

I rested the tip of my finger on Ashlee's cheek. I wanted to help her struggle and leap free, disappear into the trees. I could only hope that everything screaming through my head was wrong.

'Is she . . .?' I hesitated. 'Is she . . . OK?'

Dad didn't answer. I don't know what he thought, whether he hoped she would wake up. But I'd seen the small red marks on her neck, the blue speckles of bruises spreading out like flowers. I could see she wasn't breathing at all.

What had she been doing in the woods?

How had she got like this?

I don't know how long we stood there, with the moon and stars shining through the kitchen window like spotlights. It felt like forever. Eventually there was a creak upstairs: Mum was up.

'Everything all right down there?' she called.

Maybe she'd been waiting for Dad to return too, pretending to sleep like I'd been earlier, listening to the summer storm. I heard her slippers treading in the hall, then the kitchen door swung inwards and immediately Mum was complaining about Dad keeping us up with worry, lecturing him about staying out during thunder.

'You know how you get when the weather's like this . . .' she was saying. 'You shouldn't . . .'

Then she saw Ashlee.

She made a tight gasping sound as if she'd sucked up all the oxygen in the room at once. She looked at Dad then back to Ashlee. She stepped across and felt for a pulse.

'Who is she?' she said, her voice low. When he didn't answer, she strode across the room and grabbed Dad by the shoulders. 'What's happened?'

She moved towards the telephone on the windowsill, her eyes running over Dad's muddy face and wet clothes, then over Ashlee again. The wheezing sound from Dad's chest got louder.

'Was she in the woods?' Mum's voice rose. 'With you?' Her fingers were shaking as she pressed the numbers on the phone. Eventually she got through. 'We need an ambulance . . . police.'

I wanted to tell Mum that this was Ashlee Parker from school. I wanted to say that I didn't know what had happened, and neither did Dad, and that he was trying to save her . . . but the words stayed lodged in my throat like something half swallowed. Mum gave our address, hung up, went back to Dad. Her nails dug into his shoulders. Dad gulped air like a fish, one of his panic attacks starting. I knew I should go get his inhaler, or start talking softly to him – reminding him of where he was and who we were – but I couldn't move. I couldn't stop looking at Mum's frightened eyes.

'Tell me what happened, Jon!' she demanded.

I edged towards the open door to the garden. *Give Dad time*, I wanted to say. *Let him explain.* But Mum wanted answers, and that made me panic too . . . made me want to get away.

'Dad found her,' I whispered, saying what I wanted to be true. 'She was in the woods, walking . . . lost.'

Mum looked at me: the first time either of my parents seemed to notice me that night. 'She's dead, Emily.'

Her words sent me feeling for the door handle, for something to hold on to. Then Dad's sudden shout made me jump.

'She wasn't supposed to be there!'

It was what he always said when he came out of a flashback. The same words. He was in a flashback again, he had to be. Mum was right. It must have started from hearing the thunder, from being out in that storm when he shouldn't have been anywhere near it.

Mum brushed the hair from Ashlee Parker's face. 'Did you do something, Jon?' she asked very quietly.

I lurched forward, wanting to stop Mum's words, stop all of this. 'How could he?'

Mum held out her palm, wanting Dad to answer for himself.

'He's just in a . . .' I said. 'He's just . . .'

Dad's hands were trembling. He was panicking badly, losing it, like I'd seen him lose it so many times before. Only this time was worse: his eyes were wilder somehow, still glazed in that nightmare. Did he even know where he was? Who we were?

Mum kept looking at Dad. 'If you know something, Jon – anything! – they'll take you away, they'll ask you, over and over . . .'

'Away?' Dad's arms shook too. 'Away, away . . .' He repeated the word like it was snagged in his mind.

'Away from us. The woods. You'll be gone in a police car . . . Do you understand?'

'Gone,' Dad repeated. 'Gone.'

He looked from Mum to Ashlee Parker and then through the window to the woods like he was searching for something. Trying to remember. Trying to pull something back. He crashed to the floor like all his bones had snapped, his body juddering as he grasped at the worktop. I went towards him, but he held an arm across his face as if he thought I'd hit him.

'Sorry,' he said, his eyes watery. 'Sorry, sorry, sorry . . .' He looked at Mum desperately. 'But they were shouting . . . the soldier told me I'd done it.' He shook his head and murmured, 'Me, me, me . . .'

The same words. The same story about the soldier who'd yelled at him during that firefight: who'd told him he'd killed a civilian. Dad was remembering being in combat that last time, flashing back.

Mum realised it too. 'But this girl isn't the same,' she told him firmly. 'Not the one you killed.'

'The same!' Dad wailed. 'Same.'

He lashed his fist into the kitchen unit; blood ran down the cupboard. When Dad got like this Mum usually told me to go to my room and sometimes she joined me. We'd listen to him shouting into the night, wrecking things as he raged. Outside the rain started again, heavy and persistent, but no more thunder. Dad gasped and gasped.

'I was in the compound . . . and she was . . . she was there and I . . .' Dad tripped on his words, stopped and tried again. 'I didn't mean to . . . but the enemy, they were hiding . . . out there in the dark . . . all around . . .'

'You're not in combat now, Jon! There's no firefight! You haven't shot anyone!' Mum was almost pleading with him. 'You're in your kitchen. You're with your wife and daughter. You're an ex-soldier in a flashback, that's all!'

Dad blinked. Maybe Mum thought she had him back with us because she added, 'But you have brought home a girl, Jon, and she's dead.'

'I didn't mean . . .' Dad turned towards the rain coming in sideways at the kitchen window. Was he waking up?

'But the soldier . . . he told me. He said it was . . .' He shook his head, kept murmuring, '. . . me, me, me . . .'

2

Sunday Morning.

Damon

The sun was hot against my eyelids. Bringing my hand to my neck I felt only one dog collar. Hers? I ran my fingers over its worn leather and stiff stitching, touched the tiny rips at the edges, its cold circular tag. Then I traced my fingers over its engraved letters: **DH**.

So where was Ashlee's collar?

And what time was it, anyway?

I patted down my chest, felt over the mattress and pillow. Nothing. But I'd caught her. We'd gone all the way, just like she'd promised. So why didn't I have her collar? Or why didn't she have mine? I tried to force my brain to think, remember. Her sweet rosey perfume was still stuck inside my nostrils. I tasted mud on my teeth, in my gums; I tasted Ashlee's fairy dust. Forcing my eyes open properly, I made my gaze move across the bed, looking for Ashlee's thin, shiny pink collar. It wasn't on the floor either, hadn't fallen off me in the night. I was curved like a banana on top of the sheets, still in my dad's old combat shirt, still muddy. There was dirt and leaves everywhere, and I was wet . . . soaked through. Sweat? No, rain. There'd been a storm last night. I must've been pretty fucked up not to remember that straight up. Even my boots were still on.

But there was no collar . . . nowhere. Maybe I'd dropped it in the woods? Ashlee would kill me if I'd lost it. They all would. We'd have to get her another before we could play the Game again.

I sat up, immediately wishing I hadn't. My collar felt too tight around my neck and I fumbled to get it off, my hands still drunk and awkward. Touching my neck made me feel even sicker. I chucked my dog collar on to the pillow, then pulled my shirt off too. Pressing my hand to where my tatt started on the base of my spine, I tried to breathe deeper. Everything about me stank, but there was no sick, or piss, on the carpet, not that I could see. I remember Ed boasting once about being so drunk after the Game that he'd pissed in the corner of his room. He'd said something about being as drunk as Mack's dad, then he'd had to duck quick from Mack's fist.

I knew I should text them, find out who won.

I should text Ashlee.

I felt down my damp, clinging combat trousers, but

there was no phone there. Had I lost that too? My head hurt too much for thinking, maybe I'd drunk away my brain cells. We'd been going at it pretty hard in the car park first, and then, of course, in the woods. After Ashlee had given me that fairy dust, the woods had changed into something mixed up.

'Fairyland,' Ashlee had said, giggling. 'Just slip down into it.'

But what else had I slipped down into? Ashlee?

I stared at my boots like they could give me memories. Mud was all over them, a leaf caught in a shoelace. They looked about as battered as my brain. I could remember my face against something damp, the smell of earth . . . there were still bits of leaf and bark in my hair. I pushed the boots off me rough, kicked them under the bed. I grabbed the covers and pulled them over my face to stop the sunlight, burying myself. I wanted sleep. I wanted Ashlee to touch me and do what she must've done the night before all over again, but this time so I could remember it. I wanted a cuppa.

I lay there, but no cup of tea or Ashlee magically appeared, not even sleep. Too much head pain. I kept my eyes closed anyway. Last night hadn't been like the other nights, and it wasn't just because of the sex Ashlee had promised. For a start, there'd been that fairy dust. Ashlee had spun some story about fairies in the woods, how we'd see them once the dust kicked in.

'Just go with it,' she'd said, rubbing that stuff into our gums.

She was good at getting drugs, but she'd never got this shit before. Charlie had laughed like a hyena. I'd seen his face stretch into a snout.

'You get special treatment,' she'd whispered to me, dusting my gums so much I'd gagged.

And later, we'd been on the forest floor. We'd been going all the way. I tried to remember the feel of it . . . the feel of her. The softness of her skin around me. Her warmth.

Nothing!

What was the point of fucking if you couldn't remember it? What was the point of any of it if you got head pain like this? Had someone punched me real hard at the end of the Game? Was that why it wasn't coming back? Was that why I didn't have her collar, neither? I squinted 'til I finally saw my phone on the table beside the bed. Punched out a message to her.

What you doing sexy?

Did it sound too keen? Like I didn't care about her at all, just wanted the sex? Did I sound like an arse?

I sent it anyway. Then I put my head back on the pillow and waited for her reply. She'd send me something cute, maybe even a photo. She'd been doing that a lot lately: letting me see her in her bed, in her pyjamas, showing me the undies she had on. But right now with the way my head was, even if she just told me she'd had a good time last night, even that would do. Even if she just told me who'd won the most collars, who'd won the Game.

I dreamt she was touching me. I felt her bitten-down

fingernails across my stomach. She tasted of sugar, and her tongue darted around my teeth like a fish. Then she was putting me inside her mouth and she was making me warm. I was having her . . . almost. Then I was almost letting go. I dreamt 'til the sunlight heated me up again and a text message beeped beside my ear. I smiled. I was hard from the dream, ripe, ready for her cute words. Perhaps I'd call her and she'd talk low and dirty in my ear. Perhaps she'd remind me what we did last night.

But it was from Mack.

I read it anyway. Leaning on to my elbows, I stared at the words for ages. The longer I read them, the more I started to wake up.

You heard what's happened? You OK? Come round mate.

What was he on about?

Did I do something stupid? Was I that drunk and high? I checked through my other messages, nothing from Ashlee since last night. No reply to the message I just sent her either. Was she in a mood? It wasn't like her to ignore me for long.

I frowned. Because there was a word in my brain, coming at me out of nowhere.

Useless.

Why?

Had she called me that last night? Is that how I'd been when we'd been doing it? Too fucked on the drugs to get it up? Too fucked to care?

In the end I typed to Mack: *What you mean? I'm OK. Headache.*

Mack called. His voice was husky and lacking sleep, had an edge. 'You don't know anything? No one's been round to you or . . . nothing like that? The police?'

'Know what? What d'you mean?'

I heard him breathe in. 'You don't know about Ashlee?'

I was silent. So fucking confused!

'Come round, mate,' he said. 'Just come round. We need to work something out.'

NOW

3

Tuesday. October.

Emily

Kirsty has today's paper in her hands. Beth, Jonah and Luke are all crowded around, forming a tight huddle in the schoolyard, shutting me out. And even though Mina is tugging on my arm, trying to pull me on, I don't let her pull me anywhere.

'C'mon,' she says. 'Joe's saved us a spot in the canteen.'

But in front of me are my friends, my supposed *best* friends. They're not like Mina, who's just been friendly with me since all this stuff happened with Dad, and they're not like Joe. I've only been tight with Kirsty's group for about a year, and things have changed for me in school since then: I've got popular. Until Dad got arrested, that is, until these last few weeks.

Now they're whispering about me. Or about Dad. I can tell this by the way they are standing so close to each other, throwing glances over their shoulders towards me. I can't just ignore it. They'll be reading about Dad's plea and case management hearing, yesterday in the Crown Court. Maybe they're reading about how the public gallery was almost full, about how everyone expected Dad to plead guilty to the charge of the murder of Ashlee Parker; about how he didn't. Maybe they're reading about how Dad entered a plea for manslaughter by reasons of diminished responsibility instead.

I still remember how Dad's defence lawyers talked us through all that. 'He'll plead manslaughter because of his flashbacks,' they'd said. 'Because he doesn't remember the events of that night, because of his post-traumatic stress disorder.'

But what do my friends believe? That Dad stalked Ashlee Parker and he meant to kill her? That it was an accident that happened because of a flashback? I want to shake them, tell them that Dad only thinks he killed Ashlee Parker because he can't remember what really happened. Tell them that if he can't remember, then maybe he didn't do it at all.

Dad's body was curled from the shoulders as he stood in the dock, head down, eyes not looking at me or Mum or anyone.

'Not guilty of murder,' he'd said. 'But guilty of manslaughter by reasons of diminished responsibility.'

His words had slammed into me like a punch. The first words I'd heard him say for weeks.

'Guilty.' Mum had whispered the word too.

There was a film of tears wrapping her eyes. But if Mum felt so awful, why didn't she tell the judge that she knew Dad couldn't have done anything? Why didn't she stop arguing with Dad so much over this past year too, always telling him he had something wrong with his mind and making him believe it? Why did she tell Dad's lawyers about all the flashbacks he'd had?

The prosecution barrister had said she needed more time before she could accept whether Dad was mentally unstable enough to commit manslaughter. She said she needed to get her own psychological assessments done. So the case isn't closed yet. And Dad isn't sentenced. That gives me some hope. Maybe it shouldn't.

I walk forward, shrugging Mina off.

There's a way people look when they talk about Dad – their eyes widen, their voices go high-pitched and kind of whispery. I've heard this in shops I go into, with the teachers at school. But this is the first time I've seen my friends doing it. I focus on the back of Luke's neck, still tanned from the summer, waiting for someone to look over. I can imagine the headlines: *War Damaged Soldier* . . . *PTSD As Defence* . . . *Murder Or Manslaughter For Shepherd?* Maybe my friends can imagine Dad being a murderer, or a soldier who wanted to keep killing.

Mina is still trailing after me. 'Come on, Emily, just ignore them. They're not worth it!'

But I thought friends were meant to stick by you whatever happened; I thought Kirsty would.

I shake my head at Mina. 'I need to speak to them.'

A part of me just wants to read the paper they've got, but another part has finally had enough of how these friends are being. I want to tell them.

The whispers start again when I get near. My friends draw away as if I'm a dangerous animal, or a disease they could catch . . . as if they think I'm Dad. I get how people might be wary of me now; I'm not so stupid to ignore how people look at me like I'm a killer's daughter. But these four people *know* me, we used to speak all the time. Now they look nervous I'm even approaching. Only Kirsty meets my eyes.

'All right?' I say.

It's the first time I've spoken to her since last week, since before Dad's plea; I hear my voice shake. Her eyes widen like she's surprised I've spoken to her at all. Beth tries to hide the newspaper.

'It's OK,' I say. 'I know what you're looking at.'

'Why'd you come over, then?' Kirsty snaps the words back so fast it's as if she's slapped me with them.

I point at the paper in Beth's hands, not knowing how to explain all these feelings inside me. 'Do you want to show me too?'

Do you want to at least talk to me? — This is what I want to add. *Do you want to at least pretend I'm your friend?*

Kirsty pushes the front page at my face, but it's too close to read properly. I catch the words: *soldier . . . court adjourned . . . psychological profiling . . . stress disorder . . . combat.* It's all I get before Kirsty snatches it away again.

'Happy?' she says.

My breath catches. *Happy* is about as far from me as it's possible to be right now. Kirsty doesn't care. So I just do it – I say the words that have been screaming inside me for weeks now.

'I thought we were friends.'

I risk glances at the others, wait for them to react and, maybe, to apologise. I'm expecting Beth to go all smiley and sweet like how she used to be with me. I'm waiting for Kirsty, or even Jonah, to flash a grin. And I'm waiting for Luke to hug me again. When I look at him, he flicks his eyes towards mine and his cheeks redden. Only Kirsty keeps holding my gaze, her eyes narrowing.

'Yeah, we *were* friends, Emily,' she says slowly, '. . . friends until your creepy Dad went and killed Ashlee Parker.'

I feel the anger rise like it does every time someone says something bad about Dad. Only now it's worse because it's Kirsty who's saying it.

'You weren't there,' I say. 'You don't know what happened.'

It's my stock response and it sounds ridiculous, I know, but I won't do it . . . I won't admit my dad's a killer. I can't.

Kirsty's eyebrows rise. 'Thank God I wasn't there . . . to be murdered!'

'His plea is for manslaughter,' I correct. I can't believe she's being so mean. It's like she's never been friends with me at all.

'Whatever. Still means he killed someone. They don't hand out life imprisonment for nothing, do they?'

I shove Jonah aside so I can get to the paper. Life imprisonment? Jail? Our Family Liaison Officer told us that pleading guilty to manslaughter by reason of diminished responsibility would mean Dad would end up in a secure psychiatric hospital instead, somewhere he'd be treated for his disorder, where he could get better. I try to grab the paper from Kirsty's hands, only she holds on to it and it rips, straight through a pencil-line drawing of Dad: an artist's impression. Kirsty laughs a little and that makes me hate her suddenly.

'Oops,' she says, '. . . torn in two. You'll have to put the pieces back together.'

She pushes the bits of paper into my hands and I can see the picture as well as the whole article. I scan for the words *life imprisonment*, then keep looking at that pencil-line drawing. It's a mock up of that night – an artist's representation of Dad carrying Ashlee Parker from the woods. The artist has got it all wrong though, drawn Ashlee with her shirt unbuttoned and her shoes gone, and has made Dad's pale blue-grey eyes black. No wonder my friends believe Dad's a murderer. In this picture Dad looks like an angry psychopath.

'Ashlee shouldn't have been anywhere near that bunker.' Kirsty's voice is low, her finger jabbing at the paper. 'It was nowhere near her route home. Even if she was drunk she wouldn't have gone that far off track!'

I bite the inside of my lip, look away. I know all this.

'They're saying he stalked her,' she continues, '. . . lured her there . . . they say his screwed-up mind isn't any excuse for what happened.' Kirsty is jabbing so hard at the paper she's making it rip more.

'He didn't do those things.' I stare at the drawing, trying to keep my voice steady. 'It's just the reporters jumping to conclusions . . . making a story.' I'm repeating Mum's words now, what she says when I start raising questions. 'They don't have any evidence for him stalking Ashlee.'

Newspaper headlines are screaming in my mind though: *Darkwood Hunter . . . Soldier's Killing Woods . . . Woodland Murder.*

I sense Luke crowding in beside me, looking over my shoulder to the drawing. 'He's sick,' he hisses. 'Your dad's sick and twisted.'

Kirsty chucks the rest of the paper at my feet. I want to pick it up so I can read it all later, slowly, but I don't want to give her the satisfaction of knowing I want something from her. I don't want to give this so-called group of friends anything at all.

'Dad's not convicted,' I say.

'So, he's innocent?' Kirsty raises an eyebrow. 'He still did it! The number of years in prison – or wherever – won't change that.'

I look to Beth for support, but even she is looking at Kirsty. It's like Kirsty is some sort of gladiator about to whack me in the skull: she's even enjoying the attention.

'You're all weirdoes,' she tells me. 'I see it now: your freaky dad, your mum, you . . . all hiding out in that creepy bunker in the woods. Just another weird army family.'

Why aren't any of the others talking her down? Why isn't Beth? I want to run, escape somewhere quiet and alone.

'You know, Emily,' Kirsty adds. 'They say it runs in families. I've heard there's a murder gene — that once someone in the family has killed a person . . .'

My face goes hot and I push into her chest, wanting her to shut up. Before I know it she's falling back towards the grass and her fingers are in my hair taking me with her. She makes an oomph sound as she hits the ground.

'It's not true!' I shout. 'Take that back!'

But she won't. She tries to roll on top, maybe to hit me, but I'm suddenly strong – mad with it. I won't let her.

She scratches her nails against my cheek instead. 'Get away from me!'

I slam her shoulders against the ground. 'Shut up, then!'

I force her head back. With her neck tilted like this, she can't move. I could curl my fingers around her; I could hurt her in the same way she thinks my dad hurt Ashlee. I start breathing harder.

'Get off!' she shouts.

I make myself blink, pause. This is Kirsty. One of my best friends. Or was. My heart is beating so hard I'm surprised I'm not shaking. Perhaps I am.

'Freak!' Kirsty spits the word in my face, punches me like this. 'Scum family!'

My fingers tighten in her hair.

There's yelling behind me, jolting me back to where we are. I hear Jonah and Luke shouting, but there's a crowd around us too, people jostling for a view and screaming for a fight. One voice cuts through it all, getting closer. Then someone is grabbing my shoulders, pulling me off Kirsty as easy as if I were a piece of rubbish. That person is dumping me on the ground and, before I can roll away, he's pinning my arms still, leaning his head right up close to mine.

'What's going on?' he growls, his eyes widening as he sees who I am.

I search for air, gasp. Close up his features are blurred, but I can still make out his copper-coloured eyes, the downward curve of his lips. It's not because he's on top of me that the words won't come. It's because of who he is.

Leaning down into me, stopping my fight, is Damon Hilary. Sports prefect. The most beautiful boy in the school.

Also, Ashlee Parker's boyfriend.

4

Damon

It's not this girl's eyes that are staring back at me, it's his: Jon Shepherd's eyes, stuck in this girl's face. They're the same blue-grey eyes I saw in court yesterday: the last eyes Ashlee would have ever seen. And they're waiting, calmly. I want to slam them shut. Make them cry.

I force myself to look at her properly. Shepherd's daughter. Knowing what happened in court yesterday, I can guess what she's been fighting about. Everyone in this school's got to hate her now. My fingers grip tighter on her jumper. I could shout a million things at her; I could do more than this too. I could make her pay for what happened to Ashlee: an eye for an eye and all that. *These eyes* for *those eyes.* That's fair, isn't it? But this girl is still staring, still waiting.

Then I get why.

I stopped this fight; it's the first prefect job I've done for weeks. It means it's up to me what happens next, what punishment I give her. For a second I feel so insanely happy about this that I want to laugh. I could do anything to this girl: his girl. And I want to make her feel what Ashlee felt. Hurt her. Punish her. But for a good long moment I can't do nothing 'cept stare. Her eyes are bigger than his, nicer somehow. Thinking that makes me want to hit them more.

5

Emily

He should hate me. My first thought. Damon Hilary should want to throw his own punches, continue what Kirsty started. No wonder he was the one that stopped this.

I go limp and watch him, wait. His eyes are very serious on mine. He hasn't talked to me for a long time, not even yesterday when we'd sat only a few rows apart in the public gallery.

'What's this about?' he says, but not in his usual confident prefect voice. 'Why were you fighting?'

I can't answer. He moves off me, goes about as far away as possible while still keeping a hand on my shoulder. Maybe he thinks I'll go for him, push him like I pushed

Kirsty. I wait for him to give me a detention or refer me to the Head with a recommendation for suspension. As prefect, he could do this. I don't care: suspension is what I want, anyway. At least then I won't have to listen to people talking about me and Dad. Or perhaps he wants to do something nastier to me and he's trying to work out what. It's *me* after all, it's *him*.

He takes his eyes off me to glare at everyone else still milling around. Kirsty is standing close, red-faced, she's trying to tell Damon that I was going to kill her just now. I don't think he's really listening, his eyes are drifting around the crowd.

Freak. Kirsty's word still hurts.

Suspension will be good. That way I won't have to see any of these so-called friends. Perhaps I can get a suspension so I'm away from school when Dad's next hearing comes up, when the prosecution decide what kind of killer he is. I shiver and Damon's hand darts away from me.

He turns to the people standing around. 'Clear off! Haven't you got something better to do?'

His usual strong voice is back, but still no one moves. I know why: Damon Hilary is about to punish the daughter of Jon Shepherd, someone could sell tickets for this. I see Mina then, pushing through the crowd and pulling Joe after her. Joe's eyes are like an owl's as he clocks who's sitting next to me. He doesn't give me a goofy smile like he normally might, doesn't move closer to check if I'm OK either. When Damon spots him and glares he even backs off. The crowd gets bigger when Damon's mates saunter in too − Mack Jenkins, Charlie Jones and Ed Wilkes − the cool, tough boys of the Upper Year. They swagger about so confidently it's as if Damon's radioed them in for backup. I feel like I'm in a car crash that everyone's stopped to gawp at.

'You right, mate?' Mack calls across.

Damon tilts his head in the direction of the crowd, makes a face. 'Help me get rid of these clowns?'

'On it.'

They go to work, pushing everyone back and saying there's nothing to see. These boys seem huge compared to everyone else in the lower years, their final-year jumpers making them important. Only Joe stands as tall, but even he hunches down when they get close. No one looks like they want to leave.

'Go on, clear off!' Damon yells again. 'Otherwise I'll give you all detention. I mean it!'

I watch Ed Wilkes walk close to Joe. 'Always watching, watching, watching . . .' I hear him say. 'We should charge you money one day . . .'

Charlie Jones shoves Joe's shoulder, and Joe glares at that. Then he's turning to look back at me, shaking his head in a way I know means *Don't do anything stupid, Emily!* Kirsty shifts too as Damon starts threatening detention again. I feel every single stare from every person as they leave. Then I hear the whispers: *What's he going to do to her? I can't believe Damon Hilary stopped it . . . she'll get suspended . . . expelled . . .*

I wait, ready for whatever punishment Damon's going

to give me, but he's still watching his mates lope after the crowd. Ed turns and walks backwards, staring at Damon and me, maybe checking I'm playing nice. He grins, all teeth, until Mack grabs the collar of his jumper and pulls him away. Only then does Damon turn back to me – he looks at me in a slow and curious way, almost as if I'm a specimen he's studying. If it were anyone else looking at me like this I'd probably arc up, but I'm still thinking of how he'd sat in the row in front of me yesterday in the public gallery; how his chair screeched back when Dad said the words *not guilty to murder*; how he'd scowled. I get this strange urge to apologise, I can't hold his gaze. Does this mean I'm starting to believe it – everything? Damon's hand feels heavy on my shoulder, pressing me.

'Are you going to tell me what you were fighting about?' he says eventually. 'If you don't talk to me I can make up anything, I could take you to the Head who'd suspend you straight up.'

'Do it.' I say the words before I mean to.

If I got suspended I wouldn't have to be near Damon at all, and this would be better for both of us. I wouldn't feel this weird guilt just from being near him; he wouldn't be so angry. His jaw tightens, doesn't want to give me anything.

'I want answers from you,' he says.

There's a quick flash of something in his eyes – Panic? Curiosity? – it's there for a second then masked over just as fast. I wait for him to start firing his questions. The schoolyard is empty now, everyone gone to class, and the silence goes jagged and awkward. Is he enjoying making me wait, this power over me? He's not gloating like Kirsty was. Why didn't he just hand out a detention slip and walk away?

'You can fight,' he says eventually. 'Did your dad teach you?'

This isn't the question I'm expecting, and it's hard to answer. 'I guess,' I murmur. 'Sort of.'

'Why?'

Again there's no easy answer, no answer he would want to hear. I can hear Dad's words in my head, though, when he'd been showing me how to crouch into a fighting stance in Darkwood ages ago: *All young women should know how to get away, if they need to.*

I can't say this to Damon. Not when Ashlee didn't get away.

'He was a soldier,' I say eventually. 'It's what he did.'

Damon seems satisfied with this. 'I know about soldiers.'

I twist my face away, remembering that Ashlee Parker isn't the only person that Damon has ever lost. Maybe this is something else we share: army dads, dads who used to be heroes . . . dads who, in different ways, have been blown apart.

Damon grabs my chin, turns me back. 'Just because your dad was a soldier, it doesn't mean he gets off with pleading manslaughter. He's a murderer!'

'He's not.'

Damon watches me. 'I'm not sending you to the Head.'

'What then?'

'Detention. With me.' He says the words quickly, almost as if he's daring himself to. 'Sports detention after school.'

'You can't do that.'

'I can.'

I don't understand it; he could punish me, seriously, for what I've done. Why settle on the lowest level of punishment when he could get me suspended? Sports detention is what's given for dropping rubbish, or not wearing a uniform properly, not for fighting. It won't even go on my records.

'People deserve a second chance, don't they?' he says, but his eyes are hard. 'Anyway, we should talk.' He gets up. 'After school today, OK?'

I nod; it feels like I don't really have much choice. And I want to know what he has to say to me, his questions. 'Where do I meet you?'

He thinks. I'm expecting him to say the playing fields or the gym.

'Meet me in Darkwood,' he says instead. 'I'll be waiting at the Leap. You know it?'

'Darkwood?'

'Yeah.' He nods. 'The Leap.'

I get a flash of memory of bumping into him in Darkwood once before — by accident, when he'd almost tripped over me. I remember how the expression on his face had changed when I'd started to talk to him then. But why would he want to meet me there now? After everything?

Again, he nods. 'As soon as bell goes, go there. We'll run. Sports detention.'

Then he's gone, and he doesn't turn back. Not once.

6

Damon

Stupid. STUPID. This is what I'm thinking as I'm jogging away from her. I didn't need to do that. Why didn't I just come down on her hard, march her to the Head? Why did I need to speak to her at all?

I know why.

Because I'm an idiot!

And she doesn't believe it. Any of it! Not even after yesterday when the bastard admitted to what he'd done. Just thinking about all that shit – how Shepherd said he was guilty but didn't admit the whole story – well, it makes me want to hit something. *Someone!* Yesterday I'd wanted to push aside chairs and people and whatever-the-fuck-else just to get at him.

The boys would approve of me punishing Emily Shepherd. We'd all said it, hadn't we? That we'd kill Jon Shepherd given the opportunity, chuck him over the Leap to the sharp rocks below. Strangle him slowly. Punish him.

But she isn't him.

The most I can do is rough her up a bit, give her the toughest sports detention I've ever given. It's not enough, though: I want her to feel like I do, to understand. I want her to know what it's like to lose people who don't have a chance of coming back.

I tip into a run. I should go to Mr Smith and clear this sports detention like I'm meant to, but I won't. Course not – I decided that as soon as I gave it. Smith would never clear a detention for me and Emily Shepherd in Darkwood – no one would, it's mad.

As I turn on to the playing fields, I touch my hand to the base of my spine, feel the space where my tatt begins. My old man wouldn't like how I am right now. Ashlee wouldn't have minded, though – she always liked me playing tough. I remember what it was like to run after her, fast in the dark, to take her dog collar. I want to do it again so bad that I almost have to bend over and breathe deep to stop this feeling from rising up into coughing, or sick, or something worse like crying. I feel choked, like Shepherd is trying to strangle me too. I need to run this feeling out. I need to run Shepherd's daughter so hard that she's the one who's sick. Run her 'til she tells me who her dad really is and why he picked Ashlee. I almost pull out my phone and call Mack, even if he is in class. Because right now I need Darkwood. The Game.

No.

I can't need that again.

I close my hand into a fist and try to think of what my old man would've done: he'd have said that the Shepherd girl is scared, probably just as screwed up as I am. The fact that she doesn't even believe her dad did it at all suggests she's mental, don't it?

But even so . . . why Darkwood? Why even say that to her? It's because it was the one word that was going round in my brain as I was looking at her. And I need to go back. Because I need those woods. Need what they do to me.

And I need to understand.

7

Emily

'Why Darkwood?' Mina says when I tell her. 'Why would *he* want to go back in there? With you?'

'What's wrong with the gym or the playing fields?' Joe murmurs from the other side of me. 'Why give you sports detention at all?' He's staring straight ahead, his eyes blinking quickly like he's trying to read the board and can't see it properly.

'It's weird,' Mina adds.

'That's for sure.' Joe's eyes dart across to me then.

'But the cross-country team train there, don't they?' I ask. 'So it's not *that* strange.'

Joe shrugs this away, starts drawing cartoon figures on the side of his exercise book.

I know what I'm doing: I'm trying to make this whole crazy detention sound less weird, trying to stop the nerves that started as soon as Damon left me in the schoolyard.

'No one has detentions in Darkwood.' Joe says, making me anxious all over.

I feel Mina's nails dig into my arm. 'Maybe he wants revenge? You thought of that?'

I remember Damon in the courtroom, the way he'd glared.

Joe sighs. 'What about all the stuff we've been talking about, Em? The list we made? The theories we came up with?'

I think about the conversations I've had with Joe over the last few weeks, the theories we'd had about who else could have been in Darkwood the night Ashlee died: tramps, druggies, kids from out of town, ex-army . . . We'd made a list − possible suspects − I'd wanted the police to keep looking.

'Someone could still be hiding in those trees,' I'd said. 'They could be waiting undiscovered.'

But the police hadn't listened.

Damon was on that list, though.

'Don't go,' Joe says. 'Seriously.'

I'm thinking about how Damon stayed next to me in the schoolyard when he could have left so easily. 'He's got something to say. He won't do anything.'

Joe snorts. 'There's another side to Mr Nice Guy.'

We all shut up then as Mr Westbury shoots us a glare.

Mina looks down at the desk and adjusts her hijab, tucking her hair neatly behind it.

'You know they took him in for questioning?' she says, jabbing me in the arm again. 'Damon Hilary was one of the first people in the station the day after Ashlee died, along with . . .'

She stops, doesn't say the words that come next: *along with your dad.*

'I know.'

I remember that spark of hope when I'd heard: when I'd thought, for a short while anyway, that maybe it was Damon that killed Ashlee, that even this was more likely than it being Dad.

'They always say it's the boyfriend,' Joe had said that day. 'On the cop shows they do.'

I'd wanted to believe him.

But the police didn't keep Damon long, and they didn't press any charges. And why would he do it anyway? Everyone knew Damon followed Ashlee about everywhere, adored her. When the two of them were together they were golden – they shimmered in this school. My stomach knots as I remember the sports honour board with Ashlee Parker's name on, her locker left open after her parents cleared her stuff out for the last time, the space on stage where she'd sat in assemblies . . . the way Damon's eyes used to linger over her in break times. This school is riddled with holes Ashlee has left: shot through with shrapnel.

Damon couldn't have done that.

Suddenly I'm blinking and forcing my eyes to focus on the board. But I can't concentrate on this lesson, not even if I want to. So I nudge Mina. 'Do you think he's had counselling?'

'Sure,' she says. 'His girlfriend died . . .' *And your dad killed her.*

But she leaves off this last part. It's something I'm glad of with Mina, why I don't mind her hanging about: she never says outright that Dad's a killer, never corrects me when I say otherwise. Just like Joe never does.

I allow myself a moment of Dad, of how he was before he got discharged from the army. *That* Dad could never have hurt Ashlee Parker. Whenever I say this to Mum she says people change; she says that awful things can make brains buckle. She reminds me that only one person has ever admitted to killing Ashlee Parker and that person is Dad. How can the police ignore something like that? How can anyone?

'Sometimes people can't be who they once were,' Mum says. 'When people see a lot of horrible things they become different.'

Has Damon changed too because of the things that have happened to him? Have I?

Mina is still looking at me, concern threaded through her skin.

'Damon won't do anything,' I say, though I don't know why I'm so certain of this. 'Anyway, if I don't go, he'll refer me to the Head and Mum will know I've been fighting. I'd get suspended.'

Mina nods at that, always the good girl. But when I look across at Joe he's got his head down, ignoring me, sketching a tree blown sideways. He's angry. And maybe I am being foolish, doing this alone.

'It's time I went back,' I murmur.

And it is. I haven't been into Darkwood since before everything happened, not properly. And right now the leaves will be red-gold, the branches gripping on to them desperately. It's the first autumn since Dad got posted here that I haven't seen the leaves turn in that forest and, after seven years, that feels wrong somehow. This, at least, is something Mina doesn't understand: my pull, still, to these woods.

'I'm serious,' I say again. 'I want to go back.'

I look to Joe — to see if he understands it — but his fingers just tighten around his pen. Maybe he'd rather draw me the woods, though Darkwood will be too achingly beautiful right now to be caught in an image. It will be starting to get slow for winter, and that kind of stillness needs to be felt. I want to hear the trees groan as they steady themselves. And I have things to say to Damon Hilary too, things to ask.

When the bell goes for end of class, I get up fast and move towards the door. I need to do this before I change my mind.

'Emily, wait!' Joe says as I'm turning into the corridor.

But I've decided. 'Don't follow me, Joe.'

I go faster when I think I hear Joe's footsteps behind me. Once, Joe might have come with me into Darkwood after school and we would have mucked around and played stupid kids' games. Not today.

I change beside my locker, pulling on sports kit and a hoodie, then dump my school bag inside. It'll be hard to do detention with it banging against me and, anyway, I'm not interested in homework right now. Damon isn't in any of the bus queues, so I don't join them either. It's not far to the main entrance of Darkwood anyway, only a couple of stops, and I move into a jog: warming up. For the first time in weeks I make my shoulders drop, relax into the movement.

Going into Darkwood always used to make me feel better. It might be crazy to think that it's going to do this again now, though – when my dad has just pleaded guilty to manslaughter; when I just pushed over my supposed best friend; when I'm going to a detention with a boy who probably hates me. Still, even now, something inside me gets lighter the closer I come to the woods. Weaving between shoppers, I see a few older boys slouching on corners and waiting at the chippie, none of them Damon. He could be joking about meeting me in Darkwood; maybe I'll get there and he won't show at all. Like Mina, he probably thinks it's the last place I'd want to be right now. Maybe my detention is simply going back there, facing it.

As I move down the high street I get that familiar feeling that everyone's staring at me. Since Dad was arrested, I've got pretty good at ignoring people but it's hard not to notice the way the boys in the chippie are nudging each other as I pass, or how an old lady has stopped in the middle of the street just to gawp. I look into a shop window, stare at plastic ghosts and blow-up pumpkins. I'm part of it all this year, I live in the real house of horrors that everyone is so fascinated by. It's four days until Halloween now; that means it's less than two weeks until Dad is either convicted of manslaughter or sent to trial for murder. Both of these days will be filled with ghosts and nightmares. I keep going. The feeling that everyone is watching me still clings, worse than usual. It's as if everyone knows where I'm going and who I'm meeting. Nobody likes it.

I zip up my hoodie like it's some sort of protection, and I don't avoid the cracks in the pavement like I used to. What's the point? All the bad things have happened to me already. I keep going past the charity shops. Then past the supermarket I don't go into any more, ever since some woman shielded her kids from me and muttered *scum*. I keep my head down as the first school bus passes. Joe might be on that. I tense as the bus slows in traffic, listening for banging on the windows to get my attention. But it moves on. When the bus stops at the shelter further up the street and I see a tallish boy getting off, I don't hang about. I cross the road, dart between cars. I take the passageway between the doctors' surgery and the launderette, skirt around the town playing fields. I don't look towards the edge of the army barracks like I always used to, just turn left on to the footpath. With my hoodie up I feel invisible, like a ghost. Maybe it's like this for Ashlee – always watching, waiting.

Then I'm in Darkwood car park: the main entrance into this vast, ancient woodland. The place Damon and Ashlee and Damon's mates were drinking that night. There are soggy colourful bundles of flowers and toys that must be for Ashlee, to pay respects, like how there are sometimes tributes laid at the sides of roads after car accidents. I search for something to add, but there's nothing here but dying leaves and rubbish. Eventually I find a pale cloverleaf and place that near a laminated photograph of her. I don't read any of the cards or messages, though I do wonder what Damon left.

I walk past the few rotting picnic tables, the overflowing rubbish bins, the empty muddy car spaces. There are squashed drink cans and bundles of scrunched newspaper blowing about. But there are no people, and there always used to be at this time of day. Perhaps it's Ashlee's death, scaring everyone away. Perhaps it's because it hasn't stopped raining since the summer ended – since that night – and now this place is clogged with mud.

The last time I was here it was mid-summer, about a month before that night, before the rain started. It's odd to think that I'd been here with Dad then. But he'd been calmer that day, that's why I'd suggested the walk through the woods in the first place – just like we always used to do on Saturdays. Maybe I still thought I could coax the old version of Dad back; I could pull

Dad out of his sadness.

'Be careful,' Mum had said, pressing the phone in my hand and checking that Dad had taken his pills. 'Call me if there's a problem.'

But he'd been OK. He'd even looked up and noticed the summer migrants – the swallows and swifts skittering about.

Now I spin in a circle until the trees around me blur. I should hate these woods, just like everyone else seems to. I should never want to be back inside them again. But I can't help it. I want to be here just like someone else might want to see their family. Is that wrong? Does it make me sick? It makes me like Dad, I know that. I brush my fingers over the sign I've passed so many times:

Welcome to Darkwood Forest Nature Reserve.
Please keep to the paths and respect this ancient woodland.
Keep away from cliff edges.

I've never been nervous of going into Darkwood before, but now it feels as if this wood is more than its trees and animals – it's deeper and darker. Just thinking of going inside it makes a part of me want to turn and run back to the high street, but there's another part of me that keeps me here. The same part that makes me look out at Darkwood from my bedroom window every night before I sleep, that makes me wonder what is inside, or who.

I rest a hand on the gate and it's cool, solid, a little damp. Exactly how this gate has always felt. So I do it – I go into Darkwood to find Damon.

8

Damon

We're going the long way, Mack and me, entering the woods from near the river. I didn't want to go through the car park, not past her trinkets again.

'Still wonder if we should have told them,' I say, my voice sounding louder than I mean it to. 'About the Game, you know . . .'

Mack sucks in air. 'What's the difference? Ashlee was on her track home when he found her, we'd finished playing.'

When his eyes flick to mine, I nod. Because this is what I told the guys the next day after all: *I walked Ashlee back to her shortcut track.* It's what I did every time.

I watch Mack as he looks round at the trees. There are thoughts in my head – questions – things I don't want to be thinking about right now. Things I never want to be thinking about. So I ask if he's been back here since.

He shrugs. 'Not much. What's the point?'

He's right: without the Game, why come here? Without Ashlee . . .

The woods look different in the daylight. I'm seeing things I never saw at night: orange leaves, birds. I'm remembering how I used to play some hiding game with Dad and my brothers in some other wood near another of Dad's barracks – that feels like years and lifetimes ago. It was, I suppose.

Mack notices me being weird. 'You all right?'

'Course.'

Being back must be strange for him. Maybe images are slamming into his brain too. Maybe he wants to run to get them out.

'Might have a go for some elvers,' Mack says. 'Come with?' He squints like he's searching for the river behind the trees, like he's trying to find the spot where the elvers are. 'Should be plenty flowing down that place soon, just need to bring a bucket and scoop 'em up . . . be worth thousands if no one catches us.'

He flashes a grin, tries to. He's trying not to talk about when we were last here together two months ago, that much is obvious. I haven't told him that this is part of the reason I want to be back again now – to see if I can remember more, work something out.

I keep quiet, remembering Mack's garage the morning after, remembering him grabbing my shirt and pushing me against the wall and demanding to know what'd happened the night before. His face had been so close to mine I'd seen jagged red lines in his eyeballs.

'After the Game finished,' I'd said, 'I walked Ashlee to her shortcut track.'

The words had been out of my mouth before my brain kicked in, so they must've been right – they *had* to be.

But Mack had kept staring. 'I've just been past her house and there were coppers everywhere!'

I'd blinked, gaped.

'Ed reckons she can't have come home. And Charlie tried to get into the woods and it's all closed off.'

Charlie and Ed had been standing behind Mack, staring at me too. They'd also wanted answers. But I'd been unsure, so drunk the night before I'd still been spinning. I'd been hung-over as hell. And I couldn't remember. And I'd thought it would come back.

'I walked her,' I'd said again. 'I won her collar!'

If I said it enough times, maybe the memory would kick in.

Mack had nodded. 'She's probably just passed out somewhere and hasn't gone home yet. It's probably nothing.'

I'd gone into the toilet attached to Mack's garage and thrown up. Vomit came out so fast I'd thought I'd choke on the stuff. I could smell whisky and Ashlee's fairy dust all through it, plus something sour and evil. That was when the guilt first hit.

I'd run to Ashlee's house, the others behind me. I'd seen the police car out front and I'd banged on her door, demanded answers. From inside, I'd heard crying: not Ashlee's. The police wouldn't let me in, though, said they'd come for me next. So we'd gone back to Mack's garage, waited there, trashed some of Mack's things by chucking fishing sinkers into the air and hitting them with the butt of an old air rifle as if we was just playing cricket. I'd whacked those sinkers hard, trying to jolt my brain each time, trying to snap it into thinking of words, images . . . anything. Mack had yelled when I'd smashed a jar of his best fishing bait. But we couldn't do nothing else – not even go into the woods to look for her, not when the cops were coming, not when it was me who'd seen Ashlee last the night before.

'Maybe we shouldn't say about the Game,' I'd said.

And Mack had agreed. 'Yeah, we'd get slammed. They'd think we did something.'

Now, Mack is silent as he walks. He's learnt that off me and I learnt it off my old man: how to step so soft it's like you're not stepping at all, how to keep your body weight evenly spread across your feet. A hunter's walk, Mack calls it. A soldier's walk is what my old man said. Mack and me walk like this automatically, taking the deer tracks up towards the Leap. We know where we are without speaking about it.

'What you going to do with his daughter then?' Mack asks. 'Are you really giving her detention?'

'I'll run her 'til she's sick.'

Mack's eyebrows rise. And maybe that does sound harsh, but this appeals: making Emily Shepherd sweat, seeing what she's made of.

'Do what you need to do, man. Whatever helps. Then forget her. Seriously, forget all of it.'

'Maybe I'll push her off the Leap, then,' I say. And it's a joke, sort of, but Mack don't smile.

'Careful,' he warns.

I shrug off his stare, focus instead on the steep pathway to the summit of the Leap. When Ashlee first saw these pale rocks glowing in the moonlight – that first night she played the Game – she said they was magic. But I know from Geography that limestone rock is made from the skeletons of sea creatures, that this cliff comes from ancient dead things. I look across to its wild, rough side where the wind blows hard.

'You know, Damo, being nasty to this girl won't bring Ashlee back,' Mack says.

And that's the sum of it, isn't it?

'If only,' I say. My voice sounds weird. 'You think I'm an idiot for giving her detention with me, don't you?'

'Yeah. Total knob end.' He half-smiles. 'Just get her expelled next time, get her away from us . . . from this town.'

Mack's a mate. He knows I'm breaking up inside but he doesn't make a big deal of it. He's not like all the rest at school.

'Maybe she's a psycho like her dad is?' I say. 'Could happen.'

I'd seen the anger in Emily Shepherd's eyes as I'd pulled her off that girl today: she was a wildcat. I'd even thought she might've gone for me.

'Maybe.' Mack shrugs. 'Race you?'

Then Mack and me are off, scrambling to the summit, just like we used to. I'm ahead of Mack instantly, weaving easier through the overgrown paths. Mack barges through bracken, grabs at rocks, kicks dirt across at me to make me slow.

'Hey!' I shout.

He doesn't care. His long arms reach further around the rocks than mine can, and he pulls himself up ahead of me, slithers and disappears over the summit ledge.

'Dirty bastard,' I call.

'Dirty winner!' His face pops over. Then his hand reaches towards me, grabs me.

I lean backwards, testing him. If I used my whole weight I could probably pull him over, send us both tumbling down. If he let go of me it would just be me who'd fall.

'Stop grabbing on to my hand, ya poof,' he says. 'Get up here.'

So I let him pull me up the last bit 'til we're both lying on the summit, backs to the cold rock. This is like how things were, before I got with Ashlee, before we even started playing the Game with the others. Just me and Mack and these woods: the running together after my old man died, almost a year ago now. I've got that empty, angry feeling that I had then too.

I roll on to my stomach, look over the edge to see the different ways up here. There's the bike trail, the jagged rocks where people sometimes rock-climb, then there are the tracks the animals use. Animal tracks are how me and the boys get most places in these woods, how we stay hidden. For no good reason I dig about in my pocket for the cigs Ed gave me after my old man's funeral, light up and inhale.

'Fucking brilliant sports prefect, you!' Mack says.

I keep sucking it down, ignoring him. I don't care much about sport since Ashlee's gone, or even much about being a prefect. It's not like I deserve it now anyway – any other prefect that had been found drunk and on drugs would've been stripped of the badge straight up. I'm only still a prefect because the school feels sorry for me. I hate that shit. So now I just do what makes me feel OK. Mack knows it.

I hand the ciggie over. 'Can't kill myself alone.'

Neither of us says nothing else for a while. I just listen to him sucking down that cig.

'Maybe we should start training for army selection again,' he says eventually. 'It'd be good, y'know, start pushing ourselves . . . something to keep our minds off . . . get us back to where we used to . . .'

He trails off and I don't help him out. Joining the army seems a long way from right now, though I suppose the selection process begins in only a few months' time: as soon as school's finished, as soon as we're both eighteen. I don't feel that buzz of excitement when I think about it now, though. I take the ciggie back from Mack, drag 'til I feel the smoke curl into my lungs. Dad would've hated me doing this, would've hated a lot of things about me these days. When I try to hand the cig back to Mack he gets up and starts balancing along the edge of the summit instead, like we did when we first started coming up here.

'Could you jump?' I call across. 'What would make you?'

Pausing at the steepest bit, he looks down for so long that I start to feel my legs twitch.

'You'd have to have done something real bad to drop down there,' he says.

He balances on one foot. For a moment I want to run full-pelt-crazy, straight over the edge – join Ashlee and my old man this way. I could take Mack with me. I keep sucking down my cancer stick instead. These are crazy thoughts. I don't even know where stuff like this comes from sometimes.

'If Jon Shepherd was here, I'd push him over,' I say.

'Sure!'

I go and balance-walk with Mack. To one side of us is that steep drop, where, if I fell, I'd be skewered in a hundred different places. Mack turns, arms out, like he's balancing on a tightrope. He's loving this, even making himself wobble deliberately. But if I pushed him, even just a little bit, he'd be gone: his trainers would slip on the rock. I reach out quickly, take his shoulders. Like this, we'd both go.

'You sure you'll be all right?' he says. For a moment, I think he's meaning about me standing on this edge. Then I remember why I'm really here: Emily Shepherd.

Her detention. 'You're not going to, like, flip out or nothing?'

'I'll be fine! She might not turn up anyway.'

'If not, get her suspended, serve her right. You saw how she was going at that girl today. She's dangerous!' Mack's top lip curls, but he's hardly one to make fun of how other people fight.

Emily Shepherd will come, though. She's curious about me, I saw that in her eyes when I pulled her off that girl. She feels sorry for me too.

Mack digs into his pocket, holds his phone up. 'Well, you know where I'll be.' He grabs my shoulder real quick, wiggles me back and forth. I go limp, put my weight into his hands. 'Don't do anything dumb, Damo. I mean it.'

I step away from the edge, shrug him off. I'm surprised to feel my thighs are shaking. I've balanced on that edge a hundred times!

'Just give her detention and get the hell out,' Mack adds.

'I'm the prefect.'

'I know.'

He makes his hand into a fist, holds it out for me to lock in.

'Safe,' he says, like we're some sort of gangstas, like we've been saying for the three years or more I've lived in this place. Such a stupid ritual, but it always makes us laugh. Always used to.

'Catch ya later.'

He pretends to throw a punch but I avoid him easy. He raises his hand to his forehead in a kind of salute. Then I see him move through the trees. Maybe he'll wait somewhere nearby, checking his rabbit traps.

After I can't see Mack no more, I go back to the edge of the Leap and tightrope round it again, arms outstretched. One slip, I'd be gone. Dead. It wouldn't be hard. The thought hovers at the back of my brain. And the muscles in my thighs are shaking again, daring me. I'm tingling all through. I'm remembering leaning up against Ashlee after one of the times she'd played the Game.

'You have to notice tingling feelings,' she'd whispered, her fingers working up across my chest and giving me those feelings all right. 'Tingling means that something's going to happen.'

I'd laughed and kissed her. 'Something like what?'

She'd shrugged. 'I dunno. Like going somewhere. Somewhere like Fairyland.' She'd rolled her eyes.

'You're nuts, you are.'

I'd grabbed her quick, my hands under her top.

I blink fast to stop the memory, and look over at the rocks below. Shudder. Tingling would be nothing like how it'd feel if I dropped down there, if I smashed on to those rocks. Hitting something like them would be nothing but pain.

9

Emily

I'm trembling standing here and it's not because it's cold. It takes every bit of my concentration not to run back to the gate and leave. There are images in my head. Ashlee stumbling drunk on one of these pathways. Someone following. Hands on a neck. Dad's hands brushing her neck in our kitchen. Rain washing everything away.

Someone else might think these woods were still and silent right now, but they're not. Dad taught me that. For one thing there are two swallows wheeling high above me, which is strange because they should have left long ago. They belong to a summertime with Dad in it.

I do what Dad did to calm his mind, just make myself focus on the forest around me. I listen to a bird shaking its wings out above me. I smell earth, rotting and sweet. There's the taste of smoke and pine needles. A breeze whisks around the back of my neck promising rain. I hear the trees creak.

Once when people asked what I wanted to be when I grew up, I would say a tree. It used to make Dad laugh, and I liked that, but it was more than this too. It was knowing that, as a tree, I would only feel wind on my bark, animals on my branches. I could stretch down deep into the earth and this would be all I'd need. I breathe in, this place feels fragile and desperate. Its ancient air wants to be sucked down into my lungs, doesn't want to let go. I take a few steps towards the red-gold trees and it feels as if I'm walking into a blaze of fire.

Then I see a twitch of movement up ahead.

I squint. Stop.

There's a darker shape between the trees.

A dark shape in these woods could be anything, or anyone. A deer? A bird watcher? Maybe a tramp or a jogger. It could be someone more sinister. I take my phone out, just in case. But when I look up again, the shape has disappeared in the dappled light. Now I'm not sure I've seen anything at all. I peer to the space through the trees where I thought the shadow was but, with the branches swaying, shadowy shapes are everywhere now. Maybe I imagined it. It could be my mind playing tricks on me because I'm back here again, because I'm feeling nervous.

Then I realise who else it could be: Joe. He could have

followed me from the bus stop, it would be just like him to worry. I call his phone, still squinting into the undergrowth. I don't hear it ring but he's often got it on silent. It goes through to his voicemail; I don't leave a message. I don't shout out his name either, don't want to break the silence of this wood unless I have to. Anyway, there are shadows and shapes everywhere now. That shadow I thought I'd seen could have been nothing at all.

I walk on. I don't know this part of Darkwood so well, but I guess the edge of the quarry will be on my left soon, and then the caves, then the boulders that lead up to the Leap. Its summit has the best view of anywhere. From there it's easy to see how huge these woods are, how they stretch into and separate parts of the town, how they seep into farmland like sea on a shore, how they retreat into darkness.

Maybe that shadow I'd seen was Damon, getting up to the Leap before me. There aren't even any birds darting across this path now. Wiggling my fingers apart, I think about how it would feel to have Damon walking beside me, his fingers threaded through mine. And, before I can help it, I'm remembering that time again, late afternoon last November. That day where I'd been sat on the edge of the bike trail, waiting until dusk for when I'd go collect Dad from the bunker. When I'd been watching the first of the starlings begin to flock and form a roost.

That day Damon had appeared out of nowhere. He'd been running hard. I hadn't recognised him, just saw a madman. I'd stood up fast as he'd stumbled over me.

'What are you doing?' I'd said.

'What are you?'

He'd put his hands on his knees and his head down between them and breathed and breathed. When he'd looked back, I'd pointed out the starlings I'd been watching, explained a little as the sky darkened, as the birds turned. 'When one starling changes direction,' I'd said, 'each of the other birds does too. These birds are the most highly-tuned pack of animals there is.'

He'd calmed down then. 'That all you been doing? Just watching birds?'

I hadn't said about Dad, about how I'd really been in Darkwood to fetch him. I hadn't said I'd been putting it off as long as I could. But I'd wanted to. I'd wanted Damon to stay and watch the starlings: talk. I could tell he was thinking about it.

But then it all changed. His mate arrived.

'See you round,' Damon had said. And they were gone, running fast, one chasing the other, shouting through the trees with their voices echoing back.

I wonder if Damon even remembers all that. Remembers me.

A woodpecker makes a sudden laugh, and I jump. These are stupid thoughts, all of them, and the woodpecker knows it. Before I move off again I push upright a leaning sapling blown sideways. If it grows straight, it'll be an oak.

When I start the climb up the Leap, I get another stupid thought. Perhaps there is a different reason why Damon wants to meet me up there. In town they call this place the Jump, Lover's Leap . . . Suicide Drop. People have killed themselves falling from these rocks; there have been accidents. What if Damon is planning to jump off? It would be one way for him to escape the nightmare that must be his life right now. Pushing me off the edge might be another.

Now these stupid thoughts won't go away. I get this image of Damon throwing himself off the Leap like some sort of deranged superhero and that's it then, I just run, straight up the path towards the summit. My feet skid in mud and a branch brushes my neck and I keep going. Because I'm also thinking: Damon has lost two people, his girlfriend and his dad. Could that be enough to send him over? I'm remembering the jagged rocks on the other side of the Leap, that steep vertical slide . . . how once a person started falling that would be it.

I tumble on to the summit, my head darting sideways: looking. The light is brighter up here without the tree cover, blinding me for a second, but I see him. He's standing on the ledge, looking over. Then, as I heave to get my breath, he turns towards me and I see his face. He's angry, frowning.

10

Damon

She arrives like a bullet from a gun. 'Hey!' she shouts, so loud it almost tips me off.

She raises her arms like she's going to catch me, like she's trying to play hero. She looks so much like her dad. I could snap her thin arms that she's stretching towards me. I could step out of the way. *Keep coming,* I'm thinking, *keep coming and I'll watch you fall.* I look over the edge again, and she skids still.

'It's not me who should jump,' I say.

Her eyes dart down, stare at where my feet are: how close to the edge. I could tightrope walk the whole way around this summit, dare her to do it too. Follow the leader. It's a kind of detention.

'Reckon you could jump because of what your dad did?' I ask.

Her eyes widen. Now I'm playing with her – being a bastard – but I don't want her to come any closer. Don't want her to feel sorry for me neither. There are dark rings under her eyes. I'm glad if this means she's not sleeping: she should be suffering. She doesn't look away from me. She's got nerve, this girl.

'Why don't you believe it?' I just go ahead and ask her this too. 'If it wasn't your dad that killed Ashlee, who did?'

'Plenty of people use these woods. All the time they do! Anyone could have been there that night.' She's looking at me hard like she knows something.

'Police don't think so,' I snap. '*Your dad* don't even think so.'

Still, she keeps eye contact. 'My dad doesn't know what he thinks.'

I make this weird laugh-noise in my throat. 'He knows he's guilty. Even if he *says* he can't remember, he admitted it yesterday. Manslaughter?' I try to stare her out, try to get this into her thick skull.

She shrugs. 'He's not well.'

The casual way she says this makes me want to shake her: it's *because* her dad's not well that all this happened. Can't she see that?

'What kind of psycho would kill a girl like Ashlee?' I say. 'She was perfect, did no one no harm. The longer they lock him up the better.'

She keeps quiet.

'So which is it?' I hiss, frustrated at her now. 'Murder or manslaughter?'

Her face goes blank, switches to a mask that looks like she's practised a million times. I keep going.

'Did he meet Ashlee before that night? Because that's what the papers are saying. Did he chase her there like a bastard? Or do you believe those lies about your dad being in a flashback when he did it?'

Emily Shepherd won't tell me anything. Although, there, behind her mask, just for a second, I glimpse it: pain. Total screw-with-your-head pain. She doesn't know what to believe neither. She's hurting with it too.

'You're not tough,' I say. 'So stop pretending it.'

She sticks her chin out. 'Neither are you.'

I glare at her. 'I should give you your detention. If you're not giving me any answers.'

I consider the options. My signature sports detentions involve a heap of running and a heap more sit-ups straight after. But I need something more for this girl. She should feel scared, like Ashlee must've felt that night. She should suffer.

'My dad . . .' she says, so quietly it's like I haven't heard her at all, 'he couldn't have, he *wouldn't* . . . after the army stopped, he couldn't do anything . . .'

She reaches out and tries to put her fingers on my shirt. I leap back.

'You mean after he got discharged,' I say. 'After he got discharged for killing a civilian?'

Her mask's dropping now.

'Is *that* why he killed Ashlee?' I continue. 'He got a taste for it?'

She won't look at me. 'Dad was scared,' she whispers. 'If he'd heard someone in the woods while he was there, he would have been scared of them too. He *couldn't* have stalked anyone.'

'Maybe you didn't know your dad! Did you ever think of that?'

'It was someone else,' she says, folding her arms. 'Other people use these woods; other people were there that night.'

She stares harder now. She knows something. She knows I'm one of those other people.

'He must've talked to Ashlee before,' I say fast.

'No! He'd never seen her until—'

''Til he walked out of these woods with her dead?'

She shuts up at that. I watch the wind pull dark hair from her eyes, from *his eyes*. The guilt – again – heavy in my guts. It's my fault Ashlee was in these woods that night. My fault that Shepherd found her.

'He murdered her,' I say, feeling my mouth twist nasty. 'He watched her and he stalked her. *That's* what happened.'

I want Emily Shepherd to accept this. I want her to tell me that Shepherd used to roam around these woods at night – that he used to hang round near Ashlee's shortcut track and that he was a weirdo. I want her to admit that her dad's murder charge is right.

She waits. She's not scared of me, not one bit. Maybe she should be.

'If this is all detention is,' she says, '. . . then I think I should go.'

I hold up my hand. 'Wait.'

'Why should I?'

'Because I'm telling you to. Because I haven't said it's over.'

She frowns. 'Why should I stay here when you think my dad is a . . .?'

I wait for her to say it: murderer, killer, stalker, psycho; anything like that. When she doesn't, I tell her. 'Everyone thinks he's guilty, that he's a monster. It's obvious!'

She keeps her frown. My heart is hammering. Just thinking about her dad being innocent of murder gets me kind of panicky.

'Refer me for a suspension, then, if you're not going to do anything,' she says, and again there's that challenge in her words, in her blue-grey eyes . . . in those eyes that look too vivid, too startling, to belong to a murderer's daughter.

I'm not giving her what she wants, though, no way. I bend 'til I'm looking her square in those killer's eyes. 'Why'd you hit that girl today? Are you violent too? Are you like him?'

I want her to be, because, if she is, there's no doubt her father murdered Ashlee, no doubt that he's a liar. That they both are.

Her eyes flare. 'I didn't hit her! I pushed her and she fell.'

Now I've struck a nerve. Now she wants to push me too.

'Why don't you try it?' I say.

I want her to snap; maybe I want her to hit me so I can hit her back. I go closer, 'til I feel her breath land hot and fast on my skin. She should be dead instead of Ashlee. She should be the one hurting instead of me.

'Do it,' I say. 'Push me! Show me you got killer's blood like your dad.'

But she turns away. 'You don't have to be like this.'

She's disappointed. I see it in her eyes. Maybe because I'm not who she recognises from school, because I'm not that prefect with the perfect girlfriend and the perfect life. Not any more.

'Sports detention,' I repeat, and my voice sounds kind of empty. 'Or can't you handle it now? Aren't you tough enough?'

'I can handle whatever you want to give me. I don't care.'

There's something about her expression that *gets* me. Why can't she believe what everyone else does? Why does she have to believe nothing — not murder, not man-slaughter! Maybe it shouldn't bother me, but it does.

'A running game, then,' I say. 'I run. You chase. Then we swap over.'

She snorts something like a laugh. 'Fine.'

I take a step back and look at her skinny body, her pale skin, grey-blue eyes. I could run her 'til she's in the middle of this wood; I could get her lost; make her feel completely alone. Then she might get scared, might believe what her dad did. Then I can drop this whole thing and never have to speak to her again; stop asking these questions that she don't have answers for anyway.

Before I realise what I'm doing I feel my fingers curling into the shape of a gun, then my hand comes up towards her. It's so natural, to do this here in these woods, that I don't even realise I'm doing it 'til I'm aiming my finger-gun at her.

'You're chasing me first,' I say.

Her mouth opens a little as I aim my hand at the middle of where her ribs are. She's looking at it almost like it's a real gun I'm pointing and if she moves or tries to run, I'll shoot. I look down the barrel of my arm towards her and she's trapped in my firing line. One twitch of my finger, then *bang*. I imagine what that would be like, to see her body smash apart. I try to imagine wanting it.

'I'm It,' I explain. 'I run.'

My heart is beating like bullets, feels like I could kill her with just them. I move my 'finger-gun' back, rest my fingers against my temple this time. That's when I jerk my fingers upward in one quick movement and shoot, right through my skull. I point my fingers back at her fast and shoot again. Shoot her. Bang. Straight through the ribs. Through her heart. Still holding her gaze, I drop my arm.

'You're chasing first,' I say again.

And I turn and step off from the Leap. Right off the edge.

11

Emily

I'm so shocked I just stand there.

'Damon?'

Then I run — scramble — to the edge of the Leap. He's done it, he's really jumped: right on to the jagged rocks below. This is why he brought me here, what he was going to do all this time — I'll get to the edge and see Damon sprawled and twisted, bloody and broken. I'm not going to know what to do. What if he's dead? What if people think I pushed him?

I skid on the stone, slippery from the light rain that's just started. I've never been good with heights, just like Dad isn't, but I make myself do this. I drop to my hands and knees and crawl. I breathe in quickly and look over the edge.

He's not on the rocks. Not anywhere. It's as if he's just disappeared. Has he fallen into a crevice, slipped somewhere I can't see? The image of Damon pointing his fingers like a gun is still lasered into my mind: that wink of his left eye, his concentration. The way he'd shot me. The way he'd pointed those fingers at his head as if he were shooting himself too. I was trapped, held still by his stare. He could have killed me or kissed me then; I would've stayed.

I crawl a little further so I'm half hanging over the rock, my body juddering against it as my heart thuds. One slip and I'd be joining Damon. But I look and look, and there are only rocks below. I stay still, listen. Rain gets in my ears but, even so, I hear him . . . I hear something. It's a light breathing, like an animal's. It's coming from somewhere very close. I grab on to a spindly plant growing in the rock and, pulling against it first to check it's strong enough to hold my weight, I use it as a kind of anchor so I can lean over the edge. Directly underneath me is an opening, a kind of cave, but it's too dark to see inside straight away.

'I told you, I'm It.' Damon's voice comes back from the dark. 'I'm It and you're chasing.'

I squint to see Damon's hunched body. He's directly underneath me, just a layer of rock between us.

'What are you waiting for?' he says. 'Tag me!'

In front of the cave's opening is a tiny dirt ledge, I suppose it would be possible to jump on to it lightly and quickly and then springboard into the cave: if you had guts and weren't scared of heights, if you had the right sort of balance and had nothing to lose.

'I thought you were dead,' I say.

'Really?'

This seems to please Damon, and he shuffles closer to where I'm hanging. I grab more of the plant, painfully aware that my life is relying on the strength of a weed's root system. If this plant uproots, I'm gone. Damon comes so close I see freckles on his nose, millions of them.

'You're *meant* to be chasing me,' he repeats. He ducks out from the cave, clings to the rock face on the other side. 'Or don't you want to play in these woods after what your dad did here?'

'He didn't,' I say. 'You're not being fair.'

He thinks about this. 'Catch me and I might be. If not . . .' He breathes out fast. 'I could make your life hell for you, y'know, hurt you for what your dad did . . .' He scrambles around the cliff face, arms and legs splayed wide, until he reaches what looks like a small animal path a few metres away. 'This is your detention, remember?' he says. 'So chase me. Do it!'

He begins to run, down that path that I can now see weaves away from the sharp rocks and heads towards the bottom of the Leap; he's half out of control. I shouldn't follow him. I know he's only trying to get his own back, just like Mina said he would. I can see how full of anger he is. But what's the alternative? Stay here? Go home and find Mum already half cut on wine, sprawled on the sofa?

Damon Hilary telling on me? And then, meeting the Head in his stuffy office with Mum called in. Suspension. Expulsion? Mum in tears. Then someone leaking all this to the papers and them latching on to me as an evil psycho too: *like father, like daughter*. Then there will be more graffiti on our house. More things muttered at me in supermarkets. More hate.

Damon's running faster now, weaving down that tiny path with an ease that surprises me.

There are things I still want to say to him too.

Stomach against the rock, I slide feet first over the edge. Using the plant as support, I stretch down until the tips of my trainers touch the dirt ledge below. Then I let go, throw my body towards the cave and away from that drop and those sharp rocks. I turn and see Damon hanging on to a thin tree-trunk halfway down the hill, watching me with a hand held to his eyes. I choose my route, then run – skid – towards him.

Running down this path feels amazing, even though I could fall and slide in a tangled mess, even though this is one of the most stupid things I've ever done. It's as if my legs are moving without me telling them to, whirring underneath me. It's much steeper than Damon made it look and I grab on to dried bracken to steady myself, feeling it rip the palms of my hands. Damon pushes himself off the trunk and waits on the path. At this rate I'm going to barrel straight into him. I slip in my shoes, mud skate down, but I keep my balance somehow. As I get closer, he's off.

'You won't catch me like that!' he shouts. 'Faster!'

At the bottom he turns left on to the bike trail and I'm quicker now after him, digging my toes into the soft ground. It's more sheltered here, my shoes don't skid so much. Damon runs backwards, watching me. If I catch him, I'll make him listen to me. I'll wipe that nasty, judging expression off his face. I launch myself at him and – almost – I get him. He raises his eyebrows as he stumbles back.

'You're quicker than you look,' he says, slightly breathless, maybe even a little impressed.

His teeth are shining. When he darts sideways I'm with him, anticipating his moves. I reach out and my fingers brush his shoulder as he whirls away. There's a glimmer of curiosity in his eyes. Is he waiting to see when I'll give up? He could easily take off and leave me here, but for some reason he stays, just out of reach, scrambling out of the way when I get too close. Is this how he gives all his detentions?

'Tag!' I shout as I grab him.

He shakes his head, shakes his arm from my grip. 'You have to keep hold ten seconds. You must remember the rules from Junior School! Give up?'

'No!' Though I'm sweating and panting hard.

He shrugs. 'Catch me then.'

He runs faster down the bike trail. But I know where this trail curves, where there's a shortcut I can use to head him off. It's a shortcut I remember from ages ago, from when Dad had found an injured rabbit there. A few metres more and I dart down it: I'll be back on the bike trail before Damon even realises.

I leap brambles and branches. This shortcut is so wildly overgrown I can only focus on being fast, not quiet, on getting back to the bike trail before Damon gets there. I don't look to the sides, don't want to remember the click of that rabbit's neck as Dad twisted it dead, or the soft, limp warmth of lifeless rabbit in my palms straight after.

'It's kinder this way,' Dad had said. 'Trust me. Put it out of its misery.'

But I'd felt really sick at the way Dad had acted like that death was so necessary, that it was hopeless to even think about trying to save it.

I keep my eyes straight ahead. I'll grab Damon for longer than ten seconds and I'll make him listen: see things from my side. Suddenly I'm bursting on to that trail and I'm spinning around left and I'm waiting. Damon's coming straight for me, but he's looking back over his shoulder. My chest heaves. When he sees me he skids in the earth, waving his arms about to slow himself, his mouth opening in surprise. He doesn't have time to stop, not really.

And I don't think.

I do something really stupid.

I launch myself at him.

I feel the hardness of his chest against me, hear the air leave his throat, and then he's falling back against the ground and I'm on top, pushing. I get a flash of memory of what happened with Kirsty today, a twist of fear at what

I am. Then I'm pinning his arms, putting my knees on his shoulders. I'm doing what Dad taught me to do once: *disable the enemy as quickly as possible*.

'Dad wasn't the only one in the woods that night!' I scream it into his face. 'And Dad couldn't have chased anyone . . . not on these paths, not at night. He's scared! When he's in the woods, he doesn't leave that bunker — there's *no way* he could have stalked Ashlee!'

I'm trying to make Damon see Dad as I do — make him see how Dad can't be a killer, certainly not a murderer.

'Dad gets scared in thunderstorms,' I add. 'Loud noises give him flashbacks. And he *was* in a flashback that night, but he didn't kill Ashlee. Not murder, not manslaughter!' I push into Damon's chest so hard he can't say anything back. Not until I'm finished. 'Dad's scared of heights,' I explain, 'of getting lost, of people, he's scared of everything!'

Damon is breathing funny. Perhaps I've winded him. I don't get off him to check.

'There was someone else,' I say. 'There must've been. Dad just found Ashlee that night, he was trying to help!'

'Ridiculous,' Damon hisses.

'No! Dad doesn't remember anything — that's got to mean he didn't do it!'

Damon shakes his head. 'No one else knows where that bunker is — Ashlee didn't.'

I lean closer, place my palms against Damon's cheeks to keep his face still. 'What did *you* see that night anyway? You were in the woods, you were in the car park at least!

Why didn't you see Dad if he was really watching and stalking her? You should've been a witness to that . . . if it happened.'

Damon's eyes narrow. 'Get off me.'

I don't move. 'Why didn't you walk Ashlee all the way home, anyway? What kind of boyfriend leaves his drunk girlfriend in the woods after dark?'

'You don't know what I did.' His face is red – mad! His voice is fierce.

'You're the last one who saw her alive, though,' I say. 'So why don't you know anything? You should be the one giving me answers!'

'Get the fuck off me!'

I shake my head. 'I caught you. I did my detention.' I'm surprised at how confident I sound – surprised at the things I'm saying to him too. But I have to make him see. 'I'll get off you if you admit that it might not have been Dad who killed her, that there are other possibilities . . .'

Damon looks even more furious than he did in the courtroom. I feel his breath against my skin, see his copper-coloured eyes glaring, and the sweat beading above his lips. I watch his top lip rise, see a glint of his straight perfect teeth underneath. There's a beating feeling inside me, in my ears and chest. For a second I want to lean further into him, press my lips on his, taste his sweat and tag him that way . . . win like this. Show him. I want him to admit that I could be right. Perhaps Damon sees this because, so quickly, he's pushing me off him and I fall hard on to the track. He crawls away, breathing heavily.

'Freak!' he spits. 'Psycho! You're just the same as him —
the fucking same!'

He gets up. He actually runs from me! I sit in the dirt,
watching him go. I don't know what the hell I just did.
Why did I even say that stuff? Why did I get so mad? Why
did I want to touch his lips like that too?

I grab a bundle of damp cold leaves and squeeze them,
hard. My breath is coming heavy and fast and my hands
are quivering, and I'm thinking over and over, *Who am I?*

12

Damon

I get out of there, skidding through damp, stinking leaves with rain starting to piss down on me. What the fuck? That wasn't meant to happen; I'm not the one who's meant to be running away right now. I wipe sweat from my eyes. I want to outrun all the crazy stuff Emily Shepherd was just shouting about – it don't mean nothing! So what if her dad is scared of storms and heights and all the rest of it? It don't mean there was someone else who killed Ashlee! Don't mean it wasn't him! I should never have met her here. I need Emily Shepherd in my life right now about as much as I need a bullet in my brain.

I grab a small branch that's hanging down, knocked about by the wind. I use it to bash at things: whack the dead, dried heads off foxgloves. I can't believe she caught me! I'm never caught; not unless I want to be.

As I run, I'm checking where I am — deep inside Darkwood, Game Play. Ashlee and the rest of us would have run round here stacks of times. Maybe this is where Shepherd watched Ashlee; maybe I'm somewhere near his bunker too. That would explain why his daughter knows this place so well; he must've showed her it. That should've been her detention: to show me that bunker too, to make her go there and face the truth. 'Cause the police still ain't telling no one where it is.

I'm breathing hard: two months off the Game and I've got unfit. Emily Shepherd looked too small and weak to run that fast and far, I didn't think she'd keep up. If I was any sort of decent sports prefect I'd get her on a school team; instead I'll get as far away from her as I can.

I snap the branch, chuck the ends at a clump of bracken. The rain slides over my skull and inside my sports shirt: it's cold, winter rain that's come too early. I go faster. It feels weird running like this again, so fast and without the Game. This is how Mack and I used to run when we'd first come into these woods, when we'd run through town, sneak silently through the crack in the barracks fence as a shortcut, when we'd sprint through here. We'd lie exhausted on the forest floor after, breathing in time. Then we were brothers, part of the same pack — we was training for the army and stopping the bad thoughts inside of us same time.

'Push yourself,' Mack had said. 'How much can your

body take, how much pain?'

I'd made my body hurt so much I'd stopped thinking of anything else. For a time I did.

I turn on to a bridleway. It's not like there'll be any horse riders out in this weather anyway, but there are deer. I hear them surging through the forest to my left. There are flashes of movement in the trees as they start to run with me — same direction, almost the same speed. The thick undergrowth they leap in makes them slow. If I was with Mack and the others we'd be running after them, seeing how fast they could go. But this time I try to keep my feet in rhythm with the thud of their hooves, try to keep running as if I'm part of their herd. It'd be easy to be the stag leading those hinds away. As a stag, I could forget. I could piss off out of here and no one would notice. Emily Shepherd couldn't catch me then. No one could.

13

Emily

The rain is tipping down cold. Suddenly, being alone in these woods doesn't feel so good: I get going. I don't understand what just happened, why I'd felt so angry, why I'd wanted to push Damon over and make him listen. I don't understand why I'd wanted to touch his lips either.

Maybe I'm exactly like Damon said I am, like Kirsty said too: a freak, a psycho. No wonder people look at me strangely in the street. I *am* strange.

I go the quickest way home, on a path that passes near to where the bunker is. I should find out what has happened to it – I know I should – but I'm still not ready. Not when it's getting dark, not when shadows are slipping like unwanted thoughts between the trees. I glance left, study the dark spaces between silver birch trunks. It would be so easy for someone to stand still in there without me ever knowing. There are thoughts standing at the edge of my brain too. There are the questions Damon asked that I don't have answers for.

Today I'm glad to get out of Darkwood. I go through the wooden gate and stand on the cobbles in the lane behind our house, head bent and lightheaded. I feel like a horse just bolted, something that was wild a moment ago, caught and thrown into the light. Without looking back at the trees I turn right towards our house, keep walking down the middle of the lane to the end of the row. We have the last house at the edge of town, the last house before acres of woodland. And it's not owned by the army, it's ours. Mum used to say our house was holding the wilderness back; Dad said it was the town we were keeping at bay. I'm still not sure.

My shoes are squelching, and my sports shirt is stuck to my spine. If Mum guesses where I've been she'll be furious. But perhaps she's already on to her second glass of wine. Florence is at the back door, wet and thin. I stick my key in the lock, quietly turn it, let Florence slip in ahead, her tail winding briefly around my leg. We hardly ever use the back door now and it whinges, stiff.

'That you, Emily?'

Mum doesn't sound drunk. Quickly I shout some excuse about staying back to do homework with Joe. She might believe this more easily if I had my schoolbag as a prop, if I wasn't dressed in soaking muddy sports kit. I quickly push off my trainers. There's an unpacked shopping bag on the kitchen table with bottles of wine, a defrosting pizza and some oven chips inside. Florence is purring against me, but I'm not even stopping for her. When I hear one of Mum's quiz shows start up on the telly, I tiptoe through the hall. But she shouts again when I've got one foot on the stairs.

'Why are you so late? It's almost dark!'

Maybe I could bolt for it, make it upstairs and lock myself in the bathroom until I've washed off the evidence of the woods. I hear the creak of the couch as Mum gets up out of it. Then she's standing near me, her eyes running over my wet hair and clothes, the mud.

'Where've you been?' She leans forward and plucks a twig from my shoulder.

'Just felt like a walk.' It sounds pathetic, and anyway, I can see Mum knows exactly where I've been.

She crosses her arms very slowly, studying me. Her oversized cardi makes her look thin, her wrists like sparrow's legs emerging from its bulky sleeves. That's another thing that's happened to us in these past few weeks: we've got thin, saved on food bills.

'You've been in there again, haven't you? You've been in . . .?'

I wait for her to say one of the words she no longer uses: *Darkwood, the woods, Dad's bunker*; all the words that were once so common in this house. It's as if she's allergic to them now, though, as if she'll break out in a rash if she

84

even thinks the words. Once, Mum would say there was something about Dad and me when we'd been in Darkwood, a wild magic threaded through us. Once, she'd been happy that Dad took me there to learn about the forest. Once, she'd come with us. Now, she frowns.

'Why do you want to go back in there anyway?' She gives me this look like I've disappointed her, like I'm the freak that Damon and Kirsty think I am.

'It's autumn,' I say. 'The leaves are starting to turn. I always go then.'

She doesn't buy it. She's suspicious. Just like she was suspicious of Dad after he was discharged from the army. She doesn't trust either of us in those woods any more.

'I didn't go to the bunker,' I say.

'I don't want to hear about that place.' Her lips go tight and thin, and she's already turning away. 'I wish you'd never found it, that you'd never mention it again!'

But I wish she wouldn't switch off like this. I used to tell Mum everything about the woods in its different seasons and she used to want to hear it. It's hard enough having her switch off about Dad, but pretending the bunker and Darkwood don't exist too?

'You don't have to hate the woods,' I say. 'They're just woods, they didn't do anything.'

Mum flashes me a look. She goes into the kitchen and I follow, not wanting her to ignore me any longer. She grabs the nearest bottle of wine and twists the top off: Cabernet Sauvignon, 14 per cent alcohol, red wine now. I wonder what it would take for her to move on to spirits?

If she knew I'd fought Kirsty today? If she knew I'd chased Damon Hilary through the trees? That I had a detention?

'Don't go into Darkwood again,' she says. 'It's not safe.'

I hold her gaze. 'I thought you didn't believe me when I said someone else killed Ashlee Parker? That it wasn't Dad?'

'I don't.' Her gaze falters, flutters to the wine. 'I just don't want you back in there. I'm serious, Emily. There are other things that aren't safe in those woods too, other people.'

'You can't stop me.'

Mum meets my gaze with another sharp look. But saying I can't go into Darkwood is like telling someone else not to go to school, or to visit their friends: Darkwood is the place I belong. At least, it always used to be.

'The quicker we move away from those rotten trees the better,' she says.

I want to yell that I won't move anywhere, but then I see that her eye make-up is smudged and guess she's been crying at work again. It makes me hesitate. We're both quiet as she pours a large glass of wine, listening to how the liquid gulps and glugs. I don't want her to take a mouthful and push past me towards the telly, but this is what she does. I'd rather she shouted at me, got nasty even; slapping me across the face would be better than this. I'd rather she do anything except keep playing numb! I follow her into the lounge. This is when I see what she's done.

'Where have all the photos gone?'

I take a step inside. None of our photographs are standing proudly on top of the mantelpiece any more. All the ones of the three of us sharing birthdays and holidays have disappeared, even the one of me and Mum having a snowball fight when I was about five years old has gone.

'I don't want to remember those times with your father,' Mum says.

'But Dad's not even in half those shots!'

Mum keeps staring at the telly with her cheeks a little red. There's a tight, angry feeling in my throat, and it's a bit like how I felt with Kirsty today, like how I felt with Damon. It's hard to swallow. Ever since we knew Dad was pleading guilty to manslaughter – ever since we'd met Dad's lawyers in the city and they'd laid out the case for us – it's as if Mum wants to erase Dad from everything, every single part of our lives. Perhaps she wishes she could erase him from me too. It would explain why she never looks at me properly any more, why she doesn't ever want to talk. It would explain why she always seems so disappointed.

'Where did you put them?' I stand between her and the telly so she can't ignore me.

She raises her eyebrows to the ceiling as if she thinks I'm an idiot for even asking. I want to hate her . . . but if I hate Mum too, I'm running out of people to love.

'You have to start accepting what's happening, Emily, stop living in a fantasy world.'

'What's that got to do with the photographs?' It's all I can think of to say.

'You have to accept your father is different now!' Her voice is battling it out with the roar of laughter from the telly. 'He's not coming back! You might as well start dealing with this.'

I want to throw things at her. Tip wine over her face. I want her to stop watching television and discuss this with me normally. Instead I just glare, and she angles her head to continue to watch her quiz show around me. I swallow to stop myself screaming.

'I don't have to accept anything!'

She sighs, longer this time. 'Your father is guilty of manslaughter. He is suffering from severe psychological trauma brought about from what he saw, and did, in combat.' She speaks these words slowly and carefully, like she's spelling out something to a little kid. 'You heard his plea, what the lawyers said. You know all this.'

She doesn't look at me. Something's twisting in my guts.

'He can't remember anything,' I say, like I always do. 'So it could be someone else who killed Ashlee.'

I move a few steps towards the fireplace and she shifts to see the TV again. She frowns at a question the quiz show host asks about floorboards.

When the show audience claps she says, 'You know, Emily, if the prosecution lawyers do accept your father's manslaughter plea, the court may decide he's too mentally unstable to even be given a fixed sentence. They may put him in a secure psychiatric hospital indefinitely.'

I stare hard at the empty shelf where the photos were. 'So he might never come out?' I won't let myself imagine it. 'Why would they do that?'

'Because he could be dangerous. Because he killed someone. Because he needs help.'

'But he . . .'

'Emily!' There's that warning tone to her voice. 'Even if your father didn't mean to – even if he was out of his head and didn't have a clue what was happening – he still did it. That's not what's being argued any more.'

'But how can anyone know? For certain?'

Mum starts reeling off things she's told me before. About the fact Dad admits it. About how Ashlee Parker's DNA was on his clothes. About the psychological profiling the police have done, the flashback he was in, his trauma from combat. She looks away from the quiz show long enough for me to find her eyes. 'He was living that flashback, Emily,' she says, '. . . exactly like the psychiatrist said . . . killing, just like he did in combat.'

'It could have been anyone!'

'You haven't read the reports – his army discharge papers, the psych notes . . .'

'Because you never let me!'

Mum takes another gulp of wine. 'You know his flashbacks got worse when he didn't take his meds. And he hadn't taken those pills properly for weeks before that night.' She sounds so calm she could be reading out the news. I hate it.

'You weren't there,' I repeat. 'Neither of us was.'

She looks at me so sadly that I think she's going to suggest I see a counsellor or take pills like Dad did. This is how this conversation usually goes. She won't listen to my theories, won't talk this through. Right from when Dad was arrested she thought he'd done it, just accepted it then. She's never said this to me outright, but I know.

'Wives are supposed to care!' I blurt out. 'You're supposed to care.'

'Sometimes caring isn't enough!' She stands quickly – too quickly – and her hand shoots out to grab the edge of the couch. 'Sometimes circumstance goes beyond it.' She tries to move past me. 'The sooner you realise your dad's not the same dad you remember from childhood, the better. Then we can move on with our lives, and we need to do that.'

'You talk like he's dead.'

She breathes in sharply. 'The man we both want to remember is.'

Her voice is a thousand sharp fingers, jabbing me back into the bookshelf. I jam my spine against it and let her pass. My hands go in fists – just for a second – then I grab the nearest book and hurl it across the room, watch it splay open as it smashes against the far wall. It's a Thomas Hardy book, one of Dad's. I'm surprised Mum didn't get rid of that too. Now it lies broken on the carpet, pages wonky and sticking out at odd angles. I wish it were Mum instead.

I hear her in the kitchen, pouring more wine. I can't stay here, listening to her calm explanations, watching the facade on her face. I take the stairs quickly, grab a towel from the cupboard on the landing. But I stop before going into the bathroom. She just said it, didn't she? That I haven't read the reports? And I helped Mum package up some of Dad's things, so I think I know where those reports could be. I wrap the towel around my damp hair and pull open the trap door to the loft, climb the ladder. Last time we were up here was another day when I'd hated Mum, been angry.

The boards feel unsteady, so I move slowly to crouch near the boxes of Dad's things, reading what Mum has scrawled on their sides: *Bank Statements, Jon's College Stuff, Army* . . . I still don't understand how Mum can package Dad's life up so easily. I pull the box called *Army* towards me. Some of Dad's old combat fatigues are in this box, but there are papers underneath too. I take out one of his shirts and hold it on my lap. It feels cold and soft, doesn't smell like Dad any more. I'm still so shivery from being in the woods that I almost put it on, right over my hoodie.

At last I find Dad's letter of honourable discharge and the notes that go with it: all this stuff I've never been allowed to read. The police and Dad's lawyers must have got their copies from somewhere else, because these are the originals. I scan them quickly, nervously. There is a lot of stuff that doesn't make much sense to me, stuff about procedures and army equipment to be given back, but I see the report written by the army psychiatrist: the report Mum must have been talking about earlier. I read it fast, my eyes catching on sentences:

. . . It is my opinion that Rifleman Shepherd suffers from post-traumatic stress disorder . . . a result of an incident involving the shooting of a civilian during a firefight near . . .

I skim over the details of the fighting on the day that changed everything for Dad — I read about how it was close contact, about the injuries suffered on both sides, how civilians and soldiers and insurgents were hard to tell apart in the dust storm.

...the civilian was running towards Rifleman Shepherd when Shepherd opened fire ...

In flashbacks, Dad would often scream answers to an imaginary soldier — to the one who'd told him he'd killed the civilian that day. Dad would say over and over how he didn't mean to do it.

I read on. There are notes about how Dad couldn't cope, how he withdrew into himself, how his commanding officer had to send him back to base. There are other paragraphs detailing how Dad had behaved after he'd returned home too, a whole page talking about his 'adjustment to civilian life'.

...Shepherd replays the incident over in his mind, aggravating his fragile mental state. The symptoms suffered are of a nature and severity that there is a distinct possibility that Rifleman Shepherd will act out the flashbacks ... re-living of which could place him and others at risk ... I recommend immediate termination of all active service for the safety of Rifleman Shepherd, his fellow army personnel and civilians.

It's all there in bold letters — *a distinct possibility that Rifleman Shepherd will act out the flashbacks*. Reading this, I can see why Dad pleaded guilty to manslaughter. When Dad's lawyers read this it must have shaped their whole case. For a moment my brain just whirls with a kind of panic-noise and I can't think clearly. These reports are written so matter-of-factly, as if everything they say happened is true and as if everything they say will happen again is true too.

But I know this stuff, don't I? I know Dad was discharged for accidentally killing a civilian; I know he was diagnosed with Post-Traumatic Stress Disorder as a result. So why am I shocked? It's because there are things here that I didn't know. I didn't know that civilian's age. And I didn't know she was a girl. But there, in small print, are the details.

Local girl from K Compound, aged sixteen years, suspected as running to Rifleman Shepherd for assistance.

This girl was my age when she died — with her life in front of her and with a family and friends, with hobbies and pets maybe, and with places she liked to go when she was sad. Her death must have torn someone's whole world up. Many people's worlds.

Is this why no one's let me read this stuff? Because they knew I'd be upset? Because they didn't want me to know that this girl had been running to Dad for help? Because Dad was so ashamed of it? How is it possible I never knew? How did this information never get reported in the news either? It's like so many things out there in the world that get covered up, hidden. Secrets are made. It's too much to think of all at once.

Shutting the loft hatch quietly I go into my room, dump Dad's shirt and these papers on my desk. But my skin is gooseflesh now and I can't make sense of what I'm feeling. I'm pacing my room and trying to get warm. Eventually, I go into the bathroom and force the lock across the door, peel off my clothes and fling them anywhere, go straight under the shower. I think about the words the army psychiatrist wrote – *Distinct possibility . . . act out the flashbacks.* Mum believes Dad's done it all again, *exactly* all again. Dad's killed another girl, it's another accident. Was Ashlee just another girl running to Dad for help?

The water is hot and I haven't turned on the fan, so soon there's steam everywhere. I point my face up and let the water scald my cheeks. I want it to flush me clean, get rid of these gurgling horrible feelings inside. I think of how Mum had looked at me just now, that sadness in her eyes. Maybe she'd like it if this shower washed away the parts of me that came from Dad. Maybe she'd be happy that Dad was gone entirely then: out of this house, out of my body, removed like the photographs. Would I be any different like that, without the half of me that came from Dad? Would I still get so angry and snap into these weird moods? Do stupid things like pushing Kirsty or wanting to kiss Damon Hilary?

I'm half-sobbing, half-choking, on the shower water but I turn it hotter. I want it to be so hot that it makes me numb, outside and in. I pull the showerhead lower, force the water into my face. Perhaps it can burn me. Or dilute me so I disappear down the plughole. Then I won't have to work out what any of the stuff I've just read really means. I know why Mum finds it hard to look at me now. It's because, whatever I do, I'll always be Jon Shepherd's daughter: I'll always look like Dad. I'm branded for life, can't wash it away. But what else from Dad am I branded with? What other feelings or parts of his personality have I got?

Words Damon said are back in my mind: *Show me you got killer's blood like your dad.* He'd said that maybe I didn't know my dad at all.

Sixteen years . . .

Running for assistance . . .

Local girl . . .

I feel like fainting but I don't want to get out, not until something feels different. It doesn't seem like there's anything to get out for anyway: not for some overcooked pizza, or for a mum who can't even look at me, not even for Florence. But I do get out eventually. And when I do, I see that Joe is waiting in my room.

14

Damon

I'm almost home when my feet hit a puddle, smashing the water sideways. In tiny drops, it spreads. That's when the image comes. Dad on a routine patrol. Heat haze. Rifle across his chest and he's laughing with the guys in his unit, his head turned and looking over his shoulder. He's in front; it was always his job to look for the devices. But he doesn't concentrate, turns to laugh at a joke – some stupid joke – his detector goes sideways. He takes one step off the road.

The puddle explodes as I kick it with the other foot, the water spraying to my thighs and soaking my trainers.

I'm thinking that Dad's body must've shattered like this, turned into a human firework. Legs and ribs and bits of brain became gunk. His blood sprayed out, melted into desert air. Dad became red mist.

And it should've been Jon Shepherd.

Should've been anyone but my old man. 'Cause he never did nothing wrong.

I see drops of water land on my shoes. On the pavement. I see it spray out towards the entrance of our flat. And I know that Dad's smashed up for always now, and Ashlee's gone.

15

Emily

'What are you doing here?'

'Your mum let me in.'

Joe looks all elbows and limbs sitting on my bed; he's been waiting for me to finish. But I feel red and hot, my veins boiling from the scalding shower, and I can't be bothered to talk.

'What happened with Damon?' he says.

I remember the figure I thought I'd seen in the trees ahead of me earlier. 'Don't you know already?'

Joe's cheeks go the colour of my scalded skin. He shrugs. 'I only followed you a little way, OK! Then I took photos for my project. I'm serious!'

I glare at him. 'I knew it was you!'

I tilt my head to the door, trying to indicate that he should leave now. I want to read Dad's psych reports again, in private. And besides, I'm still in my towel! But Joe's not going anywhere. He spins around on the bed to face the wall, like we used to do when we were little kids and had sleepovers. But we're older now and I have to get changed.

'Wait outside if you have to be here,' I snap.

My eyes dart to the floor as he stomps past: it's Mum I'm meant to be angry with, not Joe. Joe's just come around to check how my detention went; he's trying to be a friend. Even if he is annoying and over-protective sometimes he's only worried about me, and not many people are that any more. But still, he shouldn't have followed me into Darkwood. I shut the door on him and look in the mirror. I'm as pink as if I'd been sitting in the sun all day, my hair as scraggly as rats' tails. I throw on some tracksuit bottoms and one of the camouflage T-shirts Dad got me once, run my fingers through my hair and try to straighten it.

'I look like crap,' I say, as I let him back in.

'You don't.'

But he doesn't look at me when he says this so how would he know? He slouches back on to my bed, pretends to be interested in the photos I've tacked on to my wall that he's seen a million times. He pushes a hand through his longish, curlyish brown hair and tries to calm it down. I remember his shape in the trees, how when I'd looked back a second time he hadn't been there at all.

'I wasn't following you,' he says again, knowing this is what I'm thinking. Then he starts digging about in his schoolbag until he pulls out his camera. He turns it on, switches it to playback mode and holds it out. 'Here, take a look.'

I'm not sure I believe him but I slouch down beside him anyway. He pushes his camera into my hands, leans over and starts moving the photos on. He shows me how he's captured the woods in shot after shot. 'I'm trying to reveal cracks of light,' he explains. 'That's my art project. The one I've been working on for months, you know?'

I nod, because I vaguely remember him talking about this. But I'm wondering if taking photos is only an excuse – did he see all the things I just did with Damon? Did he see me push him over, how I'd held my face so close? I feel my cheeks go hotter.

'Illuminations,' Joe adds, still flicking on the images. 'That's the name of it. Remember? I'm trying to find the light in the dark and the dark in the light.'

He's got photos of sunlight falling through trees, dark holes inside pine trunks, cracks in bare earth.

He holds my gaze, wanting me to understand something. Then he gets up from the bed and goes across to my window that looks out over the woods, only it's dark now and he looks out at black. I see his long, thin face reflected in the glass.

'Remember when we used to go in?' he says, meaning the woods that are out there somewhere. 'Those games we played?'

'Sure, when Dad was away.' And I get it then, what Joe wants me to understand. 'When you started your game, you mean?'

'Yeah – Cracks.'

I remember Joe's face as he'd bent to look into a crevice in one of Darkwood's cave walls, a day so long ago.

'I wonder what's in this crack?' he'd said.

That's when he'd started the imagining game.

Joe had heard there were ancient fault lines, or ley lines, in the earth that ran through Darkwood. He'd read stories that these were powerful places, where energy shot up through the ground and changed people, maybe even sucked them into other worlds. They were just stories, and we knew that, but for a time Joe had got carried away.

'Maybe there's a whole other world through the cracks?' he'd said. 'A parallel universe? Maybe it's a world where animals are in charge instead of humans, where bats are the boss of us all?' His nose had been centimetres from the gap: when he'd breathed out, dust flew into his face. 'You try next, Emily!'

I'd run my fingers over a crumbling crack that stretched all the way from the cave floor to the ceiling but when I'd peered inside all I could see was darkness. No other worlds. When I'd told Joe this, his mouth curved to a grin.

'You have to look harder to find the other worlds!'

I'd seen ancient cobwebs, hanging down like ropes. Two spiders clinging there.

'You have to imagine it!'

I'd laughed and told him that he was the one who was cracked, not the cave walls, and Joe had made a face like he was crazy.

But now it's not him, or even the cave walls that are cracked, it's me. Or Dad. Or both of us. I look over to my desk, to where I'd left Dad's stuff from the loft, and the panic-noise starts again in my head.

'We're too old for Cracks now, Joe,' I say. 'It's a kid's game.'

Joe is still staring at the darkness through my window, as if he can actually see the trees and caves inside the woods, as if he's looking into a crack right now. He's thinking hard.

'So Damon was OK today, then?' he says eventually.

I hesitate. I should tell Joe what really happened: how it'd felt as if Damon had wanted to punish me up there on the Leap. I should say about Damon getting angry. But I'm scared that if I do start telling Joe these things I'll slip into telling him everything. And the words Damon called me still sting: *Freak. Psycho.* What if Joe starts thinking these things about me too?

'We . . . we ran,' I start. 'It was some sort of running game, I guess – maybe like how Damon does cross-country training?'

Joe's face switches to a scowl. 'I wouldn't know.'

I guess he's still bitter about being dropped from the team last term.

'He shouldn't have given you detention in there,' Joe says again. 'You could have gone to the Head instead you know, another prefect . . .'

'Anyone else would have given me a proper punishment.'

'So why didn't *he* do that? You were fighting Kirsty!'

'*Pushing*, not fighting,' I correct, as if it makes a difference.

'What did he want from you anyway?'

'I don't know!'

'It wasn't just a detention, was it?'

Joe has a point: Damon did want more from me. I think I'm beginning to understand what it was, too. 'He wanted me to say Dad did it — everything he's accused of. He wanted answers.'

'Weird.'

I shrug. It's not that weird. We all want those answers. We all want to know what happened that night. I pick up Joe's camera again, flick through the photos. I pause on one of a raven clinging to a branch, its feathers iridescent.

'Em,' Joe says. 'I know Damon *seems* like a decent guy, but . . .' His trainers tap on the carpet. '. . . he's not going to be on your side, is he? He probably doesn't even like you.'

'Pretty much like how everyone else in this town doesn't like me then.'

'More than that.' I can feel Joe's eyes lingering on me. 'All I'm saying is, I wouldn't mess with him, Emily. He's probably really screwed up about all this.'

Like I am, then — that's what I almost add.

We're silent for ages. I've wondered before if Joe's height and recent quietness go together: the taller Joe gets, the more room his voice has to bounce around inside him. Once you couldn't shut the both of us up.

'Peas in a pod,' Dad called us.

'Birds of a feather,' Mum said.

Joe glances over to the photographs I've got tacked beside my bed. I see him staring at a photo of Dad and me mushrooming in the woods. Could Joe be jealous of me going into Darkwood with Damon? That thought makes my cheeks go hot, makes me feel guilty all over and I don't even know why.

'You still think your dad is innocent, right?' Joe says eventually. 'I mean, after the hearing yesterday . . . what he pleaded . . .?'

'Don't you?'

Joe's the only one left – the last one to go with me on my theory of it being someone else who killed Ashlee.

He nods. 'He's innocent. That's why I'm surprised you went into Darkwood with Damon. I mean, just because Damon was Ashlee's boyfriend, we don't actually know . . .'

Joe's voice trails off. I see a similarity then, between Damon and me: how people might look at him and wonder if he's got secrets too, if he's not who he seems. I almost feel guilty about the stuff I said to him earlier.

'The police would have arrested Damon,' I say. 'If he was involved. And it's not like he's gone on the run or anything.'

Joe is frowning. He goes back to the photos on the wall, this time looking at one from when he'd tagged along with Kirsty and me at the fun fair last year. There's no sound from Mum downstairs. She's either burnt the pizza, or she's forgotten about it. Maybe she's passed out on the couch and done both. Suddenly I want everyone to go away. I want to lie on my bed in the dark and think about everything that's just happened, make sense of it if I can. I want to work out why I feel so unsteady when I think about Damon.

'He could have really hurt you, Em,' Joe says quietly.

I remember Damon's red angry cheeks when I'd pinned him to the forest floor, how close my head had been to his. If anyone had done the hurting today it had been me. Just like I'd done at school with Kirsty. Just like I'd wanted to hurt Mum earlier too.

In the photo Joe's staring at, he's got one arm around me and the other stretched out long as it can go, holding the camera. I look so much younger, but the shot was only taken last summer, not long before Dad was discharged and came home. I'm grinning like a loon. This person is a parallel version of me, someone slipped through one of Joe's cracks into a happier, easier place.

Joe hesitates before hugging me goodbye. 'Don't go there again with Damon,' he says, his voice loud near my ear. 'I mean it, he's . . . he's different to what you think.'

This makes me bristle, how he sounds just like Mum, how Joe thinks it's OK for him to follow me into the woods but not OK for me to meet Damon there. His arms grip me tighter than usual.

'You'll break my spine, Joe!'

'Eat something, then!'

He hesitates at the top of the stairs like he's going to say some great speech, but all he says is, 'My mum cooked you guys a shepherd's pie. It's in your kitchen.'

He lopes down the stairs, goes out the front door before I can even say thank you. In the kitchen I unpack the pizzas and put them into the freezer, chuck the shepherd's pie in the oven. I feed Florence, bending down to stroke her behind the ears in the spot she likes. I don't look at the kitchen table. If I did, I would still see how Ashlee's arm trailed down from it that night.

When I take the heated-up shepherd's pie in, I expect Mum to maybe apologise for earlier. I expect a smile: we always used to joke that this meal was named after us. But I don't think she even notices it's not the pizza; she doesn't apologise for anything. She just takes the meal on her lap and continues to yell answers to another of her quiz shows.

Madagascar!

The Prince of Wales!

But she does eat. Maybe to her, each bite doesn't taste like charity.

When she falls asleep, I take the plate from her chest and watch her breathing. The skin around her eyes looks wafer thin; I can see veins under the surface. Perhaps she'll sleep talk; perhaps, like that, we can finally have a proper conversation about Dad. I turn off the telly as it switches to a wildlife documentary, the kind of thing Dad used to watch, and I wonder whether he can watch television where he is . . . whether he's watching this. I get the blanket that now lives permanently on the arm of the couch and place it over Mum, switch off the lamp next to her and find my own bed.

I don't read the psychiatrist's notes again, or even look at Dad's uniform. I don't look at the photos on my wall. Tonight, none of those smiling faces will make me feel any better. Dad's smile is a ghost's smile, and Joe's face is too close to the camera. The face I want to – need to – think about isn't there anyway.

Damon.

16

Damon

Lying in bed's the worst, these hours I don't sleep. This is when I remember Ashlee: how she'd kiss me, bite my neck, press her teeth to my shoulder blades . . . how she'd tease to go further. This is when I touch myself and pretend it's her doing it, then feel sick about it straight after. Because what kind of loser imagines his dead girlfriend's fingers on him? I remember how, one night, we'd been pressed against each other on the forest floor, listening to the Game go on around us; she'd loved that Charlie was on the bike trail nearby and couldn't see us in the dark, she'd started kissing me pretty hard, her fingers moving over my hips.

'Where's the fun if you don't take risks?' she'd whispered.

She would've *done* it with me right then if I hadn't stopped her. 'Charlie might see!'

'That's the risk!'

I shouldn't have stopped her.

It was that night she'd told me about the bunker. 'That creepy war vet hides out there,' she'd said. 'You know, that one who was in the papers for killing someone?'

And now he's in the papers again, I want to tell her. *For killing you.*

'We should try to find that place,' she'd said. 'We should *do* it inside . . . right in the middle of the Game when everyone's looking for us!'

It's like being in a maze once I start thinking these thoughts. The only way out is to think about hurting Jon Shepherd. I'd do it slowly, painfully, making him suffer. I'd strangle him over hours and days and dig my fingers into his veins. Tonight this thought doesn't help, though; my brain's too full of all the stuff his daughter yelled at me earlier. I almost feel guilty about the way I'd been. Emily Shepherd is not her father. That angry tough boy isn't who I am either, not always anyway. I listen to the cars drone by below my window. How would it feel to have one smash into me? Would pain like that be anything like what Dad felt? What Ashlee felt?

The streetlights' glow through my curtains doesn't make it any easier to sleep. Neither does the fact that the flat's so quiet. Mum's sleeping pills put her out solid these days and maybe I even miss my old man's snores, the muffled sounds of TV from my brothers' rooms. How heavy does Emily Shepherd sleep? Can she?

One of the first things I did after it all happened was go to her house. It was night, I had a lighter in my pocket. I'd sat in the gutter opposite and could imagine it all: the frames of the house cracking from the heat, the smoke, the screaming as the fire ate everything. I'd flicked the lighter on and off, stared at that flash of fire. I'd imagined living there, being able to look out of a window and see nothing but trees. I'd even felt jealous. Mum and I could easily move to someplace like that, she got a big enough pay-out from my old man's death. She won't, though, not when she can torture herself by staying here.

I turn over, thump my fist into the mattress. When I shut my eyes it's Emily Shepherd's face, not Ashlee's, I see. This time it's Emily bending over me in the woods, it's her who's laughing and teasing. I feel like a sick bastard all over again.

'Just fucking sleep!' I actually say it out loud, try to make the words sink in that way.

I make my body go still. I can't remember the last time I dreamt. I'm not sure I can even remember what it feels like to be properly awake. I've been in some sort of Neverland for a while now. If I dreamt, could I remember what happened — what *exactly* happened? Would the images come? Or perhaps this is part of the reason I can't sleep — I don't want them to. I whack the light on and start tearing up my room. It's better than just lying here. I crawl under my bed, run my hands over the carpet.

Nothing!

I've looked here before, though. Looked everywhere!

I tumble shoes about as I search in my wardrobe, rip open the shoebox where I keep the important stuff from my old man. Ashlee's dog collar isn't in any of the drawers in my desk. Or in my coat pockets. I even go through all my old sports bags again.

So where is it?

I must've dropped it on my way home that night, been too drunk to realise.

'Sorry,' I say out loud, as if Ashlee is listening. I sit in the middle of my bedroom and stare at the ceiling. 'Do you know where it is, Ash? Where I left it?'

I'm trying to remember — the feel of her dog tag, clasping it tight in my hands. But there are other things in my head now too, getting in the way. Those words Emily'd shouted: *What kind of boyfriend leaves his drunk girlfriend?*

17

Emily

I lie with my heart pounding as early sunlight soaks through my curtains and over my sheets. I'd been dreaming of Damon, he'd been yelling: *Killer's blood. Murderer. Admit it!* I'd been running to get away.

I turn over and stare at one of the photos of Dad beside my bed, see his relaxed, lazy half-smile. Shut my eyes again. But I can't sleep, not now. So I throw back the covers and sit on the edge of my mattress. What if I get to school and Damon has told everyone what I did? What if Kirsty goes for me again?

I walk over to my desk, flick through Dad's psych notes, all those bold, typed letters: **Sixteen years old . . . running to Shepherd . . . he could relive his flashbacks . . .**

It's too much.

So I pick up Dad's shirt, bury my face in it. When Dad used to come off tour he'd smell like sweat and rum and another place's washing powder. Before we sent him off again he'd smell like us and Darkwood. But this shirt just smells of dust; of cold; of something forgotten. I glance towards my window – curtains open on the woods as always. It's time to go back, and not just to the Leap like yesterday.

I get dressed in jeans and a jumper. In the kitchen I write a note for Mum: *Going to school early for a project, back normal time.* I even ring the school and tell them I'm unwell. They buy it, course they do. It's misty and crisp-cold outside our house, winter creeping nearer. I like the bite of it, the way it feels as if my body could snap as I walk the garden path. In the lane I look towards Joe's house, but no one else, anywhere, is awake, not even him. At the wooden gate, I breathe out and see my breath hesitate too.

'It could be anyone,' I remind myself. 'Someone else who killed her.'

Damon had been so certain yesterday that it wasn't: *everyone thinks your dad's guilty . . . it's obvious . . . he's a monster . . .*

I try to focus on the dull thud of my trainers on the path, and on the beech leaves that look like gold sover-eigns or foil chocolate coins: try to see their beauty. But like yesterday, I'm still checking for shadows too. I take the pathway that only Dad and I would know as one; it's more overgrown than I ever remember. Once I would've run down it, coat flapping as I leapt tree roots and branches, calling to Dad. Today I'm quiet. It's not long until I reach the thicket of hawthorn, sculpted like a perfect natural hedge. Beyond it, in that small clearing, I see the slightly raised bit of ground with the leaves and brambles covering it: Dad's bunker. The only way anyone would know it was here is if they were really, truly looking and if they knew what to look for, but we'd happened upon it by fluke. I get a memory of Dad crouched and whispering: *this is our place — a secret just for us.* Surely, he would never have brought Ashlee Parker here. It's another reason why the murder charge doesn't make sense.

I follow the hawthorn around until I find the small opening. The day we'd found this bunker was the day after Dad had signed up for another deployment out of Darkwood Barracks. Three years ago, four? We'd been walking in the woods to celebrate not having to move house and town, and everything, again. Dad's eyes had gone wide when he'd seen the edge of the rusted metal lid and realised what was underneath.

'A bunker?' He'd moved quickly towards it.

I'd started to ask what a bunker was, then realised it myself from the things Dad had told me from being in the army: a shelter, somewhere to hide from enemies, a place to fight from. 'Like they have in a war?' I'd asked.

'I reckon this one's just from the threat of war.'

Today I'm expecting the hawthorn hedge to be torn open with police tape flapping across, but it all looks the same as always. I guess the police approached the bunker from the direction that Ashlee came from that night, on that small animal track the other side. Twigs claw at me as I push through the hawthorn and into the clearing. There is still blue and white police tape half buried in the mud, one end flicking like a snake's tail. It feels colder and quieter here now, full of ghosts: *one ghost*. I walk across the clearing very slowly, kick at some of the ashes still in the fire pit. Once, Dad would have crouched here with the copper kettle he used to boil water.

'Tea?' he'd have said.

But that was in the early days of finding this bunker, back when things were still OK. I get the hugest pang to see *this* Dad again – to feel honey dribbling down my chin from the crumpets he'd cooked, to taste that smoke and sweetness. But this Dad is even further away than the one in prison. This Dad might never return, and the Dad who got discharged from combat with post-traumatic stress disorder? That Dad hardly ever got the fire going, never made crumpets. He just sat in one corner of the bunker in the dark. I dig my shoe angrily into the ancient ashes. I didn't come here to remember this stuff. I came to imagine what might have happened that night – how my father ended up carrying Ashlee Parker to our house, how she ended up dead.

Dad's defence lawyers say the thunderstorm sent Dad into a flashback, that when he'd heard Ashlee Parker in the trees he must have thought she was an enemy soldier creeping up on him, that he was out of the bunker and strangling her in an instant. Dad's lawyers say this is consistent with his psychological profiling, and that his flashback could have been building for weeks. But Dad was charged with murder, and there are others, like Damon, who say Dad stalked Ashlee and that he wanted to kill her, that it wasn't an accident at all. Either way, the forensics show that Ashlee was too drunk to struggle.

But Joe and me? We've always said it was someone else. Someone the police haven't found yet. Someone who could still be hiding in these woods: hiding right now. Time's running out to find them, though. I shiver suddenly as I look out at the trees.

I'd thought Ashlee Parker was a good girl. It's hard to imagine her stumbling through these woods, even if she had been out celebrating her exam results with the boys earlier – it's hard to imagine her being so drunk that she'd stumble this far from her shortcut home. To get here from her shortcut, Ashlee would have had to turn right on to a small animal path. She would have had to follow it all the way here. Would she have kept walking that far?

My feet move slower as I get closer to the bunker. I'm thinking about Dad in flashbacks, how sometimes he'd go motionless and stare deep into nothing. How I'd see him patrolling the garden at midnight with a hunting knife, Mum trying to talk him calm again. How, one time, when I'd surprised Dad in the bunker, he'd had me in a headlock before I could even shout. There'd been more than a couple of nights when Mum had slept in with me, when Dad had started smashing things. Once we'd even called the police. Maybe there are cracks in Dad's brain now, different cracks to the ones Joe and I used to talk about in his game. Dad's cracks lead to scarier worlds than we could imagine.

With tingles on my spine, I bend to the bunker. Dad's lawyers said that killing was second nature to Dad, what his mind and muscles were trained for.

'It's like instinct to him,' they'd said.

But Dad could do other things by instinct; he could save things too. And there's a difference between having a flashback about killing and actually killing, there *has* to be. None of the papers have reported anything about the Dad who saved things, who freed caught animals from snares and nursed them afterwards, or the Dad who once told the world's best bedtime stories.

The lid is down over the bunker's entrance, the camouflage netting still fastened over it. Like this, I could almost believe Dad is waiting inside. I look across to where they say Ashlee died – a few metres away, between here and that small animal path. My skin goes shivery. It was raining on and off that night: hot, summer rain that could hide footprints and evidence, there was the thunderstorm. Someone could have dumped Ashlee here after she had already died, maybe all trace of that could have been washed away. I'd tried to tell the police.

'What about all the other ex-soldiers?' I'd said. 'It's not only Dad who's suffered, who has flashbacks, who has PTSD. This is an army town, it's full of people like this!'

There's one thing I can't believe – that Dad is only using his post-traumatic stress disorder as an excuse, as a way to cover up what he really did, as a way to cover up murder.

I start to lift the lid, my arms shaking.

On the day we'd found this bunker, Dad had knelt at this opening; he'd pulled me close so I could look too. I'd been amazed. Under the ground was an entire buried room, just like the earth had swallowed it. Dad had jumped down into its darkness, held his hand out for me to jump too.

'What if it falls in on us?' I'd said.

'It's solid.' Dad had pulled me towards him. 'Anyway, I'm taller than you so it'll fall on me first.'

I'd jumped into his arms; he'd been strong enough to catch me then. The bunker had smelt like an unused cellar, like things forgotten, like fear. Dad had walked around it, pushing against the walls and seeing how it was made. The roof was curved and ridged like ribs. It had felt like we were in the belly of a beast.

'There are secret bunkers like this all over the country,' he'd said. 'Just in case.'

'In case what?'

He'd looked at me as he'd thought. 'In case it all starts again: the invading, fighting. People always need somewhere quiet and safe.'

But this place was more than that, even then. Maybe if I go inside, I'll be able to make sense of who Dad was that night, what happened.

18

Damon

I go the long way to school, the really long way that makes a massive detour through Darkwood. I've got that twitchy thing going on in the corner of my eyes, making it hard to see straight. Headache too. Did I even sleep last night? How many nights has it been now of lying awake? How many weeks? Have I slept at all since Ashlee died? Sometimes it's hard to tell.

The car park is empty. I go straight over to Ashlee's tribute pile. More soft toys and flowers have been placed since I was last here, making my stupid rose look like nothing. I pick it up and dried petals fall over my hand. Keeping hold of it, I sift through some of the other flowers, see who's left them: I don't even know most of these people. I go back to the note I wrote: *You were beautiful, Ashlee. I miss you.* The words don't seem like much now. Maybe I should've said *I love you*, or something like that, but we never said these things to each other when she was alive, so . . .

I untie my note from the rotting rose, slide out one of the fresher flowers from the bunch my mum made me drop off for her and pin it to that instead. What I should leave here is my collar; Ashlee would've wanted it more than flowers or toys – to have beaten me for all time. There's a lump in my throat as I walk to the place where we were all drinking that night. How long had we stayed here, an hour? Not even. How much had I drunk before I'd got into the woods? How much dust had Ashlee given me? She'd sat on my lap and wiggled her bum around in just the right way. She'd known it would make me want her.

'Just got to catch me first,' she'd whispered. Her mouth had smelt like liquor, her skin like roses and salt.

I go through the gate to Darkwood's main path, walk along it for a few metres 'til I reach the smaller track that peels off left towards Ashlee's housing estate: her shortcut home. This is where I always left her after a Game, where she wouldn't ever let me walk her any further.

'My parents don't like me with boys,' she'd say. 'You're a secret.'

I don't think she ever told them about me, not properly.

'But I'm a prefect,' I'd said. 'So that means I'm responsible, yeah? You don't need to worry!'

She'd just laughed. 'You're still an army boy, Damo.'

And now Ashlee's parents hate me. But why wouldn't they? I took Ashlee to a car park beside the woods to drink. I'm the one responsible for not getting her home. They probably want me and the rest of the boys locked up too. But what they don't know is that it was Ashlee who'd wanted to do it all so bad in the first place, and they don't believe it was Ashlee who'd brought the drugs.

I was here that night – on this track – I'd kissed her goodbye. It isn't some other night I'm thinking of, it *can't* be! I lean my head against a tree trunk, try to remember what else we'd done that night. You'd think if we'd had sex, I'd at least remember it. She'd promised we'd do it on the first full moon after exam results, during a Game.

'It'll be more fun this way,' she'd said, 'dangerous!'

But sex was sex, wasn't it? Why did it have to be dangerous?

I kick at this tree trunk, kick 'til my shoe is scuffed. But it's no good. I'm not remembering any more just from hanging around here, and I'm already late for school.

19

Emily

I think I hear footsteps, running in this wood, closing in on me, but I wait and no one comes. When it's quiet again, I turn on my phone, the light shaking thin and bluish when I hold it into the bunker to see. I'm almost expecting a hand to reach out and grab my arm, pull me down. But the bunker is empty. It's like a snail shell that's been left behind. There's some stuff on the floor, though: branches and dead leaves, rubbish. Dad's chest of drawers is still in one corner, and his old paraffin lamp has fallen on its side. These are the only things the police have left here. Apart from the drawings.

Feet first and stomach to the ground, I lower myself in, slide down until I feel the floor. The light from my phone goes off, but I don't turn it back on yet. It's warmer inside. I touch my fingers to the slit that runs horizontally along one wall of the bunker, push out the earth and wet leaves that are clogging it. Shafts of light spill in from the forest floor.

'Funny window,' I'd said when I'd first seen it. I'd been measuring its height with three of my fingers stacked on top of each other, my eyes level with the ground outside.

Dad had smiled. 'It's not for light.'

If Joe were here now he'd take a photo of how the sunlight falls through this slit; he'd say it could be one of those cracks to another world. I look out of it again to see Darkwood from beetle height; see how the moss grows on just one side of the fallen branches and how it's green as emeralds. There's an earwig, centimetres from my eyes, dodging water that's dripping from branches far above. There are a million shades of orange, a million more of brown, hundreds of red and yellow and green. But if I were looking through this crack from the other side, peering into this bunker? It would be a different world I'd find then, a lonely room built for violence. A place Dad got sad.

I turn towards its pale concrete walls. I can't ignore Dad's drawings any longer, all these dank scrawls around me. I look at one near the roof – a wolf clamping its jaws around the neck of a deer. Below is another wolf with red eyes. Near that is a sketch of a gun. The police took photographs of all this. If Dad's case goes to a murder trial, the police might say these sketches are evidence of a killer's mindset.

I remember the other dark scrawls that appeared on the front of our house after Dad's murder charge went public: the words *Killer . . . Psycho . . . Child hunter . . .*

I force myself to notice that there are other animals on these walls too, not just wolves and deer, but foxes and squirrels and birds. There are wild boar with tusks like spears; dark, detailed insects; a snake. It reminds me of a game Dad and I used to play, ages ago, when I was a kid: he'd draw an animal and I'd say who it looked like. Or sometimes we'd do it the other way round: I'd say a person and he'd draw their animal equivalent. He was so good at getting the likeness just right. I keep walking around the bunker and looking at the drawings: in one corner is a noose dangling from a branch, in another there's a dark swirling pit, there's a skull.

He should have killed himself, not her — that's what people yelled outside the courtroom. Ashlee's mum had sobbed in her husband's arms. 'He murdered her. . . that monster should be burnt!' she'd shouted.

I want to scrub these pictures away, return this place to how it looked when Dad and I first found it. I wish we'd never found it at all. Maybe then, Dad wouldn't have ended up so sad and strange. Maybe all the bad things wouldn't have happened. I sweep the dead leaves and other stuff into one corner, near an old pile of firewood that's also been left. Everything about this place feels dying and abandoned; the air is rotten.

Once Dad would have made his hands like a step so I could reach the forest floor easier; now I scramble up the bunker wall, spider-like, until I'm through the hole and sprawled in the clearing. A moth comes up with me, clinging to my clothes. I hear light rain tip-tapping on leaves high above, though I can't feel it on my skin yet.

I close the bunker lid, listening to something rustling. The logical part of my mind knows that this rustling sound is just a blackbird digging in the leaf litter for insects; the stupid part thinks it's someone watching me. I scan the trees, remembering the footsteps I thought I'd heard earlier, remembering how Joe had followed me yesterday. Perhaps someone will step towards me, someone from the list.

Or maybe the noise could be Dad, moving through the bracken. This would be the first place he'd go, after all, if he were released; he'd choose here over our house. He'd walk into the clearing and tell me he was innocent, that he'd been set free from his prison and he'd walked all the way. I stare hard at the trees. There's a fluttery feeling inside me.

Just go home, I tell myself. *It's no one. Nothing!*

But my heart still hammers as I stare at the mottled brown leaves on the ground, as I squeeze through the hedge and get back on the path home. Then I go still, a bunch of questions in my brain in a rush. There are eyes — ahead of me — and they are staring back. They are huge and brown and unblinking. They're like Ashlee's.

But they can't be.

I look properly, and this time I see that these eyes don't belong to a human. A female deer, thin with youth, is in these trees with me. She's watching something. I follow her gaze, turning around on the path until I see another deer. A stag, only about a metre back. I let my breath go, slowly so as not to scare him. Dad would have said it was lucky, seeing a stag, he'd have said it was a sign of something going to change.

'These creatures are supernatural,' he'd said once. 'They lead people places, help them find their way through the woods.'

I plant my feet and stare back. The stag's eyes flick from mine to the doe in the trees, his nostrils widening as he picks up her scent. His ears are as big as coat pockets and his antlers as still and bare as winter branches. It's like he's grown from the trees, is part of them. Stags can attack humans during the rutting season; sometimes they're too blind with lust to control themselves. But I'm not scared of him. Right now, with the way he's standing so motionless, he reminds me a little of Damon from yesterday; I can almost imagine him lowering his head and pointing his antlers in the same way Damon pointed his fingers like a gun. I look at his wet nose, his endless fur. I want to touch it. Perhaps if you touch a stag in the woods your luck turns best of all? I'm stepping towards him without even meaning to, just wanting to be closer.

The stag moves in a heartbeat, springing out of the trees and on to the path. I see the ripples in his muscles, hear the snort of his breath, watch the thrust of his antlers as he sweeps his head from being tangled in the undergrowth. He leaps past me. The young female skitters away and he's after her, melting into the trees. Then the woods are quiet again, branches swaying back into place as if nothing had happened.

20

Damon

Emily Shepherd's not at school. I'm looking across the schoolyard to where I've seen her lately, hanging around with Joe Wilder. Today he's there, and that Mina girl is too, but Emily is nowhere. I almost go across and ask him where she is – almost – but I don't want to ask nothing of Joe Wilder. Other people are staring at me too. Do they all think I know something about why Emily's not here? I didn't tell anyone about the detention, only Mack, but she might've, and word travels fast in this place. Is everyone wondering what happened? Or am I just wired from no sleep, jittery from going back to Ashlee's shortcut track and not remembering nothing? There's this feeling that none of this is real, that soon it'll be a Sunday morning and I'll wake with Ashlee's thin, sparkly collar in my hand and all this just in my head . . . I'll meet Ashlee in the woods and kiss her so hard it hurts.

I feel a thump on my back.

'How'd it go, mate?'

Mack.

I turn to find him with his eyebrows raised, reeking of smokes. 'Hypocrite.' I make an exaggerated sniff.

'Yeah, well, you make me stressed.' He grins, half shrugs, looks across at Wilder too. 'So where is she anyway?'

'I don't know! She did her detention!'

Mack nods. 'Chill out.'

He looks behind him to where Ed and Charlie are slouched against the Common Room wall chatting to some of the girls in the year below. 'Why didn't you join us anyway?'

'Didn't feel like it.'

There's a weird silence between us, and I'm thinking that there's a whole heap of stuff I should tell Mack — about how Emily Shepherd caught me in Darkwood yesterday, how she wasn't scared, how the things she said about her dad kept me awake most the night. I should tell Mack about how I returned to Ashlee's shortcut track this morning too, and how I didn't remember nothing. But I stay silent instead and feel like the worst kind of friend.

'Don't worry about it, mate,' Mack says, guessing at what's bugging me. 'Joe Wilder would be panicked if something had happened to her, he'd be yelping.'

But what if this is what I do now, leave girls in the woods, leave girls who never come out? I get a shiver. I'm remembering Emily Shepherd's angry words as she pinned me: *what kind of boyfriend leaves his drunk girlfriend in the woods after dark?*

'Come on.' Mack starts leading me back to Ed and Charlie.

But flirting with girls is the last thing I want to do now, not when I've got this gnawing inside of me. Not when my head's too full with Ashlee. Too full with thinking about Emily Shepherd also, wondering where she is.

'I'm going to class,' I say.

'I'll come with.'

Again, I think it: Mack's a mate. He doesn't make a big deal of things, just gets what I need. But maybe what I really need is to come clean about all the stuff in my head. Perhaps then Mack'll just say I'm being a dick, tell me something about that night that'll make everything clear . . . he'll fill in the gaps.

But what if he can't?

Mack salutes the other two as we pass.

'You'll be late!' I call out, try to force a grin. 'I'll give you both a detention slip.'

'Whatever!' Ed flicks me the bird, and the girl he's been talking to giggles.

Mack and me carry on towards the science block. 'So, how'd it go, anyway?' he asks. 'Last night? Get what you needed?'

I'm thinking about how I left Emily Shepherd sprawled

on the bike trail, how I didn't look back . . . not once. How I'd been so angry.

'She was pretty determined,' I tell him. 'Pretty certain her dad's not a killer.'

'Then she's pretty stupid. He's pleading guilty.'

'To manslaughter.'

Mack snorts. 'Does it matter which?'

I look across. He's got rolling papers out, right here in the middle of school. 'It matters.'

Mack pauses, tobacco in his hands and a paper stuck to his bottom lip. 'Listen, mate, one way Shepherd did it and can't remember; the other way he meant to do it all along. But it's still the same fucking result, he's still the same fucking bastard!'

And then I get it – I work out why I've been feeling so sick and angry ever since Shepherd said that plea of manslaughter in court. It really *does* matter which way Shepherd did it; it means everything.

'It matters,' I say again, trying to work out how to phrase what's bothering me, '. . . because if Shepherd didn't plan to kill Ashlee – if his flashback story's right and it is manslaughter – then it means Ashlee got to his bunker by herself, didn't she? He didn't lure her there, or stalk her, or whatever. She walked there!'

Mack shrugs. 'So maybe his bunker is near her short-cut.' He starts rolling his tobacco, licks the paper shut. 'So maybe Ashlee stumbled a little way off it and he found her that way.'

I place my hand over Mack's lighter to stop him

flicking it on, check about me for teachers. 'You know we would have found that bunker if it was close to her short-cut track – that track's in Game Play.'

'So, then Shepherd's story can't be real – simple! He stalked her after all. He got her to that bunker.' He puts the rollie behind his left ear. 'The court won't accept his manslaughter plea anyway, you'll see. Guilty bastard's a murderer, straight up.'

'Yeah, course he is.' But I don't sound as confident as I did before yesterday and even I can hear that.

Emily's determined face won't get out of my head either: those piercing grey-blue eyes. She'd been so certain of her dad's innocence, so certain of how damaged he'd become after being in combat. She'd talked about her dad almost like how I talked about mine: as if something could've been done differently, as if a person's life had been wasted, as if she loved the fucker. I clench my fists.

'Emily Shepherd's a liar,' I say.

I'm not going to feel sorry for her. She's a wildcat backed into a corner, trying to make me believe what she wants. I won't let her make me doubt everything.

Mack's watching me. 'She said something, didn't she?'

'I don't believe anything she said!'

But again, my words don't sound confident. And this manslaughter plea is still bugging me. Because I know about flashbacks. I've seen films about that shit, and Mack and me once spent ages talking to an old war vet under the railway bridge in town about his. The stuff Emily Shepherd said about her dad – about him being scared and not remembering – that sounds about right. I'd heard about another soldier who'd gone on a shooting spree in a building site because he'd thought, in his flashback, that it looked like the compound he'd been protecting overseas. I pull Mack on.

'I've been thinking,' I say.

'That's dangerous.'

And even though what I'm going to say next will wipe the smile off his face, I can't keep it inside any longer.

'What if I didn't walk Ashlee back to her shortcut track that night?'

Sure enough, Mack's smile disappears. 'What are you talking about?'

My eyes dart away. I don't want to see his expression, not when he realises I've been lying to him – without meaning to, maybe, but lying all the same.

'I thought I remembered doing it,' I say. 'And when you were all going at me in your garage next morning and wanting answers, when I was stressing about it too, when none of us knew what had happened to Ashlee, I thought I was right. But what if I . . .'

Mack's eyes narrow.

So I do it – I finally say what's been going round in my brain. 'What if I never walked her there? What if I left her somewhere else in the woods? Somewhere else, near the bunker?'

'But you told us!'

'I know I did. But what if I'm remembering another time?'

'You're getting confused.' Mack is looking around, checking no one is listening. 'Course you would have walked her there, that's what you do – always.' His eyes are up close and there's an urging look in them. 'Course you would!'

But does Mack know how drunk I was that night? Does he know how my body went after Ashlee gave me more of her fairy dust? I pull Mack on again, fast: I need to spill while I got the nerve, and this isn't the place. I stop in a passageway at the side of the gym, press him against the wall.

'I mean . . . what if I passed out?' I say. 'That night, somewhere in the woods. Maybe it's why I don't remember nothing.'

'Don't be stupid.' Mack shakes his head, pulls the rollie from behind his ear again, lights it quicker than I can stop him. 'You got home. And Shepherd came after Ashlee as she was walking back to hers. You didn't pass out. This makes sense.'

I'm thinking about Emily's eyes, her small tight mouth . . . the way she kept repeating how her father was scared of everything. I focus on a line of graffiti on the wall. Nothing – actually – makes sense. Even now. I grab the rollie off Mack, stomp it into the ground.

'Maybe me and Ashlee had an argument?' I say. 'Maybe she walked off on me? It's possible.'

And it's another way Ashlee could've got to the bunker. There's that word I'd remembered next morning too – *useless*. Why'd she said it to me? Had she got mad?

134

Mack looks down at his crushed rollie and frowns. 'You never got angry at her. Don't think like that.'

But I did, that night I did. I think I did.

'Don't let that Shepherd girl get to you, Damo. Don't let her change what's true.'

But there's doubt in Mack's eyes as he looks at me. He tries to mask it by forcing a kind of grin, but I see it: there, then gone. It's doubt about me. I feel the heat in my neck spread. We said we were brothers, and brothers don't keep secrets: they don't lie. Mack knows this too. Mack knows I've let him down, let down all of them. But I've let Ashlee down most. I didn't make sure she got out of the woods; I got drunk and high instead. I left her alone and she found his bunker. What's true?

'It's my fault,' I say.

'No! You were just too drunk to remember.'

'Exactly.'

Mack holds my gaze. 'Just shut up.'

And now I know we're thinking the same thing: what exactly did I do that night? Why can't I remember?

I repeat what Emily Shepherd said yesterday. 'I was the last person to see her alive.'

'Apart from him!' Mack shakes me.

He glances out the passageway to where students are starting to go to class. 'Listen Damo, we covered for you. We told the cops that we were drinking in the car park and you walked her to that shortcut – I even said I saw you do it! The boys and me believed you when you told us.'

'I know.'

He looks at me seriously. 'If you didn't walk her there, Damo, then we've all lied: me, Charlie, Ed! If you tell the coppers this now, they'll charge us with something, we'll get a record, we'll go to jail . . .' He's starting to panic.

I try to squeeze my brain into making more sense: try to find a way out of this.

'OK, so that morning, in your garage . . .' I try. 'I was confused, wasn't thinking straight, I couldn't remember what'd happened . . . but it didn't make sense to tell the cops about the Game right then, even you said that. Anyway, right then I thought I did walk her back. It's only now that I . . .'

I think about the boys staring at me in Mack's garage, how their faces had relaxed a bit when I'd said I'd walked Ashlee to that track.

'What do you remember, Damo?' Mack thumps me against the bricks. 'Getting home? Saying goodbye to Ashlee? What?'

With the bricks hard against me on one side and Mack pressing from the other I feel squeezed, my lungs tight. Mack's looking at me desperate.

'OK!' I push him off me. 'I remember fooling about with Ashlee someplace in the woods, I think the Game had finished but . . . I dunno really . . . I remember she gave me loads of her fairy dust and then . . .' I shrug. 'Nothing.'

'Fooling about?'

The heat in my skin spreads. I look at graffiti on the

wall, remember what Ashlee had promised that night. Sex. She'd been holding out on me for weeks just to do it then. I'd give her my collar and she'd give me . . . well, she'd give me her.

I force myself to look Mack in the eyes. But he turns away. He's got it.

'You been doing that all this time?' He looks disgusted. 'While the rest of us have been playing like we're s'posed to?'

'We haven't been going that far. Not all the way. Just messing about, like.'

Mack's top lip curls. 'Thought we told each other everything.'

And now I'm worrying about something else. Because if the prosecution accept Shepherd's plea of manslaughter, maybe there'd be another investigation. Maybe then the police won't believe that Shepherd took Ashlee to his bunker. Maybe they'd want to interview us all again, find out more of what we were doing in the woods that night. And then? The police would know we've all lied.

'Should we just come clean now?' I say. 'Tell the cops what we were really doing, about the Game and everything?'

Mack snorts. 'You're the one who said you wanted to keep this secret in the first place, remember? You're the one who came up with the idea that we were just drinking in the car park and then you walked her back.'

'But that's what I thought . . . well, the walking her back part!'

'And now you're saying you can't remember if you passed out instead?' He gives me a dark look. 'If it was your fault she was at the bunker?'

'I'm saying I don't know!'

'Thought we trusted each other, Damo!' He slams the palm of his hand against the bricks. 'But all these secrets!'

The way he says this sounds like he's swearing, like he's accusing the whole world. He looks up the passageway. I guess we both must be late for class by now. I press the back of my head against the bricks.

'What else you been keeping hidden?' Mack hisses.

'Nothing!'

'No other little games?' Mack's eyes are interrogating.

I want Mack to keep thumping me against this wall 'til I'm proper hurt. I want to wake up from this. I listen to the sound of our breathing – quick and heavy.

'I can't remember.' I hate how my voice sounds so weak, so pathetic.

There's a pause. Then suddenly Mack's grabbing me in a rough sort of hug, then he's pushing me away just as fast. 'Don't do anything, Damo. Don't tell the other guys, OK? Don't go to the police.'

'But—'

'Not yet.' He holds my shoulders. 'You don't know anything so how can you? Besides, you didn't do anything bad that night, nothing you need to feel this fucking guilty about – I know you didn't.'

I wipe my hands across my eyes and face. Suddenly I don't know anything at all.

'We'll sort this, Damo. Didn't we sort bad stuff after your old man died?'

'This is different.'

Mack pulls me off the bricks. 'Get your head together, Damo,' he says. 'That's all you need to do right now. Then you'll remember what that bastard's done.'

21

Emily

It's three days since the court hearing – Thursday now – two days since Kirsty pushed me. I still don't want to go to school. This time I use the migraine excuse and Mum believes it: Dad used to get them and I know how to act the part. My head feels fuzzy anyway and my body aches. Mum fusses around me for ages. I almost think she's going to use my excuse as her excuse for staying home from work too, but eventually I hear the front door click shut behind her. I lie very still for a long time, even try to sleep. But this anxious feeling gets worse – this horrible doubt. So I read Dad's discharge notes again, all that stuff about him shooting that civilian girl and how it affected him. But I still don't understand how Dad's manslaughter plea came from this. Just because Dad shot a girl by accident while he was a soldier, it doesn't mean he'd strangle Ashlee Parker, even in a flashback. I hate how people just assume these two things go together.

I go downstairs, sit on the couch. After staring a while at the empty space the photos have left on the mantelpiece, I go through the pile of Dad's mail. Mum's hardly opened any of it. It's mostly bills, letters from the police and Dad's solicitors. There are several letters about his overdue car tax too, one of them threatens to tow the car to the wreckers if he doesn't pay soon. I put that letter aside so Mum will see it. Already I'm remembering how Dad used to drive that car when we went bird watching, or walking in the mountains, how it carried the three of us each time we moved to another of Dad's army postings . . . how it drove us here. Mum could be driving that car now, using it to visit Dad in custody. Instead, it's just another part of Dad that is being ignored, something else I can't do anything about. But its keys are still hanging with the rest of our keys in the hall. So that's something, isn't it?

There are no other houses at the end of our lane where Dad left his old blue Fiesta, so no one is watching me. I step up to the driver's window, wipe grime away to look in – there's a crisp packet on the passenger seat, bleached white from the sun. The driver's door moans as I pull it open. It smells strange in here: a mixture of mustiness, Davidoff aftershave, and salt and vinegar crisps. Odd how these smells can still be here when Dad's gone. I get in and put the key in the ignition. Maybe I can drive this car to Dad's prison. Maybe, without Mum with me, Dad might remember more from that night, might talk. Maybe I could hide this car afterwards too, somewhere the council couldn't take it away.

I turn the key. Suddenly I feel different — like I'm doing something. *Finally.* But nothing happens. I try again — turning the key harder — same thing. I even pump my foot against the accelerator. It's no good. Battery's dead. I sigh out the breath I've been holding, thump the steering wheel. It was stupid even trying this. I probably wouldn't have been able to drive it anyway — Dad never did give me those driving lessons he'd promised. I would have crashed before I even got to the motorway. So this car will end up crushed and useless in a junkyard after all.

I settle against the headrest; shut my eyes. A strange calm seeps into me. The council will tow more than a few sheets of metal when they take this car, our memories will be towed too. Maybe that's OK. Maybe everything will be like this soon: the photos taken down, the car disappeared . . . it won't be long before Mum stops mentioning Dad altogether. Then there'll just be me left to remember him like he was, maybe the only person who ever will.

I rest my forehead against the steering wheel. I've only seen Dad once in prison. That was when the liaison officer took us, and Mum and I had sat on the other side of a plastic table and watched Dad shake his head over and over. I'd thought that was a good sign — like he'd been trying to tell us he wasn't guilty — but when Mum had asked him what he was thinking about, he'd stopped the shaking and had looked at us with fierce eyes. He didn't speak at all, the whole time we were there. That was when I realised Dad was ill – seriously ill – when I realised I couldn't ever fix him by myself.

'He's in the best place,' Mum had said afterwards. 'He's such a shell of a man.'

Now I'm crying, properly crying, for the first time in ages. Tears are smearing over my cheeks and on to the steering wheel. I'm wrapping my arms around it and holding it tight, as if it's someone hugging back. Maybe Mum is right and the Dad I remember is just a fantasy. Thinking like this makes me cry harder. Right now I want the council to tow me away too. Just how sick has my dad become? Sick enough that he's sitting behind bars admitting to a killing he doesn't remember? Sick enough that he did it?

I stay like this for a long time. When I can move again, I have a plan. I'll search through the car, take anything out of it I want to keep, then I'll let it go: this car, these feelings about Dad . . . I'll try to. Maybe it will be easier if I can forget how life with the Dad from before used to be. Maybe I'll understand. I try the glove box. It's rammed with CDs, Beatles ones mostly: Dad's favourite. I pull out a rusty Swiss army knife, flipping open various parts of it, pressing my thumb against its biggest blade. If I kept pressing, my skin would bleed. I almost want it to. Almost want that kind of pain.

There's some sort of car logbook too. It's uncomfortable looking at Dad's tight, neat handwriting inside it; it reminds me of the notes he used to stick in my school lunchbox whenever he was home on leave: *Meet you after school and we'll go to the woods. Be clever today. Love, Dad.* I don't understand how *that* Dad could twist out of shape so much, become like a plastic carton morphed by the sun.

I'm about to put the logbook away when I see what's at the back of it. There are sketches in the corners of the pages, small and delicate, a bit like the ones in the letters Dad sent back from tour. These are different sorts of drawings to the dark scrawls I saw yesterday in the bunker. Here I see larks circling up from grasses, an oak leaf, there's a detailed drawing of a fox with big, curious eyes. There's something about the way that fox is looking out from the page that makes me think of Joe. Seeing this reminds me of that drawing game Dad and me played once, so long ago – strange to think of that again after yesterday. And now I'm remembering how Dad once drew Mum as a cat with green eyes and a small, neat mouth; how he'd always draw me as a grey squirrel – messy fur, hiding in trees. I'd always guess the person he was trying to depict in the animal. It hurts to think about it all again.

I close the book and try to shut these thoughts away too. But a loose sheet of paper falls out, and of course I look at it. It's another sketch, but this one isn't like the others. At first I think the sketch is just a deer, mid-leap in a forest: a deer being chased by a wolf. But when I look more closely, I know there is something different about it, something familiar. I study the deer's face. There's some-one I almost recognise in it — an expression, maybe — it's like Dad's game again, trying to pick it. I look at this deer's features carefully, trace its ears with my fingertips. With a gasp, I realise who I'm seeing. I go cold, make sure.

This deer looks like Ashlee Parker. It has the same huge brown eyes, the delicate ears and high cheekbones, the confident, excited expression. I see it all. This creature is beautiful too, like something from one of Dad's bedtime stories. It's half girl, half deer. Ashlee.

I wrench my eyes to the creature that's chasing it: that wolf. It looks savage, like the wolves on the bunker walls do. But as I look at it more carefully, I see that it looks excited too. There are other wolf shadows in the trees behind it. What does it all mean?

There's a thudding feeling in my ears. Dad hasn't been in this car since long before Ashlee's death. The police took him straight from our house that night. So when did he draw this? Why? I go back to the deer's face, but no matter how hard I look at it I can't stop seeing Ashlee in it now.

The wolf isn't as human-looking as the deer; I can't see anyone in its expression. But all the newspaper headlines of the past eight weeks are rushing back at me, all the stuff people have yelled: *He watched her! He's sick! He's a murderer! Woodland Stalker! Monster!*

I try to keep myself calm. But I'm breathing quicker. And I'm remembering once when Mum said Dad was like a wolf, back when he went quiet and strange after being discharged, back when she'd got angry at him and said he preferred being in the woods alone to anything else.

'You're a lone wolf,' she'd said. 'You're turning wild!'

But Dad doesn't look like the wolf in this picture. Does he?

I open the door and hang my head outside. I breathe in the cold air, stare at the gutter. How would the police interpret this picture? Would they see it as evidence? Evidence of everything they've accused Dad of? Evidence that he watched and wanted Ashlee Parker? That he's a murderer as charged?

I'm grasping at it, crumpling it, but something stops me before I tear it up. I shove it deep into my coat pocket instead. This is only evidence if I show it to someone. And it might not even be evidence at all.

Even so, there's a weight pressing on my shoulders, making me slow and hunched as I walk to our house. Maybe I'm wrong. Maybe this sketch has nothing to do with the game Dad and I used to play. Maybe Dad has just drawn a deer, some woods, a wolf. Maybe someone else wouldn't see Ashlee Parker in this deer's face. Maybe I'm just panicking.

I want to be wrong.

But I feel different and heavy and strange as I crawl into bed. It's like I'm falling, tumbling into a deep, dark pit, getting closer to something. Something I don't want to see.

22

Damon

She's still not at school, that's two days now. I grab Joe Wilder's arm as he slinks past me in a corridor, just go ahead and ask him.

'What do you want her for?' he says.

I study his face to see what he thinks of me now: it might be the first time we've talked since I dropped him from the cross-country team. First time I've stood this close to him since that day in the woods. He still doesn't meet my eyes.

'Just checking she's OK, that's all,' I say. 'Thought you'd know.'

'Why do you even care?'

He turns away, and I'm suddenly thinking about that

day in the woods all over again, when I'd wanted to hit him, when he'd run. What would happen if one of us told the police about that day? Which one of us would the cops think of as a weirdo then?

'You been watching anything in the woods lately?' I ask him. 'Following anyone?'

He pinks up. 'Get lost.'

'Hey, I haven't finished talking to you!'

But he doesn't care. Already he's hurrying towards the canteen, joining up with that Mina girl again. I'm glad I kicked him off the team. He wouldn't make it this year anyway, wouldn't take it serious enough: he'd spend too long with his head behind a lens concentrating on things he shouldn't. Perhaps I should've punched some sense into him while I had the chance.

'Wilder!' I call out. 'Wait!'

But he's proper ignoring me now, hurrying up to his friend.

I go in late to Biology, don't apologise. Charlie shuffles over from where he's saved me a seat. I'm buzzing after talking with Wilder, angry. Maybe I could've got some answers off him. Wilder knows Darkwood. He knows a lot.

'What's up?' Charlie says, noticing.

I don't know whether I should tell him all that stuff I said to Mack yesterday, or whether I should keep quiet 'til I've figured things out. As I turn to him, Ms Mitani comes over to our bench.

'Charlie!' she warns. 'No talking!'

She ignores me, though, teachers give me an easy time these days. I look out the window, don't even pretend to concentrate on the book open in front of me. Once I would have cared about stuff like this. Now, learning about photosynthesis seems a bit bollocks. When Ashlee used to sit next to me in this class she'd draw hearts on my arm, press her thigh against mine and whisper in my ear. She'd always want to go further with whatever experiment we were doing: always wanted to know what would happen next, wanted to test the theories a little more. If she wasn't so clever we'd never have got away with it. I think I learnt more in biology from the stuff she did by accident than the stuff we were meant to be doing. There is still one of her long, blonde hairs caught in my textbook: I haven't opened up Chapter Five because of it, don't want to lose it. I clench my fingers into my palms. These thoughts aren't helping anything.

So I think about Emily Shepherd instead. What's she doing away from school? Is anyone else even bothered that she's not here? When I missed school for a week, not long after everything happened, the school was ringing just 'bout every day, and a counsellor and a doctor came round to check on me. Maybe killers' daughters don't get the same treatment.

Ms Mitani is handing out what looks like weeds; she drops a few scalpels and a pile of toothpicks on each bench too. As she strolls around the lab, she's describing a plant's sex organs, explaining how to open ovaries. She says the word pistil really slowly and someone sniggers.

She's gone mad if she thinks our class can have any sort of serious lesson on this. If Ashlee were here, she'd be leaning over and repeating pistil really low in my ear, her fingers digging under my shirt at the base of my spine and pressing at where my tatt is.

'You do it,' I say to Charlie, pushing across the plant.

He bypasses the toothpicks, cuts straight through the middle of our stem with a pair of scissors. Yellowish pus spews out. When Ms Mitani is at the other end of the lab I lean over to him. 'You ever found Shepherd's bunker? You ever seen it when we were playing the Game?'

He shakes his head, frowns. Perhaps he's wondering why I'm asking this now, here.

'It's got to be somewhere in the southern section,' he says.

But that's as much as anyone knows. That's where the police were looking the week after Ashlee died, the section where the woods were closed off. I watch Charlie scrape slimy stuff from the plant to the bench.

'It's near Game Play,' I say. 'Has to be. Maybe it's even in Game Play.'

Maybe it's near Ashlee's shortcut home too.

Like the missing collar, the location of Shepherd's bunker is bugging me. If I could work out where it is – if I knew how close it is to Ashlee's shortcut track – something might make sense. Maybe I could work out how Shepherd could've watched her – how she got to his bunker – maybe something about him would make sense too.

'It's weird we never came across it,' I say again. 'Weird we never saw Shepherd in the woods either . . . I mean, if he was meant to be watching Ashlee all that time.'

Charlie gives me a look like I'm an idiot. 'It's a bunker, that's why. And Shepherd was a soldier. We *wouldn't* see him, would we, *wouldn't* find it.'

I look out the window. Just because Charlie's from an army family he thinks he knows everything. But my old man was a corporal, higher up than Charlie's dad, and decorated; Charlie's dad hasn't even got an active service role. And just because my old man's dead . . . I'm still an army kid. I know about bunkers.

'Why'd you want to find it anyway?' Charlie says.

Now he's looking at me like I'm some sort of sicko, like he's thinking that if it was his girlfriend who had died there he wouldn't want to go and see it. But what if that bunker is where Ashlee's collar is? What if this is why I can't find it? What if I didn't take it from Ashlee's neck that night at all, and Shepherd did? What if he kept it as a souvenir? Because they say that, don't they, about murderers . . . that they take souvenirs of who they kill? The police might not have picked it up either; they wouldn't have known it was important. Finding Ashlee's collar near that bunker would be proof Shepherd did everything.

I push the plant guts about in front of me. Then I pull my phone out of my pocket, don't even care that Ms Mitani might notice. I click on to the internet and go to one of the pages I started looking at last night when I couldn't sleep. It's about memory, all the different ways you can lose it. *Alcohol-induced blackouts don't stop the memories entirely* — it says — *rather your ability to access them.*

Is this what I have, an *alcohol-induced blackout*? And does this mean that I can still get the memories back somehow? *Access* them? Does it work the same for fairy dust-induced blackouts too?

I scroll down the page on my phone. I read comments from people who've managed to get their memories back after they've been drunk or drugged. There's a section that gives tips on how: *Talk to someone . . . write down everything you can remember, revisit where the memory took place . . . relive what you were doing at the last point you remember . . .*

When Charlie looks over I shove the phone back in my pocket. But I've decided — I've spent long enough sitting around waiting for these memories to come back by themselves, I need to force them. I need to find answers for the questions Emily Shepherd was asking me. I need to be certain.

'We should play the Game again,' I say.

Charlie stares. I'm thinking that he's going to say no — that playing the Game again would be the last thing he'd want to do now.

'It'll be different without Ashlee,' he says slowly. 'You really want to?'

I nod. Charlie *has* to agree, they all do. If that article is right, playing the Game again might be the only way to remember where I last saw Ashlee in Darkwood, what happened to her collar, how I got home.

'Maybe it's time to start training again,' I say, remembering Mack's words about this from the Leap. I turn my head to the window. I actually don't give a shit about training to join the army no more; I'm not sure I even give a shit about pretending to. 'Or maybe we just play it to remember Ashlee.'

Charlie thinks about this. 'Kind of like our own private funeral, you mean? Like a *let go*?'

'Yeah, kind of.'

Charlie nods. 'Letting go is good.'

I watch him swallow. I see stubble and shaving cuts on his neck. I try to remember when I'd seen Ashlee's collar there too. He hadn't won it very often, probably the least out of all of us boys.

When I ask him why, he shrugs. 'It's not like I held back or anything. I played hard like she wanted.' He looks down at the desk.

I suddenly feel jealous that he'd played with her at all. That he'd played hard. Fought her.

'Most times I couldn't ever find her,' he says. 'She was always after you.'

I turn to watch a rugby match get going on the playing fields outside, see the teams bash against each other in the scrum. I'm waiting for Charlie to ask me about Ashlee's collar – because I'm thinking it too, ain't I? – that maybe we should bury that collar in the woods, in the place we always start the Game, that this would be a proper let go.

If I had it to bury, that is.

I remember when Ashlee came into the pet shop with me to get it. She'd chosen the collar that was pink and sparkly with fake diamond things on it and fluffy padding inside.

'It'll be too easy to see you with that on,' I'd said. 'You'll get caught straight up.'

She'd wanted it anyway; she was stubborn like that. She'd chosen a heart-shaped dog tag to get her initials engraved on to. I'd paid.

'Don't go all scaredy-cat on us,' I'd said. 'The boys play rough.'

I'd been grinning, half-joking. None of the boys would play rough with her; they wouldn't play proper rough. She'd get caught whatever collar she had on. But she was real serious about wanting to join, ever since the first time I'd accidentally blabbed about the Game to her. Eventually she'd worn me down to play, and eventually I'd bought her the collar.

'I can handle it,' she'd said. 'I'm as tough as you — it'll be fun!'

She'd said that, since she wanted to join the army like we did, it was only fair that she had a chance to play too.

So where did her collar go?

Charlie's prodding a scalpel in my arm. 'Damo?' he's saying. 'You OK?'

I rest my head on the lab bench. 'Peachy. Don't I look it?'

He laughs and goes back to the plant. I hear him snipping the petals off. This bench smells like dead things and formaldehyde, it's hard against my cheekbone; I'm so desperate for sleep that I try shutting my eyes. Maybe if I can sleep, I'll dream, and if I dream I'll remember. And I almost do it, almost slip. My head sinks down, heavy. And there, for a moment, is something: Darkwood; running; chasing Ashlee through the forest; her kissing me hard and saying *do it . . . do it . . .*

Useless . . .

But already I'm out of the dream before it's even started. I'm coming back to class, hearing the voices and laughter around me. Maybe they're talking about me — *look at that poor fucker that everyone dies on . . . look how he's not coping at all.*

I open my eyes. There are broken bits of plant all over the lab, people laughing as they chuck pieces at each other when Ms Mitani's not looking. I see the ripped petals on our bench, the spewed out seeds . . . the destruction.

I've realised something, though — that internet article is right. The more I force my mind on to Ashlee and that night, the more I do remember. It's a start.

'Tomorrow night,' I say to Charlie, sitting up from the bench. 'There's a full moon then, near enough. Tomorrow we'll play.'

He nods. 'Sure, mate. If you like. One more Game to remember Ashlee then.'

23

Emily

I don't leave my bed. I sink to somewhere deeper than sleep. Mum comes in a couple of times offering food and cups of tea, smelling of booze. I don't tell her about the sketch I found in Dad's car – I can't. I don't tell her anything about what I've done today. Though it's as if she guesses something.

She smoothes my hair back from my forehead and whispers, 'It's fine to admit things – to let go. No one's going to judge you for it.'

She thinks I've finally accepted that Dad's a killer, that his manslaughter plea is right. Maybe she thinks it was the argument we had two days ago, bringing it all out. But I can't accept anything, not out loud anyway, not yet. I can only sink.

Manslaughter?

Murder?

Just thinking about saying these words out loud and my throat closes over.

When Mum leaves I untack the photographs from my wall, snap them shut in my bedside drawer. Now I understand why the ones downstairs are gone too. They're reminders of how much things have changed, reminders that life now is spoiled and strange. And it's easier anyway, without Dad's smiling face beside me.

When Joe comes, he brings homework. 'People have been asking about you.'

I don't believe him; the only text message I've had was from Mina and that was just asking how the detention went. Joe's only come to see me because he thinks he should, because he lives down the road and can't ignore me. Once my other friends wouldn't have left me alone if I'd missed school for two days; Kirsty would have been round by now bringing gossip and chocolate.

Now Joe sits awkwardly in my desk chair. My coat is draped over the back of it. If Joe dug his hand inside its pocket, he'd find what Dad drew. Maybe he'd be able to tell me that it doesn't mean anything – that Dad didn't sketch Ashlee Parker at all, that he only sketched a deer, but I can't open my mouth to tell him to look, can't take the risk.

After a while he digs inside his own pocket, pulls out the crumpled list of possible suspects we'd made.

He still has that, then.

'Do you want to go through it again?' he asks. 'Try and work out scenarios? Better than just lying here?'

What's the point, though? The police aren't going to change their opinion because of our ideas, we know that already. And then I almost do it, almost tell him about the sketch. I take a breath to. But it's too big, too terrible. If I tell anyone about it, even Joe, everything will change. There'll be no turning back then. So I turn and face the wall, keep quiet until he leaves.

I sleep.

And sleep.

And sleep.

When Mum comes in next she tells me, 'You've been asleep for over sixteen hours, Emily. It's Friday morning!'

She goes to the window, opens it. A rough wind blows in, rattles things on my desk. I see a grey sky that's the same colour as the walls in Dad's prison visiting room. It feels like only a second since I shut my eyes when Joe was here, not sixteen hours. Time is moving strangely. It's more than four days since we'd listened to Dad enter his plea for manslaughter, isn't it? It has to be more than one week before the prosecution decide if Dad is guilty of manslaughter.

Mum picks her way unsteadily over my piles of untouched schoolwork, washing, junk . . . the room feels very small, crowded with feelings and things unsaid. She doesn't even ask if I want to go to school, she just places a cup of tea on my bedside table and glances out of the window at Darkwood. It's already almost ten so I guess this means Mum isn't going to work today either. For one crazy moment I want her to crawl into bed with me like she used to, wrap her arms around. Like that, we could both sleep . . . hibernate like dormice until winter's over.

'I've been thinking,' Mum says eventually, with a tone that almost sounds like an apology. 'All this isn't really your dad's fault, not entirely – you should know that. Maybe I shouldn't have sounded so firm the other night. Your dad saw things in combat he could never talk about, things that twisted his mind.'

Dad's sketch is less than a metre from where Mum stands. If I showed her, would she still believe that Dad killed Ashlee by accident? Would she still believe it happened because Dad was suffering from PTSD? Or would she look at that sketch and see things differently – Ashlee as a deer. Dad watching her. Would she see it as evidence of murder?

And maybe, if she did, she'd hit the booze even harder – maybe it would be enough to send her right over the edge. Because imagining someone you love is screwed up is one thing; thinking that he meant to do something terrible is different. Really different.

She draws her mug of tea closer. 'They should have been checking he was taking his pills,' she murmurs. 'There should have been more help. Someone else should have noticed the way he was going.'

She looks at me with eyes so big and questioning I have

to nod. I've heard her say things like this before: she feels guilty about who Dad's become, she thinks it's her fault. I prop myself up against the pillows so I can see the woods too.

Mum tries to smile. 'Feeling any better? Your headache? Do you want to eat?'

I shake my head. I see that it's a dark sort of autumn morning, the hunkering down kind, with tree branches bending from the wind and leaves splintering away and spinning like tops. I watch them and think of Dad splintering away from us too, of everything getting further to reach and claw back. I've read cases on the internet where prisoners have got as few as five or six years for being convicted of manslaughter. I know, also, that being convicted of murder is a sentence for life. If I tear up Dad's sketch no one else will ever know about it, it can't be evidence for anything. And maybe, if Dad got convicted of manslaughter, he'd be back with us in no time.

But all this still gnaws at me. Because, if this sketch does mean that Dad was watching Ashlee before that night, can I hide it? If I do, what does this make me?

I feel as bare and as stripped as the trees in front of us, as if I'm losing everything that once made me who I am. I watch the wind push a tree so far backwards it's as if its trunk should snap. Another tree curves forward into a tight fist. The whole of Darkwood is churning, mixing up like a brew. All these leaves spinning away.

'Will you ever go in there again?' I say.

The question surprises both of us. Suddenly I have a

memory of Mum in the woods, so clearly, showing me the tiny snow-white mushrooms that grow near the caves. She'd said they were fairies' umbrellas, something to stop their wings from getting wet. Once, Mum loved these woods as much as me. Today she walks over and snaps the window shut. She sits on the end of my bed with a serious face.

'We need to move away,' she says. 'From Darkwood and all of this. Just as soon as the conviction's over and done with — get away from all those trees.'

I think of autumn leaves the colour of fire, the different kinds of mushroom there'd be right now, all the creatures getting ready to hibernate: all the things we wouldn't see if we left.

'We can become a new kind of family,' she says. 'Just us.'

I stare through the glass so hard my eyes ache. *Shellshock*, they used to call the thing Dad caught from combat . . . but right now, I think I've got it too; I think Mum and I both have. *Shellshock* from what happened that night, from what everyone says Dad is.

'I was thinking we could go up north,' she's saying. 'Maybe live with Granny and Grandpa for a while? Just until things calm down.'

She's suggested this before. When the brick came through our front window, a few days after Dad's arrest, Mum even talked about changing our names.

'We could be Hughes? Go back to my maiden name?' she'd said.

But if we move up north to become Hughes with Granny and Grandpa, what does this mean? It's easier for Mum; she becomes a daughter again with two parents to look after her. But me? I become someone I've never been: a one-parent child, someone with a buried past that can never be talked about. I lose my name and everything that currently makes me *me*: Darkwood, Dad, my friends. Unlike Mum, who can get another name and another husband, I can never forget what it means to be Dad's daughter. He's inside me. Like the woods are.

'I can't,' I say. And Mum looks like I've slapped her.

'It'll be good,' she tries to reason. 'Something new . . . a sort of . . . chance.'

She's half-hearted now, though. She'd probably love to move us into some sparkling new flat in a gated housing estate, somewhere it's colder and wetter and where we'd never want to go outside. But leaving Darkwood is like pulling out a part of me. It's like removing a lung. Having Dad gone is like that too. Thinking that Dad might have – actually – done this thing, thinking that he even *meant* to do it, is like having my heart strained through my ribs.

'It's not going to get any easier after your father's conviction,' Mum says. 'If he's convicted of manslaughter, everyone in town will feel sorry for us, or think we're strange. If it's murder, they'll hate us even more.'

I can tell by the way she's glancing at my door that she wants to be back downstairs, away from me and nearer her booze, closer to something that gives her the answers she wants. She tucks me in, her freezing fingertips against my cheek for a moment.

'Rest now, Em. Just sleep a while. Things'll be easier then.'

Her voice is like a tiny animal, and it claws at me. And even though there are still a hundred questions and worries in my mind, somehow I still shut my eyes. Somehow I sink down again into that pit, into that quiet, dark place where it feels like things will never be easier, no matter what Mum says.

24

Damon

I'm getting that buzzy feeling as soon as I'm travelling down the high street. The pubs are busy – it is Friday night after all. I take a wide berth of The City Arms, where Mack's dad drinks. If he catches sight of me, I know how it'll be: he'll place a sweaty arm round my shoulders, sneak me past the bouncers, and put a piss-warm ale in front of me and say it's for my dad. Or maybe he'd place two beers in front of me tonight and say one's for Ashlee. That's the last way I want to remember her, by drinking and only remembering the good times.

I need to remember that night.

I move quick, weaving through a crowd of swaying army boys out on the pull. Their eyes land on the combat shirt I'm wearing under my duffle coat — *Dad's shirt.*

'Hey, fighter boy,' one of them says. 'When you going to join us on duty?'

'Nice shirt!' I hear from someone else.

I flip the bird, glare at them. 'Piss off!'

I don't care if they get lairy; I can handle myself. I need to wear this shirt now, need to do as many things as possible the same as that night. That's what the article said. I'm not stopping to explain nothing.

I cross the street, push through a few students dressed up for Halloween already. A blonde girl with a big pretty mouth reaches out to touch my arm, then giggles. It would be easy to stop and let her touch me more, she's already moving closer and she looks a bit like Ashlee. Maybe being with a girl like her could help me remember?

'No,' I say. 'You're drunk.'

She pouts and tries to look sexy, but just stumbles on her heels. Already I see her girlfriends closing down on me, glaring like I've done something wrong. I get out of there.

Tonight's about Ashlee. Only Ashlee. It's about getting my head straight and working out what happened. Wearing this shirt is just the start. I jog, and immediately feel better. Darkwood always was our own kind of Friday night pub, my own kind of addiction. I have to slow as I hit the main drag of bars, though. Something's stabbing at me, some-where behind my ribs, and it's not because I'm short of breath. It's because I shouldn't be excited about playing the Game again. It's because if Ashlee had never played our Game, she'd still be alive. This ache hurts so much I have to stop in a shop doorway. I focus on the Halloween stuff hanging in the windows just to think of something else. It doesn't help. Halloween's not something easy to think about, either. I can still see Ashlee's excited face when she'd said we should play the Game on Halloween.

'We'll dress up,' she'd said. 'There'll be loads of freaky people in the woods so it'll be better . . . risky . . .'

I breathe in deep. Halloween's tomorrow.

I see my face reflected back at me in the glass, my eyes empty-looking. I glare. In the window my cheekbones stand out, and there's stubble on my chin. Only it doesn't make me look hard, like I thought it would. I look like someone pretending. Ashlee would've laughed. She'd laugh at how much of a pussy I'm being right now too. She'd be teasing me, saying she was going to catch me tonight, saying she'd take my collar.

'Gonna get you,' she'd say.

She never could get me, though, not really; she wasn't strong enough. I'd go along with her fighting me so I could start kissing her quicker, pretend she hurt me more than she did.

But she's got me now. By being gone, she's really proper got me. If this was her Game Plan, it was a good one. I touch my collar in my pocket, think about touching hers instead . . . unbuckling it, not wanting to do it too soon or too quick . . . not wanting it to be all over. I lean forward 'til I feel the cold glass on my forehead. I try to remember what it was like to be on top of her, *inside*. The police never asked if we'd had sex that night and they check for things like that . . . don't they? And, much as I want to, I can't remember it. Is that why I'd been angry? Because I'd wanted to do it and she didn't? Or was I too drunk and she got mad? Did we not, actually, do it at all? I want to press my head so hard into this window that its glass smashes and cuts me, that alarms go off.

There's an old couple gawping at me – probably thinking I'm another teenage alcoholic with too much cider in my belly, about to be sick and slump in it in this doorway. Life would be easier if that was all I was. I stumble past them, playing up to it, knowing Ashlee would've laughed at this . . . wondering if maybe she is, somewhere. Then I keep going for the woods.

I slink straight through the empty car park and on to the main path in Darkwood, don't even look at Ashlee's tribute pile. I focus on remembering how we'd walked into the woods that night. We'd been laughing and joking, high already. It's a full moon again tonight, like how it always is when we play. Even so, I'm still stumbling on the rough ground. An arm shoots out and grabs me when I'm nearly at the clearing where we start.

'Damo?'

'Jesus, man!'

My heart's hammering like a frickin' machine gun as Mack pushes me against a tree and holds his face close. He's checking my expression. 'Are you sure you want to do this, Damo?'

'I'll be fine.'

He digs about in his inside coat pocket, takes out a small bottle of the hard stuff, the stuff that burns your throat as you swallow . . . the stuff Ashlee liked.

'I don't even know why you suggested this right now, Damo. It's too soon. Least wait until after the trial. There might still be coppers in here!'

'They left ages ago.'

Though I'm not sure about this.

Mack holds the bottle out to me, but even the smell makes me feel ill. I think of my vomit in the toilet in Mack's garage that morning after. But I take a swig anyway, big as I can without gagging, because that night I was drunk, crazy drunk. And I want to remember everything.

Mack keeps his face close, checking me.

'I need to do this,' I say. 'It's important. One last time. Just to . . . just to settle things.'

And, for whatever reason, Mack backs off. He runs a hand across his neck. 'You know, you and I could just play, without the others. Like we used to?'

This option is tempting — it's easier. But I want everything to be as close to how it was that night, want to give myself the best chance like that internet page said.

'Don't go easy on me,' I say.

'The Game as it used to be, eh?' Mack nods. 'Maybe that's what we all need.'

He tries to smile. I realise then that Mack has been different these last few weeks too — quieter and tenser, doesn't talk about the army so much, or about Ashlee, or even about getting away from this town – all that stuff he used to say constantly. Maybe this Game tonight will snap him out of that, snap us all out.

Mack cuffs his hand round the back of my neck, pulls me on. Right now, with just the two of us here, it feels like how things used to be, when Mack and me first played, before the other two joined, before Ashlee: when one of us had a twenty-second start and the other one chased. When we'd fight 'til someone called surrender, punching hard, trying to hold out longest. After my old man died, fighting and running with Mack was the only thing that ever made me feel any better. Until we started the Game anyway. Until Ashlee. Fighting with Mack was about getting rid of something inside, that hard, angry ball that sat deep, bringing it out. It was like our own private Fight Club in the woods.

'It'll be like this on the front line,' Mack had said, 'withstanding pain, just reacting . . . surviving. It's practice!'

Maybe I need to feel like that again. Maybe a good fight would knock some sense into me. Because when you feel pain – actual physical, hurting pain – you stop focusing on the inside stuff so much.

We walk the last few metres together to the Game clearing. Charlie and Ed are already there, leaning either side of a pine tree. When we get close, Ed pushes himself off and starts bouncing on his toes. Mack doesn't get the hard stuff out for them and I'm glad; seems like they've had a couple of cans already. But Ed takes out a little packet of white powder, exactly like the one I remember Ashlee having that night: fairy dust. How'd he get that? He holds it out like an invitation, and I'm thinking about it and I'm even wondering if I should – whether that'd help me remember – but Mack grabs it fast and stomps it into the mud.

'We're not doing that shit any more,' he says firm. 'Not in this Game. Not when we're meant to be training for the fucking army!'

I breathe out slowly, relieved. Maybe it was the fairy dust that sent me crazy that night. Maybe I can't remember anything because I did too much of it.

'Mack's right,' I say, backing him.

Ed shrugs, picks the packet out of the mud, wipes it on his shirt and shoves it into his pocket. He doesn't meet my eyes. I'm about to demand where he got it from but Charlie steps between us.

'What's the plan, then?' Charlie says. 'How we playing?'

'Original rules,' I say.

I look around at the three of them. The atmosphere's different tonight, different without Ashlee. The boys look harder somehow, more serious. More like soldiers. But it doesn't feel like the early Games before she joined us either.

'Collars,' I say, and we pull them out of our pockets.

The boys already have their own, so no one hands back anyone else's or boasts about being the winner of the last

Game. Guess they must've talked about that Game without me, they must've already given back the collars that were won. No one says anything about Ashlee's missing collar.

'One more Game,' I say. 'To remember Ashlee. Like our own kind of . . .' And I'm about to say *funeral* but it doesn't feel right.

'Celebration,' Mack says fast. And I feel myself colour up from not even thinking of this word. 'Celebration of her life.'

'She'd want that,' Charlie says. 'A final Game.'

Ed nods too, shuffling his feet.

They all look at me, maybe to check if this is what I want too. I get a sense of all of us being in this together, like brothers, I almost open my mouth and tell them everything. These are my best mates after all, so why shouldn't I just come clean about what I don't remember from that night? Maybe we could even work it out together.

Before I can, Mack steps forward and takes the collar from my hand, wraps it around my neck. He finds a hole to put it on, one that's loose so it'll be easier to get off. When Ashlee had put my collar on, she'd pull it tight enough to feel like it was choking me. She'd brush her fingers down the inside of my arm after, almost like an apology . . . or a promise.

Mack steps back and does his own; its tiny silver studs glint in the moonlight. I glance across to Charlie's collar: black and thin and hard to remove. Then Ed's: worn leather that's kind of scratchy, a lot like mine. I know how they all feel wrapped around my neck, and I remember how Ashlee's collar always felt too tight. Perhaps that's why she'd chosen it; she'd known it'd feel uncomfortable around our boy-sized necks. I'd buckle it gentle and loose each time.

'Tighter than that,' she'd say. 'It'll fall off.'

Maybe it did. Maybe that's why it was never found.

The boys are staring at me, waiting.

'One hour,' I say. 'You know the rules: keep your collar, get the others, person with the most wins. Play 'til our phone alarms go; message if you sign off.'

Then I hesitate. I'm thinking of Shepherd's bunker, wondering if I can find that while we're playing tonight, wondering if there are other places out here that might give me answers too.

'Meet back here after?' Mack fills my silence. 'Or just go home?'

Charlie shrugs. 'We'll find each other anyway. We usually do.'

Usually.

Not that night, though. Least, I don't think we did.

There doesn't seem much else to do other than call it. Apart from one thing. I get Mack's lighter, flick it and make a tiny flame.

'For Ashlee,' I say.

The others echo it. 'For Ashlee.'

I see Mack staring at the forest floor, looking 'bout as upset as I feel. I sense Ed shuffling again. Charlie coughs. Perhaps we all need this Game tonight, even if it's just for the running in the dark. Maybe we'll remember how Ashlee meant something to each of us, how she's left a gap. The lighter flickers, burns my fingers.

I make my hand into the shape of a gun and I call the order. Without Ashlee here, I point my hand first at Ed, and then to Charlie, then Mack. I make the sound of a gunshot as I fire it at my own head last. I think about how I'd done this with Emily Shepherd too, up on the Leap, how she'd stood wide-eyed as if I was really going to shoot her with only my fingers.

Ashlee used to wink at me when I'd fire. On that night she'd poked her tongue out slowly and I'd wanted to taste it. I remember that.

I take my phone out and set the alarm for one hour so the others can see; they do the same. Mack's watching me with eyebrows raised, still checking I'm fine. Then we huddle in close and I begin the count.

'One . . .'

I falter. This is when Ashlee would've run. She'd get the best head start — only fair. I can see her, almost, running away, smiling as she'd disappear down the path. I blink; breathe in, start again louder.

'One . . .'

Ed goes instead, taking off quick into the trees with a howl.

'. . . two, three, four . . .'

I know where I'll run: down the bike trail and deeper into the woods, like I did at the beginning of that night.

'. . . seven, eight, nine, ten . . .'

At twenty seconds it's Charlie, howling like a banshee and heading in the same direction. At forty, it's Mack. He grins before he goes, makes a fist for me to lock into.

'You'll be OK,' he says, more a statement than a question. 'Just play it like it used to be. Use the Game to forget about things for a while. Relax!'

But I want to remember.

He makes a long quiet howl, moves off slower than the other two, looking around as if he's expecting them to pounce straight up. Then it's me. It's the most risky spot being last – you're more likely to be jumped on and lose your collar immediately – but when I call, I always take it. When Mack calls, he takes it too.

'Bigger the risk, better the training,' he says.

But the bigger the risk, the more you can't think of nothing else. You can only think of the Game, of not getting caught. But I'd called myself last that night too, so . . .

I stop counting after a while, leave it longer than I'm meant to, listening to how the trees are moving so much from the wind it sounds like traffic. Eventually, I pick a different direction to the way any of the others went, howl once and soft, and melt into the trees like a shadow.

25

Emily

I dream of Damon.

He's in the woods, waiting for me. The forest is bright with moonlight, and I'm running fast down tiny pathways, following his trail. I stop and listen, but all I can hear are words in my head . . . singsong.

If you go down to the woods today . . .

It's something I recognise, something from when I was a kid.

. . . you're sure of a big surprise . . .

The words get louder as I run deeper into the trees.

If you go down to the woods today you better go in . . .

I go past all the places I know. Faster.

For every bear that ever there was . . .

. . . will gather there . . .

I get on to a tiny track. There's something else . . . a panting noise. It's as if someone – or something – is running behind me, chasing. And still, the words . . .

Today's the day the teddy bears have . . .

It's a voice I know. This song is something Dad used to sing when I couldn't sleep. I'm gasping as I turn to face him.

Dad's in army fatigues, and he's walking towards me with arms held out.

'There's no use running,' Dad is shouting. 'I'll always find you.'

Beneath the trees where nobody sees they'll hide and seek as long as . . .

I slam my hands over my ears. But Dad keeps coming. There is a fur hanging over his shoulders – an animal skin – bloody and scraggly. Too big to be a rabbit's pelt.

'I'm sorry,' he says, smiling a wonky grin. 'It's only natural, you know, to kill.'

There's blood soaking into the sleeves of his fatigues, dripping over his fingers. It's dark red, almost black, coming from the fur on his shoulders.

I force my legs into a step forward, towards him. I could run to Dad, barrel into his arms and hug him like I used to. I could push him away too, into the dark beyond the trees. My choice.

There's movement behind me, a rustling. There's another person here, waiting and watching. I sense him step out from the trees and fall into line behind me. Damon. He touches the back of my wrist with warm fingers. He's solid. Ready to back me up if I need.

I take a breath, tilt my face up to look into Dad's eyes. And together, Damon and me, we walk forward to meet my dad.

26

Damon

She's running in front, darting out of reach into the trees. I spin round and she's beside me too. I try to touch her but my hand goes right through. She's silver-grey, invisible. She's in my fucking mind! I blink, try to get her out of there. There's this sound of laughter. Hers? Everything around me feels alive and watching, the trees moving and swaying like dancing girls, whispering.

Catch me . . . catch me . . . do it . . .

Useless.

It's my stupid wanker of a brain doing this, making this up.

I step off the path and rest against an upturned tree, roots pulled out from a storm. I need to get a hold of myself. I need to remember exactly what I was doing that night and do it again, need to keep calm. But I should get more hidden. I run my hands along the bark of the fallen tree 'til my fingers are dirty with gunk, smear this on my face as camouflage. From somewhere close I hear a shout. Charlie?

I hear Mack's low laugh. 'Not a chance, mate, not a chance. Can't creep up on me.'

There's the muffled thud of someone getting hit.

If I was playing the Game proper I'd be after them, chasing, jumping them in the dark and trying for their collars same time . . . darting away before they got mine. But that night I hadn't wanted to fight either; I'd wanted to save my collar and myself just for her. I'd led Ed to the edge of Game Play then I'd stayed still in the dark, watching him look for me.

I walk slowly now, sticking close to trunks, searching for Ed's skinny body and hunched-over walk. If I can find him and lose him like I did that night, would I remember chasing Ashlee afterwards? I'm listening for the others too. Now and then it sounds like someone's behind me, tracking me quiet. I climb a tree and wait, but no one comes past. Is this how it always was for Ashlee? Listening extra hard for someone to catch her? She was good at staying hidden, probably even as good as me. So why was she found that night by Shepherd? It doesn't make sense that he stalked her.

I listen for footsteps, cracks from branches, the swish of clothing through bracken. I try to make my brain think.

Another fight breaks out. I crawl away, quiet. I'm looking everywhere, searching for clues, for something that feels right. It's about half way through Game Time, about when I'd usually catch up with her.

I turn right down a track none of us use that often, just because something about it seems familiar. There's this weird pull, something like a sixth sense. That night my mind was still spinning from the fairy dust we'd taken in the car park. Now it feels like I'm spinning again, hovering somewhere between what makes sense and what doesn't, what's real and not. There's a silver shape in front of me, flickering. There's laughter. A feeling. There's something daring me on.

And I remember – I know where I'm going. There's a hollow, a small scoop into the ground just off one of these tracks: it's not far.

She'd called back to me that night. 'I've got the perfect place!' She'd stopped on the edge of this track and launched herself at me. She'd whispered against my cheek. 'It's where the fairies fuck!'

Then she'd reached for my collar. When I'd reeled away, she'd punched me to the side of my head.

I'd caught her hands. 'You're getting better at this. Not such an A student now!'

She'd laughed. 'Was I ever?' Soon as I'd tried to grab her collar she'd gone, running ahead down the track. 'Come join the fairies!'

She was high as a freakin' balloon! I'd looked round to see if anyone else had heard, then I'd run fast after her.

I start running down the track again. The faster and further I go, the more it feels right. Her words are coming with me, all the conversations we'd ever had in these woods — it's like I'm remembering parts of them all. I can almost sense her beside me too, whispering them. I remember her telling me how Darkwood was on a fault line, saying it was fairy magic that made the limestone cliffs rise up from nothing. She'd said the fairies came up from gaps in the ground too. She'd tapped her nose like she was letting me in on a secret.

Maybe the fairies really got Ashlee that night. Maybe that's why none of it makes sense. I breathe in hard. I must be flying again to think like this.

The air smells different in this part of the woods, feels heavier. I'm near the river. I move like I'm hypnotised, almost by instinct. Is Ashlee here, somehow, telling me where to go? If I found her, could I touch her?

And there, up ahead, the ground falls away and the trees arch backwards: the hollow. That night she'd run, laughing, down this bank and into it. She'd leant with her back against a tree and looked up at me. She'd wanted me, she'd had those sort of eyes.

I slide down this bank again, the ground tacky and soft with mud. I don't remember that, but maybe the storm started later that night and the ground was still hard when we came down here. Tonight I smell the damp mustiness of the autumn everywhere. That night I'd had sweat on my spine, the first drops of rain had felt like a relief. I remember these trunks that stand like an audience in the dark.

I move forward. Leaves, ankle deep, now cover this ground. It's cold, frost coming. That internet site had been right about retracing my steps — maybe my entire memory from that night will return just from being here. Then I get the stabs again and I don't know why. What am I scared of?

I bend to the bank, run my fingers through leaves and mud, search for Ashlee's collar. I can almost see her in front of me — underneath me — see that challenge in her eyes. When I'd tried to get her collar that night, she'd spun its buckle away. Her fingers had been cold on my neck as she'd almost taken mine.

'Not yet,' I'd said. 'That's no fun.'

'Catch me then.'

She'd kicked out, crawled across the forest floor. I'd been after her, pulling her back by her legs. She'd squealed with laughter and slapped my face but I'd held her firm.

'There are other ways I can get your collar,' she'd said. 'You know that.' She'd kissed me, really slowly, like she'd meant it.

That was always her Game Plan: to get me so worked up that she'd take my collar before I'd even realise. Or she'd make a deal: a kiss for a collar, and not always on the lips.

But my Game Plan that night had been to go all the way. I wouldn't let her take my collar so easy.

It hurts to remember this. Hurts more than any punch. But Mack's wrong — this is the sort of pain I need, not the physical kind, all this stuff that's coming at me confused and tangled.

Resting my head against leaves, I even try to smell back the memories. An earthy fug gets into my nose instead. But I do remember her lips, slippery . . . bending my head to hers and touching her tongue. She'd smelt of booze and ciggies. I'd stopped reaching for her collar and started feeling her up instead. We'd been half fighting, half touching, half serious, half not.

I fall into these leaves again, pull them to me in a pile as if they're her, as if I can make her body again from them. My hands had been reaching around the back of her. I'd felt her hard, hot spine, arching. My hands moving down her stomach, into her panties.

'Do it,' she'd whispered. 'Dare you.'

Had she meant touch her, or take her collar, or keep pretending to fight?

I'd kept going with what I'd wanted, pressed the tips of my fingers into where she'd been warm. She'd sighed out low into my ear.

Want to go to Fairyland?

Her words, or mine? I can't remember.

I'd felt her breath on my neck. I'd wanted her, all of her – her fit body, her warm breath, the sweat on her spine – all of it. Once I'd taken her collar she'd come for me next. I'd swap my collar for going all the way – just like she'd promised.

I'm remembering it now – what'd happened, the start of it anyway. And I've got this buzzing anxious feeling as the memory gets stronger.

As I'd touched her, I'd started undoing her collar with

my other hand. She hadn't stopped me, not while I'd been touching her same time. I'd pulled it, so slowly, over one buckle hole at a time. She'd stopped struggling and shook against me instead, went wet at my fingers. She'd sighed like something angelic. Like one of the fairies she talked about.

'Caught,' I'd said.

I'd started to slide her collar out from round her neck, but she'd realised what I was doing and moved beneath me. She'd been quick, reaching into her pocket and pressing more fairy dust to my gums, a whole ton of it. Enough that I'd gagged, reeled away.

She'd whipped on top of me fast. 'My turn,' she'd said.

She could've done anything to me she'd wanted; I wouldn't have struggled. But she'd known what she'd promised.

'All the way for your collar?' she'd whispered. 'But you haven't got mine yet. You still owe me, you know. You still got to do something back.'

She'd pushed me against the leaves, panting. I'd tasted sweat on her neck as I'd kissed it. She'd slapped my face, tried to get rough, turned from angel to devil in a second.

'You don't have to push me,' I'd said. Though I'd known she was only playing.

But she'd known I could snap too – hadn't she seen it with Mack and me a hundred times? One minute we'd be normal and mates and then – boom! – that flare up with anger, a punch.

She'd moved my hands into fists and pushed them into

her stomach, wrapped her fingers round my neck, played with my collar without taking it off. 'C'mon! Are you going to fight me properly?'

Fight me?

Fuck me?

Which was it?

My head had been whirling, just like it is now.

I could get mad if you like. Had I said that? Had she?

I'd growled into her shoulder, well fierce. She'd stuck her tongue behind my teeth: put more fairy dust there. And it'd hit me. I'd felt my brain spin, shoot up over us and glow like the moon.

Do you trust me? . . . Trust yourself? . . . Do you?

She'd been pressing me, laughing. I'd howled like an animal. I'd felt her teeth in my skin. And then . . .

Shall I tell you something?

There'd been a pulsing feeling in my veins. She'd laughed and it'd sounded like a stream. I'd seen the forest floor stretch out as carpet, glowing red coals.

It might make you fight me.

I'd been trying to ask. Trying to blink. Trying to focus.

Her eyes had been reflecting the moon, had turned orange like a creature's. Her sweat had made her face swim, made her slippery and wet and hard to hold on to. Who was she? I'd felt her fingers in my trousers, reaching for me. Her other hand on my collar. I'd needed to claw back my brain so I could do stuff to her.

Are you ready? . . . Are you? . . .

Shall I tell you something?

The forest had been spinning and I couldn't hold on. And there'd been something else. She'd said something else.

My eyes snap open.

I've heard something. Now. A crack of a branch.

Someone's here, *right here*, somewhere in the dark. I squint, see nothing. But I hear soft steps in the leaves. I'm a rabbit in headlights like this, something about to be caught. I get a sudden lurch that it could be the cops, following me and wanting more answers. But it has to be one of the boys. Tracked me here. Who else?

I swallow, and the collar round my neck feels too tight. I hope no one saw me with my head down in the leaves, grasping at them. I stand, face the direction I thought I'd heard the noise. Someone comes at me and pulls me backwards. I shout like a fucking idiot! I don't mean to, but that hand feels like a cop's hand. I whip round to face whoever it is, ducking because I'm expecting a punch. But he just stares at me calmly.

'Ed?'

It would be, wouldn't it? Perhaps it's only right that he's found me this time. But he's stopped my memory of Ashlee, all these images and thoughts! What if I never get them back? Never put them in order? What if it's all Ed's fault if I never remember any more than this?

'What are you doing out here?' he says.

I sweep his hand off me. 'Why'd you come here after me?'

He looks at me puzzled, head on the side. I'm still

trying to think, still trying to claw back those images. What had been real? What had happened?

Ed's dark eyes are on my collar. He's already caught Charlie; both his own and Charlie's thin, black collar are wrapped round his neck. He's winning the Game then. If he takes mine it's an easy victory. Ed's eyes go back to my face, narrowing. Perhaps he's hesitating because it's me: he doesn't know whether he should play the Game proper or not. But this was always my Game and I call the shots. And he's just ruined everything by interrupting.

I step back, make my arms wide to invite him. 'Go on, then.'

He doesn't hang about. He's at me, one of his bony arms punching into the side of me and the other already grabbing for my collar. He's quick. I throw a punch at his stomach but my brain's not turning off like it used to; I can't go into fight mode. I'm still trying to think about Ashlee.

I get my hand on Ed's collar, feel the buckle and start to undo it; he coughs as I pull it tight. Then he right hooks me to the face and it fucking hurts.

'We're not meant to hit there!' I shout. 'Game Rules!'

Not that I ever cared about it when Ashlee did.

I punch him in the guts: punch him for interrupting everything I was trying to remember. Punch him for bringing fairy dust tonight and thinking we'd want to do it again! Punch just because I can. I try for his collar when he's bent over. But whatever I do, I can't make this fight like how it used to be.

What did Ashlee tell me that night?

Then I'm falling and Ed's holding me down. I'm not calling surrender, though. If he wants this collar he'll have to work for it. If this is the last Game I ever play, I can't bow out like that. I sink my teeth into his shoulder, play dirty. I use the moment to flip him over, see the frustration in his eyes that I can still do this so easy, even with two months off.

Did Ed play like this with Ashlee too? Did Ashlee play like this with all of them? How did she really win those collars? Charlie's words from Biology are in my head now: *It's not like I held back . . .*

I can't believe I never asked her.

Ed gets the palm of his hand under my chin, pushes. 'You're fighting like a pussy. Punch harder!'

'Shut up!'

I bring my hands to Ed's neck. I try to undo his collar but he moves away each time.

'Useless!' Ed says. 'Come on!'

I pause. There's that word again.

I see my hands on Ed's neck, pressing. I see his brown eyes bulge with surprise, brown like Ashlee's eyes. I want to pull his collar tighter. Punish him for everything.

And that's when it happens.

I feel my fingers tighten around Ed's neck. I feel the pulse of his veins. I see his eyes are staring at me wide. Asking. Demanding?

Do it . . . do it . . .

Are you going to fight me?

Shall I tell you something?

I've done this before. I've pressed my hands around someone's neck like this before.

I stop the pressure.

Ed's coughing. 'Jesus, man!'

I try to roll off him, but he's after me now. He grabs me and holds me still and I'm reeling too much from these thoughts I just had to do anything about it. Ed snaps off my collar. I feel the friction of it go. He pushes me aside into the leaves.

'Caught!' he yells, whooping.

But Mack's out of the trees like a demon, barrelling into Ed and starting the fight all over. He must have been watching, ready to have my back.

I sit in the damp leaves. What just happened? My head's still spinning from Ed's punch. I lurch forward, dizzy, feel cold mud on my face. I don't even care if the other boys are watching me lose it like this. I can still feel Ed's pulse beating beneath my fingers.

When I look up again, Mack's staring at me as if I'm a madman. He comes out of the shadows, stretches down a hand. 'What's going on, mate?'

I can't look at him. I don't know what I'm thinking, what I'm feeling. I don't have a clue what's going on!

Fight me. Fuck me. Which one? Which one first? What did I do to her? What did I *really* do?

Ashlee's voice, teasing and teasing. Daring me.

What did she tell me that night?

I see the wide-eyed shock on Ed's face, Charlie's too as

he comes out of the trees. They're all staring at me like I've cracked. I crawl away and Ed passes my collar to me, as if that would make something better, tries to force it into my hands.

'I don't want it,' I drag myself backwards. 'I'm not playing any more!'

I get up off my knees, stumble away. That's when I hear all our phone alarms go off at exactly the same time.

'Game Over!' yells Charlie.

'Damo!' yells Mack. 'Wait!'

But I'm gone.

27

Emily

I breathe out so I can hear myself in the dark.

A nightmare, another one.

I stretch my fingers through blackness, grasp at air. I have the strangest feeling of brushing fur with fingertips. I'm home, in my bed. But something woke me. There was a noise, something that had sounded like an animal. I'm used to the sounds of the woods at night – the yip of a fox, the moan of a stag, the screech of a barn owl – but this was different.

I pad to the window and press my fingers to cold glass. This is like how it was two months ago when I was up and waiting for Dad to return. Like that night, there is a full moon again, pretty much. Unlike that night, my dad is not in Darkwood. If he were, I might race down our garden path and through the gate. I might pelt down tracks towards the bunker. I might launch myself at Dad. And she might have run.

I open the window, gasp in the cold air. It's like I'm starting to believe, all of it. I get a glimpse of understanding of why Mum's drinking every night. Right now I want to forget these thoughts I've been having too, forget what I found in Dad's car . . . everything.

I look down the row of houses. No one's lights have gone on, the back gardens are still and grey. If I crane my neck I can see the very edge of Joe's garden at the other end of the row. When we were younger Joe would stick his hat on a fence post to show me he was home and free to play. Now his fence post is empty. There is no one walking on cobbles in our lane either, no glass shards tinkling against each other as another brick goes through another of our windows. No shake and hiss of a spray can as someone scrawls out their hurt on our walls.

I go back to bed and light a candle. Once Dad would tell stories by candlelight until I fell asleep. Now I watch the candle's shadows on the walls, leaping and lurching like demons. As the flame flickers I start to drift. And, just for a moment, I think I hear it again: that noise that woke me. It's something like a howl, something far away. I try to keep listening but my brain is heavy. What's real and what's in my dream feels the same, I'm sinking. But this time someone is sinking with me, watching me breathe. I can feel him waiting too.

28

Damon

The moon shines down hard and I don't know where I'm going but I let my feet take me. I need to run 'til this roar inside me is quiet, 'til I get answers for these questions. I wake a huddle of crows – a massive murder of the things – send them screeching and squawking into the night. I run through the feathers and leaves raining down. Then I crash through a small wooden gate and I'm on a cobblestone lane, behind a neat row of houses. I'm somewhere on the edge of town.

I know this place.

I stand, heaving. It would be this place, wouldn't it, that I find my way to now? My eyes dart up and right to find her bedroom, or the one I imagine would be hers. There's a flicker of light behind her curtains. Candlelight? So, Emily Shepherd can't sleep. Somehow that's good to know. A little part of me wants to climb up to that window and crawl inside it. But why the hell would I want that? To see her? Talk? I get an image of her sleeping, her blue-grey eyes shut. I imagine telling her everything I just thought about in that hollow. I breathe, deep as I can. The air is sharp enough to razorblade my throat.

If I did climb up to her window, I really would be a madman. She'd be on the phone to the cops in a second. My skin twitches, trembles. Emily Shepherd won't tell me what I want to hear, she won't tell me nothing. The only thing she'll say is that her dad is innocent.

I hear footsteps, coming out of the woods behind me. It's one of the boys, following — Mack — coming to check I'm all right. I turn to face him. But as I do, I hear the footsteps are slow and careful. It don't sound like he's in a rush to find me. I wait. I'll ask him everything — about Ashlee, about how he played the Game with her, about what happened to the rest of them that night afterwards and whether we all met up. I'll make him help me work out these thoughts.

I see his tall body coming down the path. He's loping, almost casual. Maybe he can't see me properly with the moon at his tail because suddenly he's barrelling into me, all tall and skinny and . . .

It's not him. It's not any one of the boys. When I see who it is I get this strange urge to laugh.

'Joe Wilder?'

His eyes go big behind his glasses.

I step up close. 'What are you doing here? Were you following me?' I try to make my voice nasty, but I'm too shocked.

He's got a camera hanging round his neck. He stares down at me with his eyes huge. I want to wipe the glasses off his face, stop that goggle-eyed way he's looking. Then I realise what he's staring at – I have gunk from that tree across my cheeks. And how hard did Ed punch me? Can Wilder see that damage too?

What else has he seen?

I move forward to grab him, shake him, but Wilder trips backwards. He moves away, stumbling on the cobblestones. This is the last thing I need! Wilder, of all people, knowing I'm flipping out. Knowing I been in these woods again!

'I was just . . . I was . . . ' He's holding up the camera round his neck. 'Pictures!'

'You what?'

I get a memory that this was his excuse when I found him with Ashlee all those months ago, another time when I wasn't expecting him to be in Darkwood. But he's gone before I can ask him about it, racing away into the dark.

'Wilder, come back here,' I say. 'What you been doing?'

I'm trying to keep my voice low; I don't need Emily Shepherd or her mum to come out here either after hearing all this noise.

I start following Wilder 'til he skids up a garden path into a house. I hesitate, looking in. He lives on the same street as Emily Shepherd? Really? Now I know I should've grabbed him, stopped him and made him spill. What the hell was he doing in the woods anyway?

I go round to the street out front. It's still as stones here, all the curtains closed and house lights off. I crouch beside cars, try to see myself in their side mirrors but can't get much visual. It's freezing, car windows starting to frost up, and I'm knackered-tired, but it's a long way home from here. The quickest way is straight through the woods and out the car park again. But when the guys are still in there wondering what the hell just happened to me? When I ran off like a loser? When I don't even know what I'd say to explain it?

A hall light goes on in a house, and I move – crouching behind more parked cars – shivering. I don't know where I'm going, what I'm doing. I want to call Mack, but I don't know what to say. I try to make some sense of it in my fugged-up brain.

But there's nothing – *nothing!*

Just Ed arriving. Just my hands on his neck. My hands on a neck.

The door of the car I'm crouching beside is open slightly, unlocked. And because I'm too cold to do nothing else, I get in. It smells funny inside here, all aftershave and mustiness, but it's warmer at least. And there's a mirror. I check myself in it, wipe off the tree gunk and see if I've bruised up. There's a mark under my left eye already, can't tell how bad it's going to be yet, though. I find a freezing can of de-icer under the seat and hold that against my cheek to take the swelling down. Bloody idiot, Ed! Maybe I'll wait here a few hours, just 'til I've got my head together . . . just 'til the buses start up. Mum will think I'm at Mack's anyway.

Again I look over to where Emily Shepherd's house is. What would it be like to walk up to her door and ask to speak to her? I could do it. I could make her help me work this out. She could tell me how her dad fits in. She could show me where that bunker is too. I could find Ashlee's collar.

Maybe.

I shut my eyes. Every single inch of me wants to sleep. But I can't, because I'm thinking about the boys and how we don't keep secrets from each other. And I'm thinking that whatever Ashlee had told me that night couldn't have been about them, couldn't have been so bad. And I'm thinking that I've been keeping secrets, secrets even from myself.

29

Emily

Saturday morning and I'm browsing through the newspapers online. There are hundreds of articles about the death of Ashlee Parker. Most just report the facts that the police have revealed, but some articles have an opinion on whether Dad meant to kill Ashlee, or whether it was an accident because of a flashback. Some articles say he should get a murder sentence, others say it was manslaughter. There are whole discussion boards devoted to what kind of killer Dad is, whether he should get special treatment because of the things he'd done in the army. But not one article or blog post, or even comment on a discussion board, thinks he didn't kill Ashlee Parker at all. Not one suggests it was someone else who did. I stare at one of the photographs of Dad that's been used in some of the articles. In it, Dad is wearing battle fatigues and he's squinting at the camera lens. Other articles have used Dad's mug shot from the police station – the photo where his eyes are half closed and it doesn't look like him.

Ashlee looks sweet in all the photographs that come up of her – happy. Especially in that photo where she has the blue check scarf tied around her neck, where her long blonde hair is straight and pretty around her face – that photo the whole world has probably seen by now. She's laughing in that photo, even her eyes are smiling. She's totally breath-catchingly beautiful, someone who has her whole life ahead of her.

Only she doesn't.

I take out Dad's sketch of the deer being chased by the wolf and hold it next to this photograph of Ashlee. Both the deer and photographed Ashlee have huge beautiful eyes. They both look excited: free. And they both seem to come from another place – are too beautiful for this real, dark world I'm stuck in. A heavy, horrible feeling starts in the pit of my stomach and works its way up to my throat. Dad must have been sketching Ashlee when he drew this – who else?

Mum's still asleep when I go downstairs and into the garden. I hiss at Florence who's got her tail up like she's stalking something, scare her off it. Then I almost chicken out when I'm outside Joe's back door. I look up at his bedroom window and just will him to see me out here so I don't have to go inside. But it's too late, his mum's already throwing open their back door and bustling me in, all fake smiles and trying to feed me before I'm even inside.

'You'll catch your death,' she says, then realises the words she's used. She mumbles something quickly, rubs her hands on my arms to make me warm.

'Can I go upstairs?' I say, already moving for the hall.

Finn, Joe's little brother, stares at me from the doorway of the living room, almost as if he's trying to work out how close to me he can get now. Before everything, I might have bared my teeth and played a game with him and he would have laughed and loved it. Not now.

Joe's heard me coming – he pulls me into his bedroom when I get to the top of the stairs. 'Are you here because of Damon?'

I frown at him. 'What?'

Is Joe still bothered about that detention I had? Really? Joe has dark rings under his eyes, which isn't like him. He's also got one of his school sports jumpers on with his jeans, which looks odd, especially on a Saturday, but which is like him. I sit on his bed, realising I haven't been into his room for ages. He still has the same things on his walls, though: the photographs of the birds and the sweeping shots of Darkwood taken from the top of the Leap. There are piles of schoolbooks on his desk, and his computer is open to where his photos are stored. Joe clicks out of this when he sees me looking. I touch the sketch in my pocket – I have to tell Joe about it while I've got the nerve. It's why I came.

Before I can, though, Joe sits close beside me. 'Did Damon tell you he was going back into the woods? Did he say it the other day?'

My fingers freeze on the sketch. 'What are you talking about?'

'Damon Hilary being here last night, in the lane, Damon Hilary in Darkwood! Didn't you see him?'

'Hang on. . .' And my brain is now turning. Damon in the woods? Last night? Damon in the lane behind my house? Just thinking about that gives me a little jolt and I don't know why.

As I look at Joe, he sighs. 'It was almost midnight or something. You didn't see him? Really?'

I shake my head. 'How did you?'

'My art project!'

'What?'

'Last night it was full moon, almost, and that makes the best cracks of light.' He throws his hands up like he's trying to convince me of something. 'I was taking photos?'

But I still don't get it. 'What was Damon doing there?'

'Not taking photos, that's for sure.' Joe bends his head to mine. 'But maybe, maybe he was taking something else?'

Joe looks at me like he wants me to understand something.

'What?' I say again. 'What are you even on about? Why is it so strange that Damon was in there anyway?'

Joe's so close I smell the soap on his skin.

'Why isn't it strange?' He sighs again as he looks at me. 'OK, so how about this? What if Damon was in Darkwood last night . . . to take away evidence, to hide it better?'

'Evidence?'

'Have you forgotten everything?' Joe rolls his eyes. 'Evidence could be used against him in a trial, yeah? Evidence could prove he was involved in Ashlee's death!'

'But why would there be evidence against—'

Joe shakes his head to keep me quiet. 'What if Damon wants to hide evidence before the police can find it? What if he's trying to cover something up?' Joe lowers his voice like there are people listening, like he's in some sort of film. 'C'mon, it makes sense, and you know it. No one *really* knows what Damon was doing with Ashlee that night – only his mates – and you know how tight they all are, they'd lie for him. What was he doing back in the woods alone if not hiding something?'

I breathe in, move away across the bed. 'Damon was drinking in the car park that night. They all were. That's what he told the police. The police believe it.'

Joe raises an eyebrow. 'But do you? Really? You didn't once.'

'It doesn't matter what I believe,' I say, I hear my voice falter. 'Or what you do. The case is good enough decided.'

For the first time since I've got here Joe's quiet, thinking. I'm scared that if I don't say something about this sketch soon I won't have the guts at all. But still, my lips won't open, the words won't come.

'I think Damon's panicking,' Joe says eventually. 'I think

he did that detention with you because he wanted to find out what you know. And after he'd realised that you're not going to believe what he wants you to? Well, he's hiding something, he has to be.'

I hold up my hand. 'Joe,' I say. 'You don't need to do this.' I'm staring at him, but he stays serious. Stubborn.

'I think we should go to the police.'

I chew on my lip, look at his carpet. I remind myself of why I'm here: not to talk about Damon or any more theories, to talk about Dad. To tell Joe about this sketch. 'Joe, we've been over all this stuff about Damon,' I murmur. 'A hundred times.'

'We haven't been over everything.'

'You don't have to do this.'

Joe's only doing this to get me out of this slump – to stop me lying about in bed all day pretending to be sick. But it's not fair to Damon to pretend he's a suspect any more. It's not fair to anyone.

'Listen,' I add. 'The police never charged Damon with anything, so . . .' It feels like there's something very big in my throat, stopping me swallowing. I try to talk through it. 'The police don't think it's anyone on that list we made – you know that, so maybe we should stop pretending.'

Joe's jaw is tense. I'm surprised by how committed he seems to this idea, how he's not letting this go. I put my hand back on the sketch to take it out of my pocket.

'Your dad didn't do anything,' he says firmly. 'It's someone else. And Damon Hilary's the obvious choice.'

I stare at the pulse beating in Joe's neck. Can I still have this little bit of hope, even now, this tiny sliver of belief that Dad is innocent? Is it still possible to believe that someone else killed Ashlee? Even after what I've found? Even if it's Damon that's the *someone else*? I shake my head roughly.

'You need to stop this, Joe.'

'But, Emily . . .'

I shush him quiet. 'No. You need to help me with something.'

I take out Dad's sketch before Joe can say anything else. The paper shakes as I lay it across Joe's knees. I make myself explain it. I tell him about finding it in Dad's car —I'm talking fast just to get the words out.

'Do you think it's possible we've been wrong about Dad watching Ashlee?'

'What do you mean?'

'Look!'

But Joe doesn't look at Dad's sketch, not properly.

'Can you see what Dad's drawn?' I say. 'Can you see how it might be her?'

Joe pushes the sketch off his lap. 'What's got into you? Did you even listen to what I said? Last night Damon was in Darkwood! He had dirt on his face and he was wearing a combat shirt! You don't think that's weird? Maybe like he was high on something? Or panicking? He's freaking out, Emily! It's suspicious!'

I feel something tense inside me. How can Joe keep talking like this after I've shown him this sketch, after I've admitted everything I've been thinking – how can he not even look?

'So what if Damon was in the woods?' I say. 'And if he looked upset? He *is* upset! His girlfriend died.'

I'm thinking about how I, also, went into the woods a couple of days ago — how I went back to Dad's bunker. I'm thinking how, if anyone saw me do that, they might think that was suspicious too.

'Maybe Damon needs to go back,' I add. 'You thought of that? Maybe being in Darkwood helps him somehow? Maybe it's where he can think about her, by himself.'

I feel strange defending Damon. Shouldn't I be clutching at anything right now — anything that doesn't point towards Dad? Even this? But something has changed inside me after seeing this sketch, after doing that detention with Damon — after seeing the desperation in his eyes. Some tiny candle I had has sizzled out.

I bring the sketch to Joe's face. 'You need to look at this.' I feel the heaviness inside me as he does look this time. 'What do you see in it? Who?'

He shakes his head, annoyed. 'It's a deer, one of your dad's animal pictures.'

His eyes don't stay on it; they go back towards his computer screen. Suddenly I'm blinking back tears and I don't even know why. I thought Joe would listen. It took all the nerve I had to show Joe this and he's acting like it's nothing. But isn't that what I wanted him to do? Shouldn't I be relieved?

'Can't you just look properly?'

But he's not bothered, not about anything apart from

his stupid theories about Damon. Suddenly I'm more annoyed at Joe than I think I've ever been. I'm annoyed at how Joe is always trying to be helpful and always getting it wrong. I'm annoyed at how he doesn't see my life careering off kilter and how he always seems to think things will be alright again soon. I'm even annoyed at how nothing bad has ever happened to him and his family and probably never will. Joe will never know how it feels to be scared every day that his dad is a killer, will never know the fear of having killer's blood inside him.

'Just look at it!' I shout.

When he still doesn't look I rip the sketch from his hands, stand up fast.

'It's because Damon dropped you from that stupid sports team, isn't it?' I say. 'That's why you hate him?' And these words are harsh; I can see by the way Joe flinches that they hurt. But I don't care. 'It's not fair, Joe! None of this is fair!'

And it's not. It's not fair to anyone.

This time when Joe comes towards me I stumble back over a pile of books, scatter them. Downstairs, Joe's mum is shouting something. I hear her coming up the stairs. I can hear Finn crying too.

'It's not because I hate Damon that I think he's being suspicious,' Joe says fast. 'Of course it's not! And you're an idiot if you think it's because of some stupid sports team. An idiot!'

My mouth drops. Joe's never called me that before. He's never called me it and meant it.

'It's because Damon Hilary's not right in the head, Emily!' he continues. 'It's because he's got a screw loose!'

I'm blinking back tears – I feel them there, hot and waiting. I feel the anger just beneath the surface of my skin. 'You're just making stuff up!'

'I'm not! I'm just saying this because I . . .'

I glare at him. How can he even think I'd believe this junk? How can he even think it would make anything better to say it to me?

Mrs Wilder is banging on his door now. 'What's going on, you two? You're upsetting Finn!'

Joe flinches. 'Look, I'm saying these things because I care about you, all right? I don't want you to get hurt!'

I see the colour in his cheeks, his eyes blinking fast. For one strange second I want to hug him, but I can't. Not now.

'You don't get it,' I say instead. 'None of this.'

He looks away from me quickly.

'Emily, sometimes you just have to go with what you feel,' Joe says quietly.

'And sometimes you can't keep living in fantasy land!'

He bites his lip, quiet. And I hate myself, because I sound like Mum.

And because I don't want to upset Joe. I don't want to get this angry. It's like that horrible thing inside me is taking over again, making me someone else – someone who rages. It's like I can't stop it.

When Mrs Wilder comes through the door, I push past her fast. I've got to get out. I can't stay here and risk saying something else nasty, I can't let this anger out properly. As I take the stairs fast, I know I've just got to find somewhere to think. I need to look at Dad's sketch and decide what to do with it myself.

30

Damon

There's this sound – dragging. Something moving through leaves. Through mud. There's rain too. A weight on my shoulders. A heaviness. I'm trying to move forward, trying to see. I smell something like pine, feel something like cold. A stinging frozen cheek. Eyelids that don't want to open.

I've been sleeping. Dreaming?

I focus on my little finger, try to make that move. But I can't open my eyes, not yet. And there's another image, a memory.

Detectives. The two that faced me in that interview room. A hard-faced man across a shiny table. A woman with her arms crossed. They're asking about us all drinking in the car park. There's sweat on my back. The man leans across and asks if Ashlee and I had been fighting, and I want to say yes. Because, right in this moment, I've done it — whatever it is they're trying to get me to confess to. These detectives know about the Game, they can see how I'm panicking. I wait for those words you hear on a hundred TV shows: *We're arresting you on suspicion of . . .* Because whatever has happened to Ashlee, it's my fault.

The detectives don't arrest me, though, just open the interview door for me to go. And in a room I pass on the way out is a man with his head in his hands. Just by the way he looks I know he's the guilty one. Jon Shepherd. I breathe out, relieved. And I sink back again into blackness . . . and cold . . .

I'm in a car.

It's freezing.

I still can't open my eyes.

But there's a tapping sound — loud. Beside my right ear. I turn my head, painfully sneak one eye open. Through the window is a face. Frowning. Behind her I see that it's morning. Grey-pink. I shut my eye and open it again. She's still there. Still angry. And now she's yanking open the door I'm leaning against. I'm starting to fall towards the road. I grab the doorframe, stop myself. My body is numb. Perhaps I didn't sleep at all, perhaps I passed out with hypothermia instead. When I look up she's shouting something, pushing my shoulder.

'What are you doing in my dad's car?'

It looks like she's been crying; looks like she could do it again. I pull myself up straight as I can, try to ignore the shooting pain that's running through my arms, the dull throb of my cheek, the hunger in my belly, the way my head's so fuzzy. I try to fix my eyes on Emily Shepherd.

'It was unlocked.' My voice sounds heavy. 'It was freezing outside.'

'Why are you even here?'

She's shaking my right shoulder, making more pain shoot through it. She's looking so mad perhaps she's about to call the cops. And why shouldn't she? I'm a freak: I've been sleeping in Jon Shepherd's car. No wonder she's mad.

And there are images, still, in my head, even as I look at her. I don't think I'm properly awake. There's still that sound, that dragging. There's an image of shoes being caught on tree roots. A flash of seeing my hands on a neck. There's laughing. My chest is thudding hard.

I follow Emily's gaze, see the can of de-icer still in my hand. She's frowning at it, looking around at the car then back.

'It's not a spray can,' I say, turning it so she can see. 'It was here.'

She frowns even more. I watch her grey-blue eyes focus on my left cheek, the place where Ed hit me. I hold the de-icer can up to it, wince from how freezing it feels. Her face goes softer then – least, I think it does – and maybe that makes me bold or something because I open my mouth.

'I need to speak to you,' I say.

And this — I realise — is true. I breathe out. I think I'm even glad she's here, that she's found me like this, that I found this car without even meaning to. Maybe it's a sign. But what the fuck of, I don't know!

She bends down, crouches so her eyes are level with mine. 'And I need to speak to you.'

31

Emily

I make Damon shove across. This is too weird, he shouldn't be here. What Joe was just saying is buzzing in my brain too: *He's not right in the head . . . he's got a screw loose.*

Is this why Damon was waiting in my dad's car? He really is nuts?

He certainly doesn't look right. His eyes are big and dark and red rimmed. There's dirt on his skin, and something else that looks like a bruise. He's shivering, freezing.

'What happened?' I'm looking at the mark on his cheek.

'Walked into something.' I must look sceptical because he adds, 'I was in Darkwood last night; there are a lot of trees there.'

He glances across. For a second I think he almost smiles at the stupid thing he's just said.

'I know where you were,' I say.

'Course you do. Joe Wilder told you, didn't he?'

I'm surprised he's not denying it. Surely if he was feeling guilty about being back in Darkwood — if he was hiding evidence like Joe says he was — he'd be trying to keep quiet, trying to throw me off the trail. I look around the car to see if he's got a bag with him, anything he might have used to carry evidence away. I look at his face and check for guilt. There's nothing. Damon is staring through the windscreen as if he's only just realised it's daytime. He looks exhausted.

'Have you been in here all night?' I say. 'In my dad's car?'

He blinks. 'Maybe.'

I see how his hands shake. Perhaps Joe was right when he said Damon was on something last night. Maybe Damon went back into the woods to get out of his head. To forget the things that have happened to him. To escape.

'You look kind of desperate,' I say.

He shrugs. 'Kind of feel it.'

I keep looking at him and he doesn't seem to mind. He looks like I feel — he's the human embodiment of the mess that's inside me.

He turns to me slowly. 'Last night I was looking for something . . .'

I freeze, remembering Joe's words about the evidence.

'I didn't find it.'

Now he's looking at me like I'm some sort of answer, like I'm a rope to pull him out. If I wasn't so confused by this boy, if I wasn't still thinking about what Joe just said, I might want to keep hold of that look, store it to remember later.

'Joe thinks I should stay away from you,' I say.

Another shrug. 'Maybe you should.'

It's not the answer I'm expecting, but he doesn't give me any more. The combat shirt he's wearing is muddy and torn, I see *Hilary* on the name badge. His dad's?

'Joe thinks you know something,' I try again. 'Something about that night. Something you haven't said.'

I don't know why I'm saying this. Am I testing him? Testing myself? I wait for him to get angry – to get confrontational like how he was on the Leap. But he just stares at me with tired eyes. The fight's been taken out of this boy and I don't know why. I don't think he hates me any more, at least.

'Wilder would think that,' he says eventually. 'Wilder doesn't like me too much.'

He rests his head back on the seat. I wonder then whether Damon doesn't really like Joe too much either, whether there's more going on between these two boys than just the cross-country team.

'But what do *you* think, Emily?' he says with his eyes closed. 'Do *you* think I could hide something? Am I like that?'

He opens his eyes and turns to me, the chair creaking as he shifts. The last time I was this close to Damon –

holding his gaze like this — I was pinning him to the forest floor after he'd told me he could make my life hell. What's happened to him? Why isn't he demanding answers about my dad any more? Why is he acting so strange?

'Anyone can hide things,' I say.

He looks back through the windscreen. And I get it suddenly, why Damon might have been in the woods last night, what he might have been looking for.

'You'd never find that alone,' I try. 'Not if you didn't know where it was.'

He frowns, there's a wisp of a smile straight after. I know I'm right about what I thought.

'Show me, then,' he says. 'Please?'

It's the *please* that gets me. I nod, not because I want to take him there but because he's so desperate-looking. Because I see how much he needs this. Because I still feel this odd kind of guilt every time I look at him, this odd kind of *something*. Since I've found Dad's sketch, this feeling is worse. I nod, because the anger I'd felt at Joe's house is starting to drain away just by being here. But, most of all, I think I nod because, despite everything, I don't want him to get out of this car. Maybe that makes me kind of desperate too. But Damon said it, didn't he? That he wanted to talk? Maybe that's what I want as well.

I stare at Damon's copper-brown eyes. I know Joe is wrong with the things he said about Damon. Damon isn't suspicious, he's just someone who's not coping at all. He wants to understand what happened that night like I do. And there's something else I know — Damon would see

Ashlee in that sketch. If she's in it, it's Damon who'd know. A shiver skims down my spine as I think about going back to that bunker, going back with him, showing him the sketch.

'I need to see that place,' he says.

There doesn't seem to be much else to say, so I get out of the car and just walk. If Damon wants to, he'll follow. I lead him around the side of our house and to the lane out back. I go through the gate. As I walk into the woods he's close behind. I remember the touch of Damon's fingers against my wrist in my dream – how he'd walked forward with me to meet Dad. I also remember that other time I'd seen Damon in these woods. Not the time on the Leap the other day – that time months before, almost a year ago, when he'd been running hard. The time I'd shown him the starlings. That day he'd looked tired and desperate too. I hear him brush his hand against a trunk behind me, tap his fingers against bark. Maybe it does make sense why he was running so fast that day – why he'd looked upset. That day had been just after the bomb that killed his dad.

There's a slight whirring sound as wind moves through branches somewhere above us. It reminds me of how wind rattles the razor wire on the army barracks' fence in town. I look back to Damon and wonder if he thinks that too.

'Do you think our dads knew each other?' I say. 'They must have been in the desert the same time.'

Damon frowns and I don't think he's going to answer me, but he shrugs eventually. 'Maybe.'

I think about my dad and Damon's dad in an army base together — whether they ever talked. Maybe Damon's dad unearthed an IED that my dad could have stepped on. Damon's dad could have saved my dad's life without anyone ever knowing.

'Do you wish it'd been my dad who died?' I say, the words out before I even mean them to be.

Damon doesn't answer this. But there are answers going around in my head. Because, maybe, if my dad had been the one to die on duty, nothing bad would have happened later. Maybe Ashlee would still be alive. Maybe this thought is enough to make Damon hate me for the rest of my life.

I focus on the rustle my shoes make in the leaves, and I get this strange feeling it's not Damon I'm walking here with, but Dad. I'm almost listening to hear him talk about the hard fern and wood blewit and devil's bit — all these things I can see in the ground as we walk. I'm waiting for him to tell me how when the trees breathe, they give us life — how, without them, there'd be no oxygen on Earth at all. But it's quiet behind me. No Dad mumbling about nature. And anyway, if it really were Dad there, I wouldn't go to the bunker. I'd go deeper into the forest, somewhere with sunlight, and I wouldn't leave him by himself. Not again.

The whirring wind around us gets louder, spins leaves down. I walk faster. It's such a grey day, one of those days that never really gets light: rain coming. I think about Dad that night, walking through here just by moonlight. I think about him with Ashlee in his arms. I shiver, then flinch away as Damon grabs my shoulders.

'Sorry,' he says quickly, his hands darting back. 'I was just trying to . . . you must be . . .' He starts taking his duffle coat off. 'Here, do you want this?'

I shake my head. 'You're OK.'

He hesitates like he's going to say something else, his eyes are flicking all over the place. I feel Dad's sketch in my pocket. It's on the tip of my tongue to tell him. All of it. To see what he says. To see if it's something different to what Joe said. Do I dare?

'We won't stay long,' I say.

I turn on to the track I used to run down, and the wind kicks up in a cold angry gust. I'm breaking one of Dad's rules to bring Damon here but it doesn't feel so terrible to disobey him, not now. Several times I look back to check Damon is still behind me – he moves like a cat. Each time his eyes are roving around, as if he's looking for something, or searching for a part of Darkwood he knows. He looks lost. And like he's thinking about every tragic thing in the world. It makes me wonder whether people other than soldiers can get post-traumatic stress disorder. Could Damon have it because two people he loved died? Could I get it over what's happened? Could Mum? Maybe this whole town has it, everyone touched by violence somehow and suffering? I hear a rumble of thunder.

'Do you want to keep going?' I say. 'We're almost there.'

Damon nods, determined. A few more steps, though, and the rain starts. I feel the drops on my cheeks, soft and light and irregular at first. I'm surprised at myself. In this past year I thought I'd got good at watching for storms, for being prepared for when they'd arrive, always being hyper-aware because of Dad.

At the hedge before the clearing, I turn back. Rain has plastered Damon's hair to his cheeks; his lips look thin and a little blue. They remind me of how Ashlee's lips looked that night too. I look at the bruise under his eye and see it's gone puffier. The rain goes up a notch, turns to cold, hard bullets.

'We should shelter inside the bunker.' I raise my voice. 'Just until this stops.'

I'm too cold to think properly — I must be — because I'm grabbing the sleeve of Damon's duffle coat and I'm pulling him through the hedge and the rain is falling and we're slipping on wet leaves. Damon slows as we go through the clearing, his eyes on everything. He wants to stay and look.

'It's too cold,' I say. 'Look later, after the rain. We need to get inside!'

I drag him to the bunker entrance and pull back the camouflage netting. Then I lift the bunker's lid and tumble down into its blackness, pulling Damon in after me. We hit the floor with a jolt, one after another. I'm shivering too, but at least in here the rain's not on us. I turn back to pull the cover over, only then realising that I'm trapping myself inside with him. Joe would go mental if he could see this. So would Mum. But I'm on my own.

32

Damon

Emily is shouting something. Torch. Do I have one?

'I'm not a freakin' boy scout,' I snap, giving her the lighter in my pocket. She takes it, goes away quick.

I don't mean to be nasty, but suddenly I'm weirding out and I don't even know why. I thought I'd be fine coming here. I thought I'd realise something – that I'd just feel it. I thought I'd know, without any doubt, that Jon Shepherd did everything he's accused of. Maybe I'd get that strange feeling again, like the one I got in the hollow last night. Or maybe I'd see Ashlee's collar hanging on a tree and that would be proof. All I'd need.

I get a pang as I remember last night – how it'd felt, just for a second, like Ashlee was running with me in the woods.

But there's no collar here, none I've seen. And I didn't recognise nothing as we walked here. I don't think this place is near Ashlee's shortcut track, either.

I slide down the wall and sit on a concrete floor that's dusty and damp at the same time. Ashlee would've loved this place. She'd have thought it was the perfect place to hide. I think about it – pushing her against the bunker wall, touching her, *doing* it while the Game was on. She'd have loved that too.

I can hear Emily moving around. And I can't help it, I think about doing it with her too, making our own heat. Emily'd be softer than Ashlee somehow, more unsure, I don't think she'd tease. Maybe she's never even done it at all, not with no one. Maybe I'd be her first. I stop and realise what I'm thinking – these thoughts are sick, they're worse than that. But, here in the dark, I can't shake them. Because I'm thinking that when a girl like Emily does it with someone, she probably means it. She probably wouldn't play games.

There's a sudden flash of lightning. I see weird shapes on the walls, then dark again. I stretch my hands into it, I can't really see my fingers but, like this, I can imagine them pressing, into someone, against a neck. I can almost feel it.

Another rumble.

I'm thinking of my fingers on a pulse. Anger.

Something clatters from where Emily is. Another rumble of thunder. Another flash. I get a vision of this place as a small square room, Emily crouching in the corner. It's strange to be in a bunker now, before even joining the army — strange to be in this bunker. My old man's bunkers would've been bigger than this, stopped up with sandbags and boiling hot during the day. He'd have slept with his boots on and his gun beside him. Even though this bunker's never seen any combat, it still smells like rust and spent shells and waiting. Maybe bunkers always do.

There's light — gold spears on the wall — Emily Shepherd with an old lamp in her hand. She puts it down beside me, then clears out what looks like a gun slit, lets in light from the forest floor and some sideways rain.

'Are you OK?'

She's looking at me careful. Do I look like I'm freaking out? Or is it because I'm sitting here like an idiot, not doing nothing?

'I'm fine.'

I'm not, though. I'm thinking that someone else wouldn't have passed out drunk on a forest floor and left his girlfriend alone. A cold drip of something slides down my neck, clings to my spine. For one crazy moment I want to tell Emily everything, about last night and the images I'd had, about how I don't remember what'd happened. I want to say how her dad's plea might be right after all — because if I passed out, because if Ashlee walked back home past this place . . .

Emily's staring at me like she wants to tell me something too. She's got this really intense look in her eyes. I think about all the things I'd said to her the other day on the Leap and I look away.

I can see this place properly now: a small concrete room with a corrugated iron roof. And those drawings! There are animals, swirling dark lines, stick figures hanging from trees, a gun, a twisted-up face. They're everywhere. So, Jon Shepherd really was screwed up!

'This used to be an Operation Base,' Emily tells me.

But, of course, I know this already. She keeps explaining how there are bases like this in woods all over this country, built for a war that never got here. 'They built it so civilians could fight too, so they could wait for when the enemy arrived like a secret resistance.'

I think of my old man waiting – all those months overseas – only to be blown apart by something he never saw, by another kind of secret resistance.

'My dad used to wait here,' Emily says. 'Ever since he came back from combat, he stayed out here in the dark.'

Her face is close to mine, I feel the faint heat from the lamp, her blue-grey eyes still asking questions of me: *What happened that night? What do you know? What can you tell me?* I used to be good at keeping my cool, but now . . . now . . . can she see my skin twitch? How I can't meet her gaze? This is what being on edge is: not playing the Game like Mack thinks, not even joining up for the army . . . *this.* It's not knowing what I did that night. It's knowing I should tell someone. Knowing I can't.

Emily's fingers are reaching out as if she wants to touch me; I don't move away. 'This bunker is at least ten minutes' walk from Ashlee's track home,' she says. 'Did you know that?'

So I was right with the distance thing. 'You still think someone else did it, then?' I say. 'Someone set your dad up?'

Her fingers hover in mid-air. 'I don't know.'

And I'm surprised by that.

I remember Joe Wilder coming out of Darkwood last night, the shock on his face when he'd seen me, how he'd told Emily Shepherd to keep away. What else has he told her? How else does Emily think Ashlee got here that night? Has she made any connections yet?

'Ashlee could've got here by mistake,' I say.

But I can't say no more. I can't say how Ashlee could've got here because of my mistake.

I stand, press my hands against the lid covering the exit. I feel like I'm being buried by this place. I need to be outside, searching for Ashlee's collar and phone. If I find them here, it means that Shepherd stalked Ashlee and tried to hide the evidence. Doesn't it? It means that I can stop this guilt. I want to crawl up the wall and tip out into the rain, start searching.

'It's too wet,' Emily says, watching me. 'There's lightning.'

'Just like that night too.'

Why doesn't this make me remember something? How could I have been so drunk that I slept through a storm?

Emily presses her fingers to my arm. I look down. A

part of me wants to snap those fingers off me, still wants to hurt her. That part wants to be gone and running through these woods, searching 'til I find Ashlee's things. That part wants to run further – out of Darkwood and all the way up north. Away from these mixed-up thoughts. But I don't listen to that part. I stay and look at Emily's fingers, and I want to hold them. I don't understand how I can both hate and want this girl at the same time – how she can be two people at once. How I can be, too.

Emily's saying something about calming down, about how we can't leave yet. I stare at mud on the bottom of her jeans, mud like stains, like blood. I feel dizzy, rub my hand across my neck. Then I pause with my fingers wrapped round it. What kind of pressure would it take? Could it be done by accident? I think of that first day with Mack in the woods – that first time I threw a punch. I'd wanted to know how hard I'd need to press to do that too. I try to breathe deep, I can't flip out here. Not with Emily watching.

'You're freezing,' Emily's saying, coming a little closer. 'You're shivering.'

But I don't feel cold. I move away. If her fingers stay there any longer, I really might grab them. I might grab them and hold her. I might tell her everything.

I bend to search the bunker. I pull open drawers from a chest in the corner, then lurch on to the floor and run my hands into the edges of this place. There's dirt and bird crap and things blown down from the trees, a bundle of logs that I tip over as I push through.

Emily joins me. 'What are you doing? You're messing it all up!'

'I need Ashlee's things,' I explain. 'Need to know where he put them.'

'There's nothing here! The police took everything except the stuff you see. They searched all around!'

'They must be somewhere!'

She shakes her head. 'The police think she lost her phone before she got here, in the woods.'

Her phone. Course. Emily doesn't know about the collar. No one does. Just me, just the boys. Just Shepherd . . . maybe.

I run my hand along the gun slit. I am shaking — I can feel the movement of me but still can't feel the cold. There's no phone. And no collar. Nowhere.

'He hid it somewhere in your house, then?' I try.

'The police searched.'

'It's not just disappeared!'

Emily shrugs. Maybe the police are right, and Ashlee dropped her phone in the woods, and maybe I dropped her collar someplace else. There are a hundred reasons why these things haven't been found yet. They're submerged in mud. A fox had them. The storm buried them in leaves.

But if they were here . . .

Emily is stepping towards me again and I still don't know if I want her to hug me or shove me. Instead she pushes something into my hands. A piece of paper, crumpled. I open it. It's some sort of drawing. It's like the ones on the walls, only smaller and more detailed.

'Maybe you should look at that,' she whispers.

And she's different now — scared — won't hold my eyes.

I don't know how long I look at this bit of paper, but the bunker seems to roll round me as I do. It's like I'm in a ship, sinking. Because this thing — this picture I'm looking at — it isn't an ordinary drawing. Ashlee's face is staring back from it. Only her face is also a deer's face, and that deer is running through woods. She's beautiful, half-wild. I blink, look at all of it, make sure.

There are wolves chasing this Ashlee-deer too, drawn in dark detailed lines. There's one wolf in front, bigger than the others. More desperate. Enjoying this chase.

'My dad drew this,' Emily says. 'He must have drawn it weeks, maybe months ago, before Ashlee died . . . I found it in his car . . .'

Her words drift away. I look at the wolves' faces, the excitement in the deer's eyes. I have a feeling about what Shepherd was drawing. Does Emily see it too? Did her dad tell her about it? Did Joe?

I trace the muscly shoulders of the wolf in front of the pack, the way its mouth stretches back into what could be a snarl or a smile. Shepherd must've looked out from this gun slit and seen us, heard us all. He got the movement right, that feeling of running through this wood. The darkness. The chase. He got *her* right.

Emily is still staring at me really intensely, like she knows something, like she's waiting for me to tell her everything. It's freaking me out. Now I'm proper shaking.

Because I'm thinking – when Emily looks at this sketch, who does she really think chased Ashlee here that night?

What does she really think about me?

33

Emily

His eyes are wild. But what was I expecting? That he'd be relieved? That he'd see the sketch and be OK? Tell me it doesn't mean anything?

We both flinch when thunder cracks. Damon is shaking, *really* shaking; he's looking at the pictures on the walls then back at the sketch. He's seen Ashlee in it, he must have done – why else would he be reacting like this? But has he seen Dad there too? Does he think this picture is proof that Dad watched Ashlee in the woods? Is it evidence that what happened that night wasn't an accident? I move away from him, let him be. He buries his face hard into the wall of the bunker.

I want him to tell me this sketch means nothing.

He keeps quiet.

When he sits up, his eyes are dark holes, the bruise like a shadow on his cheek. He's stretching his fingers forward, they're shaking, he's stroking the dark lines of the wolf in that picture.

I stay silent. Because, after all, it might not be my dad he's seeing. And if Damon can't see Dad in this, like Joe couldn't, then maybe I can relax.

Damon breathes out so slowly his breath waits too, hangs in the bunker air. 'This picture . . .' he starts, his voice husky and quiet. 'It's not . . .'

I watch him. His eyes flick to the gun slit and he frowns as he thinks. Then he stands, goes to the slit and peers out.

'Your dad was looking out at the woods from in here, wasn't he? That's how he saw it all?'

I lower my head. Damon's got it. He sees everything in this picture I've been scared about. There's a sharp twist in my guts, and it takes all I have to stop a sob from escaping. How can I pretend this sketch means nothing now?

'Ashlee in the woods,' Damon murmurs. '. . . months ago. And Shepherd saw it . . .'

He's trying to understand. I bite hard on my lip, taste blood. *You were right about the killer's blood*, that's what I should say, *you were right about it all*. Now I wish I hadn't shown him this sketch. Wish I'd never found it. I should have torn it up. I should have believed Joe when he said it meant nothing. I am an idiot. Stupid!

'Have it,' I say, pushing it at him. I don't want to see it any more.

And maybe this is a mistake, but if Damon has this sketch, it will be his decision what to do with it next. Not mine. And if he tells the police? Then it's not my fault if Dad stays in prison for life. I don't have to feel guilty. My throat goes tighter. I want to throw things.

'Why are you showing me this?' Damon says.

But that's obvious, isn't it? Because it can't just be me who sees, this *evidence* can't just be up to me. Damon's face is pale as he watches me, the hollows under his eyes loom. Again, he looks like I feel.

'You need to get warm,' he says. 'Fast.'

He reaches across and touches the side of my neck. I gasp. His fingers are like streaks of ice. He frowns as he looks at me. Whose face is he seeing right now? Mine or Dad's? Mine or a monster's? Why is he being kind?

I press my hands to the floor, try to steady myself. I'm half expecting to touch mouse fur or moth wings or the curled up legs of a spider . . . something dead. Damon finds a candle, lights it and holds it close. It doesn't make me warmer. But it does make the walls glow orange. I feel like a trapped animal, shivering.

Very slowly, he crawls towards me. I hear the rustle of his coat as he lifts his arm and places it around me. 'Are you warmer?'

I don't answer. But I shut my eyes. I try to will myself warm. I think I hear Damon's breathing change, get lighter. I know it shouldn't feel good to be this close to Damon, especially not now. I know he's only doing this to make me warm, so I don't die of hypothermia. I know he must hate me even more after seeing this sketch. But, even so, I could stay here, just like this, for a while I could. I could concentrate on how Damon smells like damp clothes and dirt. I could listen to him breathe. Just for a few moments. Just until I'm warm. I feel his heartbeat making a rhythm like the rain. We're quaking like leaves now, both of us. And I don't know why we're leaning like this, against each other, why he'd want to. Shouldn't he be running with that sketch, running to the police to change everything?

Maybe I should tell Damon about Dad's scruffy, unkempt hair, the wispy, greying beard. Maybe I should say how, in those last few months, it was almost as if he'd been trying to look like a wolf.

'Your skin's like chilled meat,' Damon says. 'You're freezing!' He shuffles away to pull off his soaking duffle coat. 'Have this.'

'It won't help.' But my teeth are chattering too much to get the words out properly. I see something else as he's struggling with the coat. 'Wait!'

The combat shirt he's wearing has ridden up and I can see his skin. There are goosebumps and bruises all over him, but there's something else too. There's a huge tattoo at the base of his spine. I reach out and almost touch it.

'Can I?' I say.

When he nods, I lift his shirt a little higher until I can see that spreading out across his entire back is a tree. There are dark curls across his shoulder blades, winding branches stretching towards his armpits, dark and intricate leaves and tiny inked birds. It's swaying as his body trembles. I almost forget about Dad's sketch and what it has to mean, forget that Damon and I are even in this bunker. I just see his skin. See him.

'That must have hurt,' I whisper.

'Like hell.' Damon pulls his shirt down quickly, covering it. 'It's the same tattoo my old man had, exactly. I've copied it. He had a thing about oak trees.'

I think he's babbling now, nervous, talking in a rush so there's no silence between us. He's turning towards me and holding his duffle coat out. I see that his lips are trembling.

'You think it was my fault, don't you?' he says. 'Why Ashlee was here, why she . . .?'

I know I should shake my head. Because if this sketch does mean that Dad was watching Ashlee before that night, then it's not Damon's fault about anything. It wouldn't matter if Ashlee had been in the car park that night or any other night. It means Dad would have done it anyway. Like the newspapers say. I'm shivering hard.

I want him to rip up this sketch and burn it in that candle. I want him to tell me we'll find someone else to blame. But Joe and I already tried that and it didn't get us anywhere. I want more of his warmth.

I smell the mud on his duffle coat, the damp in its collar. I watch him lick his bottom lip. I want him to see how I'm not like my dad too, want to show him.

I notice him go tense. He's seen me watching him. I

feel like an idiot now, like the freak again: like how I did when I pinned him to the forest floor.

I stand up fast, try to, only I stumble with cold, stiff muscles and have to steady myself on the wall. I let his coat drop. I should keep away from Damon, like Joe says, I shouldn't screw with his mind. Shouldn't screw with mine.

I'm moving my legs on the spot, getting life back into them. Pins and needles shoot up my calves. Then we both hear it, the rain slowing, slowing, stopped.

'I'm sorry,' I whisper. 'For everything.'

And I don't know if I'm saying this because I'm sorry about me, or about Dad, or because of this whole messed-up situation.

34

Damon

That girl surprises me again — she's away and out of this bunker, too quick to stop. As I pick up my coat and put it back on, I hear her feet pounding on the forest floor. I don't understand her. Why did she just show me this picture? Why did she leave it?

And why did I hug her like that too?

Idiot!

I breathe out in the dark, blow the candle, try to get the lamp turned off. What does Emily Shepherd know? And what is she going to tell? And her last word, still ringing in my ears — *sorry*.

Why?

When I stand, I try not to look at Shepherd's drawings

on the walls, try not to see the wolves everywhere. I'm so damn cold — can hardly think with it. Emily's expression is still in my head, her eyes focusing on my face, her fingers on my arm. Who is she, really? What does she want?

I take the picture of Ashlee. Wedging my shoes into the corners of the entrance, I stretch up and out, then skid over ground that's gone wet and muddy since we've been inside the bunker. Maybe Emily Shepherd's playing me. Giving me this drawing could be some sort of trick to make me go to the police. I got no clue about this girl at all.

I kick through leaves and search, look up in branches too — anywhere a phone or a collar could be stashed. I still hope. It's like I'm moving without my brain's say-so. Like it's not even me in my body and I'm looking down on this strange person doing strange things from above. On the other side of the clearing from where we arrived, I find a small animal pathway. It's well worn, maybe from the police investigation, or the animals that use it, or . . .

I turn my head and check, both ways. I know where this path leads, both sides of it. Course I do! This path is one of the edges of Game Play: a boundary. I pause to take this in. All that time we'd been so close to this bunker! No wonder Shepherd drew what he did.

Then it sinks in where exactly this path leads, both sides of it. If I turn right, I'd get to that hollow Ashlee took me to that night. And if I turn left? Well, that way I'd link up with the main track of Darkwood. And if I crossed that and kept going? I breathe damp, heavy air as I realise it: this path turns into Ashlee's shortcut track home – it's the very same path! I take another breath. I turn left and walk a little way. This means that this path is a direct route between the hollow and Ashlee's shortcut, this means that Shepherd's bunker is in the middle of them both. Did Ashlee use this path to get to her shortcut that night? Is this how Shepherd heard her?

I could've used this path to get home that night too.

I kick through dead leaves, look in branches, still hoping for that collar and phone. Nothing! There are deer prints on the ground too, though, pointing me on like arrows. I follow them and keep going towards Ashlee's shortcut, towards my own way out of here, towards Mack who I got to speak to more than ever now.

There are still things I don't understand – that dragging sound I'd thought about in Shepherd's car, the anger I'd remembered feeling that night, Ashlee's missing collar and phone. It's like there's something big I'm on the edge of understanding. Something I'm scared of pressing at. Something *more*.

I walk a few more metres down this path, and that's when I see it – it's got to be the biggest, widest oak tree in Darkwood. And it's got branches stretching out to me, waiting. I go towards it, almost like I'm being pulled there, stumbling off the path. My fingers crash into deep, ridged bark that smells sharp. Tree sap sticks to my fingers. It's strange, but something about this tree feels safe. I touch the bark and it all feels so familiar. I dig my fingers into it, see parts of it splinter off and get under my nails. I've held on to this tree before. It's like my skin is remembering it.

Why?

I wrap my arms around the trunk and I kick it. Over and over. I grasp at it like I can pull it from the ground. I want to shout. I'm going mad to think I know a fucking tree!

That's when the tips of my fingers catch on something. There's a hole here, round the other side of this trunk. I pull my face away to see. As I look at it, I'm getting hit again with that strange, heavy feeling. Like I'm knowing something. Like I'm remembering.

I step round so I can peer inside. There are feathers and twigs and dried leaves, but the hole goes deeper than this. There is something else inside. I stretch to reach it, and this heavy sense I've got gets worse. I know what this is, what it has to be. It's been hidden here.

I pull it out.

In my hands is a pink sparkly dog collar, soft wool on its inside. Hanging off the side of it is a heart-shaped dog tag, small and silver. That tag has two letters on it – two letters that were engraved into it in a pet shop and paid for by me: AP.

I run my finger over them, wipe dirt off the dog tag 'til it shines again, 'til I see my ugly, shitty face staring back.

Ashlee's collar.

Finally.

Here.

I look back into the hole. But there's just this collar. Nothing else. Her phone isn't here.

I squint back towards where the bunker is. Shepherd could've come down this path and hidden this collar here. But why not the phone too? I turn the collar over: it's stained with dirt. I press my nose to it, but her smell has gone.

Nothing feels right about this. I've got this weird sick feeling winding around inside me. I have to walk. I shove the collar deep inside my cargos pocket, take it with me, though part of me wants to forget I've even seen it here at all. I don't feel no relief in finding it like I thought I would. I walk the path towards Ashlee's shortcut track, towards the main car park too, towards town, and towards Mack.

35

Emily

My phone beeps. A voicemail, someone must have left it when I'd been in the bunker. I pull my phone out and check. Joe. He's apologising for the way he was earlier — he must be. He won't want me to stay angry with him for long. I lean against a tree and listen. His voice is hesitant, quieter than usual, but not apologetic.

'I'm right about Damon,' he says. 'He is suspicious, not who you think.' He breathes in and I can tell he's trying to work out what to say next. 'Just call me back, Emily. You need to know something.'

I press myself to the damp bark behind me, remember how Damon's arm had felt heavy and warm around my shoulders in the bunker. I think of Damon's tired eyes too, how sad he'd looked when I'd shown him the sketch. It was so obvious what Damon saw in it.

It takes me a while before I return Joe's call. It's going to be hard to tell Joe everything that just happened – because this is it then. Joe's the last person to believe in my dad. I feel like a traitor, a kind of Judas. I'm almost glad when I hear that Joe's phone is turned off now – I don't leave a message. It's weird, though. Why would he turn his phone off if he wanted me to call him back? Come to think of it, why is he being so odd about everything?

I start walking for his house, realising that if Damon does show the police that sketch, Joe needs to listen to me, and fast. I also need to tell Mum.

36

Damon

People get out of my way, all down the high street. People are parting to let me pass. They're staring. Maybe they think I'm one of those crazy, drunk war vets that hang out under the railway bridge. I keep my head down, cover up my old man's shirt with my coat. I keep hold of the picture in my pocket. When I start thinking about Emily Shepherd's eyes again, I stomp through a puddle. I go straight past the entrance to our flat and I don't buzz the intercom. If Mum was bothered about me she would've called my phone. I think I'm going mad with all this – literally, fucking MAD. If I don't straighten out something soon I'll be like those figures in those drawings on Shepherd's bunker walls – the ones of the hangings, the guns against the heads, the disappearing into dark, swirling holes . . .

Maybe.

I need to see Mack. Get warm. Things'll make sense after that.

I go straight to Mack's garage and bang hard on its side door. He don't answer for ages and I'm almost about to bang again, when I hear the lock turning. He opens it a crack, I see immediately that his eyes are bloodshot and he's just woke up. He stinks of booze.

'Been waiting for you to show,' he says.

He don't look happy. He don't even look like he's going to let me in. I push past him anyway, heading for the couches. I'm about to launch into what just happened with Emily Shepherd and what I got in my pocket — I'm even about to pull out Ashlee's collar — when he grabs my arm and turns me back.

'What happened to you?' He's speaking in a hoarse whisper, frowning at my clothes.

'Got wet, didn't I?'

'I meant last night.' He chucks me an old towel. 'You haven't been in the woods all this time, have ya?'

I shake my head. I smell cigs and whisky and hangover in his breath. I wonder how long him and the boys stayed out for? Did they play another Game? Drink in the car park?

'So, where'd you go?' Like the people on the High Street, he's looking at me like I'm a full-blown Crazy. 'Why'd you run off like that?'

This is my chance, to tell him about being with Emily in Shepherd's bunker, to explain all that stuff I'd thought last night – those images I'd had.

'Just let me sit down at least!'

His eyes are narrowing in confusion. I want to tell him – and I will! – but right now I want to get inside properly, I want to sit on one of Mack's couches and get warm, just want to not be hassled for a moment, let the words come when they're ready.

'We looked for you,' Mack whispers. 'Me and the boys – for ages.'

Now I see why Mack's annoyed – because I ran off from them last night, because I didn't explain, because that's the sort of thing a soldier would never do in a real combat situation. And why's he whispering anyway?

'Could've called my phone,' I say. 'Could've come after me.'

That uneasy feeling's back as I remember who did come after me. Wilder. And that's as strange as the rest of all this.

I go across to where the telly and couches are. I just want this to be an ordinary Saturday morning; I want to be playing video games half the day and go into the trance of it. I don't want to have to think or work anything out. But I have to, don't I? And it hits me like a hammer to the skull all this stuff I got to think about. *I fooled about with Ashlee in that hollow. I think I passed out. I think she walked back past Shepherd's bunker.*

I found her collar.

I knew it was in that tree.

'Emily Shepherd knows,' I blurt out. It's a start.

I hear Mack stop behind me. 'What?'

And I'm about to tell him everything – even about that dragging sound that's still going round in my brain, even how it'd felt familiar to have my hands tightening round Ed's neck – but I see the others. Ed's sprawled on the big couch, his coat over him like a blanket. Charlie is curled up tight in the beanbag. I'm so surprised to see them that I just stand there, staring. I'm jealous of the way they can sleep like that.

'Heavy night, then?' I say.

Mack tries a smile, which I don't return. Because that should be me sleeping there; those two never used to stay over after a Game. I start backing up, away from the boys and the telly, back to the main part of the garage. What was I thinking anyway? Playing video games all day like nothing's up? Like I'm normal?

'What are you on about, *Emily Shepherd knows*?' Mack says. 'Knows what?'

I lean against the bench, but there are three dead rabbits there – fresh, like the boys caught them last night. Mack steps in front of me before I can check them out, forces me to look at him instead. 'I thought you were staying away from that girl, anyway?'

He's trying to say this casual, almost like it's a joke, but I know he's freaking out, I can tell by the way his temples are pulsing and how his jaw's gone tight. I run a hand through my hair, rest my forehead against a shelf of

Mack's games. I could shut my eyes. I could faint from this tiredness. Again, I get that sense that I'm looking down on me from above, watching the movements I make: tracking me like I'm a criminal in some film.

'Emily Shepherd knows about the Game,' I say eventually. And my voice sounds kind of spaced.

Mack takes this in, watching me. 'You sure? She told you?'

'Not as much, but . . .'

I feel the picture in my pocket, the collar next to it. What do I show him first?

'Come on then, explain.' Mack pushes a rabbit across the bench towards me, he slides a skinning knife across too. 'Do this same time.'

I look at the rabbit's draping back legs, the rigid neck. I don't pick it up, or the knife.

'She knows,' I say again. 'I got proof.'

I take out Jon Shepherd's picture and hold it out.

'Shepherd drew this,' I say. 'Months ago. Emily found it in his car. And there are other drawings in his bunker, ones like the wolves . . .'

Mack's eyes flick to mine when I say the word *bunker*. 'You went there too? With her?'

I shrug. 'Wanted to see.'

Mack sucks in air through his teeth. 'I'm worried about you, mate. This is morbid, what you're doing. It's wrong!'

So I explain the picture how I see it. 'Shepherd's drawn the Game . . . there's Ashlee, the rest of us . . .' I point out the deer and the wolves, but Mack still doesn't look like he's getting it. 'I'm chasing her,' I say, my finger hovering over the wolf in front. 'Through Darkwood. Shepherd must've seen me do it, seen all of us. He must've been looking out. His bunker's on the edge of Play!'

Finally, Mack takes the picture. 'But this is just a wolf, a deer . . .'

'It isn't.' I step forward and point out what Mack hasn't seen yet, what I've hardly admitted to myself. 'That wolf is wearing a collar.' I pause. 'And that deer looks like Ashlee!'

'Ashlee?' Mack shakes his head fast, too fast. 'Nah, mate, you're seeing things.' He throws a glance towards the couches, goes back to the picture. 'Firstly, that collar is just a darker line in the drawing. Secondly, how can a deer look like a person?'

'I dunno.' I shrug. 'But it does. Look properly.'

He keeps staring, but again he shakes his head. 'You gone mad, mate. Why are you even worried about this? It's a picture of animals!'

I remember the intense way Emily stared at me as I looked at this sketch. *She* knew. *She* saw it.

'It's Ashlee,' I say. 'It's us. Emily Shepherd gave it to me because she knows about the Game too. She even said she was sorry . . . like she was sorry she knew, or sorry she was going to go to the police or . . . I dunno, sorry about *something*. It was odd.' And now I'm feeling really mixed up.

Mack waits, frowning.

I throw my arms wide. 'If Emily does go to the police with this, then the police'll come after me, and I'll have to tell them . . . tell them . . .'

My head reels as it hits me: what else I'd have to tell the police once I start . . . how I'd been in the woods and chasing Ashlee just like in this picture. How I'd lied about walking Ashlee to that track that night. How I don't remember what'd happened at the end of the Game.

And about how she'd said something to me that had made me angry? What about that?

About how I'd found this collar?

It's like something has unbolted in my brain: it started after talking to Emily on the Leap. It's like I've widened a door and everything's whooshed inside: all these images and mixed-up thoughts. I go back to the picture.

'The police will think I chased Ashlee to Shepherd, ' I say. 'They'll look at this picture and think it's my fault she was there!'

Mack stares at the rabbits. 'But you walked her back to her shortcut. Remember! That's what you told them.'

'I don't remember it, not one bit. I don't even remember the Game finishing. I was too drunk, Mack, and you know it!'

I'm thinking about being in that hollow. Fooling around with Ashlee. I'm thinking about how much dust she'd given me. I wouldn't have even been able to walk straight, let alone walk her back to her shortcut.

Mack reaches towards the bench, grabs the skinning knife. 'You walked her back,' he says firmly, waving the knife at me. 'You're a fool if you say anything different.'

I'm touching the collar in my pocket, wrapping it

round my fingers. I'm thinking 'bout how I just knew this collar was inside that tree. I should tell Mack about that too.

'Give it me back,' I say.

But Mack holds Shepherd's picture away from me. 'Listen, Damo, no one except you is going to look at this picture and see the Game in it. Seriously. Not even Emily Shepherd!'

He's staring at me.

'Then why did she show me?' I say.

'I dunno! 'Cause she's trying anything? She's desperate? She wants you to go to the police and get the heat off her dad?'

He grabs me round the back of my neck, which feels weirdly soothing, like how a cat would pick up its kittens.

'You've got to stop this,' he says. 'Shepherd has admitted. And whatever you do, or don't, remember it won't make any difference now.' He squeezes the back of my neck until I look at him. 'You're a good person, Damo. The best! If your first thought was that you walked her back, then you walked her back. You don't lie.' He leans closer, his eyes pleading. 'Go home and chill. If Emily Shepherd goes to the police, she goes to the police. You'll be all right, I mean it.'

He lets go of my neck. But I don't feel *all right*; I don't feel like *the best*. And I *am* someone who lies. I'm remembering Emily's intense gaze, the words she'd said to me on the Leap: *you were the last person to see her alive* . . .

'You know, she could think it's me,' I say. 'It's possible. Emily Shepherd could think it's me that did everything.' I

250

choke on air as this thought sets in. 'She could think her dad drew this picture as some kind of, I dunno, like a warning or something . . . if she tells the police that, if she convinces them I'm in that picture and so's Ashlee, and that I'm chasing her, then . . .'

In one quick movement, Mack takes the skinning knife and slices the picture.

'That is crazy,' he says, scrunching the two sides into tight balls. 'Don't you even think that! It's the stupidest thing I ever heard.'

He's so determined, I shut right up. He aims the bits of the picture at the sink. One goes in, one doesn't.

'Stop going mad,' he says. 'You know what's true. Shepherd wanted to kill her — he's been charged for it.' His eyes hold on to mine. 'It's not the army you'll end up in if you keep up with all this, Damo, it's a loony bin.'

He walks round the other side of the bench, then pulls one of the rabbits towards him like the conversation is over. He makes a cut at the back of its neck, starts ripping the fur away. I flinch like an idiot. He's trying to act normal, I know he is, he's trying to act like it's a normal Saturday and we're doing normal things, but the pulse in his temples is beating stronger now, and he's doing the skinning too fast and rough. He's ruining that pelt.

Maybe I am just going mad. Maybe Emily Shepherd is just trying to set me up. Or maybe there is something else. Is it Mack who's not saying something? Not wanting to believe it? He's got the knife clasped in his hand so tight his fingers are white round it.

I think about that animal path. The bunker in the middle between the hollow and Ashlee's track. I think about Shepherd watching us all those months ago.

'Why did he even draw it?' I say. 'Why did he even watch?'

Mack stops pulling the skin over the rabbit's shoulders. 'He didn't!'

Ed turns over on the couch then, and we're both quiet. There's so much I got to say, but I see now Mack's not going to listen. He's hellbent on sticking to that story I threw them the morning after.

'I didn't walk her back to that track,' I say, quieter this time, watching Ed bury his head into a cushion.

'You didn't do anything bad either!' The knife – wet from the rabbit – is waving in Mack's hand. He holds it up towards me as he speaks. 'If you even start thinking you've done anything, you've ruined yourself. Your life's over. Good as. You wouldn't be able to live with it. No one in the army's going to let you in with doubt like that. Don't you see?'

And I wonder, for a second, whether this is just about the army, whether it's just about us serving together someplace – staying brothers for always, teammates. Mack chucks the ruined rabbit into the sink on top of the ball of Shepherd's sketch. I watch rabbit blood seep into the paper.

'You know what this is?' Mack says quietly. 'It's grief. Sadness!' He nods at me. 'I get it! I understand why you feel guilty. You brought Ashlee into our Game, you were the one who was meant to look out for her . . . but *mate!*'

I look away, my eyes hot and weird-feeling.

'Mate, sometimes things happen that we can't control.' He moves his head so I'm looking at him again. His eyes look red and sore too. 'Damo, we can't always be every-where.' His voice is lowered, and serious. 'Sometimes people do their own thing and sometimes you can't do nothing about it. This isn't your fault.'

'I could've done something,' I say. 'I could've . . .'

'You're a good person, mate. I'm looking out for you. And I know you just need to sleep. That's all.'

'I can't.'

Everything about me is aching, though, wants to be lying down. My stomach is a hollow, hungry hole. Over on the couch, Ed mumbles something. Mack walks over to him and digs into one of his coat pockets. 'You go back to sleep and all,' he says.

When Mack comes back he's holding out one of Ed's joints, fat and a little squashed and fragrant. 'This help?' he says. 'Or I got some sleeping pills somewhere too, or some of my dad's antidepressants? Booze? Or Ed's other stuff? Walking pharmacy, me!'

I almost grin. Because this is the old Mack; it's not the Mack I just been seeing right through, who I know is almost as worried as me. But I still got my hand on that collar in my pocket and a hundred questions in my head.

'You did what you said,' Mack repeats. 'Even if Emily Shepherd goes to the police, it'll be all right.'

I don't hold his gaze.

I wonder what he really thinks of me. What he believes. Maybe, like me, he just doesn't know any more.

So I take the joint. Because now I got an idea how I could use it.

37

Emily

The closer I get to our lane the worse I feel. I start to run. It was different, in that bunker, being so near to Damon with no one else there, watching him shiver, having his arm around me. It had felt like I'd needed to show him that sketch. Now, the further I'm away from him, the more I'm not so sure.

What have I done?

I slam open the wooden gate to our lane, hear it bash against a tree trunk, bash into the thoughts in my head too. The thoughts that say — so what if Dad drew Ashlee as a deer? So what if he'd seen her in these woods before that night? Even this doesn't make him a killer. It just makes him someone who liked to draw people as animals, like he's always been. It makes him someone who watched. Who waited.

Why didn't I think this through before? Why does my mind jump around so much with what it believes?

Again, Joe's mum sees me coming and ushers me into their kitchen, rubs a teatowel or a towel or something up and down me to get me dry.

'You're soaking,' she says. 'Where've you been? The woods? Does your mum know?'

And I'm nodding and I'm trying to evade her. Because I'm looking for Joe, and I'm already moving for the hall.

'He's not here, love,' she says.

And that stops me.

'I thought he was with you, to be honest,' she adds.

I must look really confused because his mum comes towards me again and wraps an arm around my shoulder. 'Why don't you wait for him upstairs? Stay and get warm at least?'

And I don't have any other options right now apart from go home and explain to Mum about the mess I just got myself in. I hear Joe's dad and Finn in the living room, singing songs, but they don't come out. I wonder if Damon gets this too, people avoiding him. I wonder what he's doing with that sketch.

I'm grasping on to the banister, pulling myself up so fast I'm tripping on the stairs. It's Joe's fault I showed Damon that sketch. It's Joe's fault because he didn't listen to me this morning, and I got mad. It's Joe's fault because he's meant to be my friend and now everything's changed.

And where is he anyway?

As I try Joe's phone again, I pick through things in his room. On his bookshelf I see a ticket stub from when we went to the cinema months ago and saw that dumb sci-fi film. I find a note I passed him in class. When I flip through his half-done homework, I see the games of Hangman we'd played on the sides of his exercise books. We'd done all this when we'd been proper friends, months ago. Why didn't I just make Joe listen to me?

'I'm waiting in your room,' I say into his voicemail this time. 'You need to tell me what's going on. And I need to tell you.'

I'm sick of secrets. Sick of not knowing what everyone is thinking – not knowing the whole of it. I slump into Joe's desk chair and my hand is in a fist before I realise, pressing into the desk. His computer screen comes back on with a jolt. Investigations should be about interviewing every single person who ever knew anything about the victim, putting it together in some genius, objective machine that calculates the right story. Maybe we'd get to the truth then. Or maybe there would still be secrets lurking someplace, dark cracks through it all?

I thump my fist on the desk, and the screen shakes. It's strange that Joe's left his computer on – wherever he's gone, he must have gone in a rush. I start clicking on things. If I sit here any longer, just waiting for Joe, I'll go mad. I need something to do. Because, right now, I want to get in a taxi and go to Dad's prison and apologise, talk and talk. I want to go to Damon's house and get that sketch back.

I click into Joe's photo programme. I've seen most of Joe's photos before, but never all of them. And I need to think about something else – *see* something else – something other than that sketch. Something other than Damon's shaking lips in the bunker, the way his eyes had darted to mine. I need to calm my mind before it panics big time – before I start thinking I've just done the worst thing I've ever done in my life.

But Joe has hundreds of photos of Darkwood on here, so my mind isn't going anywhere new. I flick through picture after picture. Joe really is obsessed, capturing the trees in all the different seasons, day and night. His pictures make the woods look powerful and mysterious and huge, like the woods in Dad's bedtime stories.

There are a couple of photos of the bunker too. My hand quivers over the mouse as I look at them. I've never shown Joe the bunker, though I have told him about it. Did he follow me there to find it? Follow Dad? In these photos the entrance lid is open, and the hole looks like a dark pit. Joe could have sold these shots to the papers. I shift on his desk chair, suddenly uncomfortable. Why would Joe hide this from me? What else has he hidden?

I'm curious now. So I start to go through every folder, even the trash, which has hundreds more shots of trees and leaves. And that's where I find it: a photo of me. I'm side on, face serious, the shot taken a little distance away. I'm going through the gate from the lane into Darkwood, maybe I'd been going to collect Dad. As I keep clicking through, I see more shots of me in the trees, all of them shadowy, half in focus. And I'm swallowing hard now and trying not to chuck the computer keyboard across the room – because I don't know when Joe took all these photos. And because there's a photo of Dad here too. In it, he's curled forwards, crouching in the woods. His head is bowed towards a pile of dried branches. He looks empty, totally alone, like a hollowed out tree trunk hit by a storm.

Joe took these shots without ever asking either of us?

I click through more photos of dark, overgrown passages through the woods. But there's no more shots of me or Dad or the bunker. Maybe they were one-offs. Could he have snapped them when he'd been with us after all?

I stop on another picture.

At first I think it's of me again, but the girl in this picture is taller and curvier, the sun glints gold on her hair. I gasp, can't help it. This time it's Ashlee Parker who is slipping through the trees. And it looks like she's unaware of her picture being taken too.

I stare for ages. What is she doing there? Why is Joe watching? The next shot makes me breathe in harder. Because, in this photo, Ashlee Parker is posing, staring into the lens and leaning forward. Her lips are parted slightly and her eyelids are half closed like she's trying to copy some sort of sexy model pose, like she's trying to look seductive. Her eyes glint, sparkly make-up smeared around them. She looks sexy and confident – like a kind of bad girl rockstar – not like the Ashlee Parker at school.

How has Joe got this shot? Why?

My hand is shaking as I try to move the mouse around the screen, as I furiously try to find the date that these photos were taken. I click on info and see it: June, not long before we broke up for the summer holidays, two months before Ashlee died, round about the time Joe got dropped from the cross-country team. I click through the rest of the photos, but there are no more of Ashlee. No more of me or Dad either. No more of the bunker.

I go back to that close-up of Ashlee. I've seen so many pictures of Ashlee Parker in these past few weeks, but there have been none that look like this. Strangely, the picture of her that seems closest is Dad's sketch – where she's half wild deer. I gaze at her, I'm practically willing her to open her mouth and talk. *Tell me what happened* – that's what I'd ask – *tell me what happened that night. Tell me why Joe has this picture of you!*

There are bits of twigs and ivy threaded through her hair, mud on her cheeks. If it weren't for her stylish signature scarf draped around her neck, she could have stepped from some survival film.

I grab my phone, start ringing Joe again. Looking at this photo is making me nervous. Because now I'm sure that Joe is hiding something, something big. Because suddenly it feels as if I don't know him at all. But as soon as his phone starts to ring this time, his bedroom door is opening and there he is, inside this room and walking towards me.

'I got your message,' he says, all in a rush. 'I tried to wait for you earlier, but . . .'

And I want to know where he's been, and I want to ask him, but now that he's here, so tall and right in front of me, I can't find my words. I stumble up from the desk as he steps closer.

'Emily? What's wrong?'

Joe's frowning, looking around. It's not long before he sees what is open on his computer screen. I watch his face turn pale.

'I can explain that,' he says quickly. 'That's what I've just been telling the police about. All of it.'

38

Damon

As I round the corner to our street I see there's a cop car parked outside where our flat is, and I freak then – really do – because even though I know I got to go to the cops with all this stuff in my brain, I know I'm not ready for it yet. Because maybe this means that Emily's done it instead. Can cops move this fast? Could they be looking for me already?

I skid to a stop and back up against some shop window. I breathe in cold air, feel the sting in my throat. Maybe they've been tracking me, seeing where I been going and how I been acting. I start shivering all over, still not proper warm from earlier. My stomach is empty as fuck.

I rub my hands over my eyes. I know what this is: the

cops just want to fill me in on the case, that's all. They're probably even DC Kalu and DC West – the ones who interviewed me; the ones who've been checking in with me pretty regular. They just want to keep me informed about how everything is going. But they've never arrived in a regular cop car before.

I pull Ed's joint Mack gave me from behind my ear and stick it in my pocket instead. I can't think about that yet. But soon . . .

A crowd of kids dressed as zombies stalk past me then, jolting me, talking about some party they've got going on tonight. I move round them and out on to the pavement so I can look up at our kitchen window. Mum's not at it. She'll be in the living room instead, offering the detectives tea and saying I'll be back soon. And I want to be back soon. I want to be back in my flat with no police there, asleep to everything. And I almost do it . . . almost just keep walking to the door and buzz the bell: I could just tell Mum where I been and what I been doing. This could be a chance, these cops being here. I could go inside and straighten out everything in my head. It could all be OK like Mack says.

I could also write my own prison sentence.

I need to be sure before I go through those cop station doors. I need to remember. Everything.

I hesitate, watching those zombie kids 'til they go round the corner. What kind of idiot tells the police the stuff that's going round his head?

So I stay, undecided, watching a crisp packet being

blown across the road. When my phone rings and I see that it's Mum, I turn it off. Get the panics all over again, only ten times worse. It feels like they're coming for me . . . the police, Emily, Mack, Mum . . . everyone's closing in. It's like I got to work out my story, and fast. It's like I've only got one more chance.

39

Emily

Joe is pulling me down the stairs, and I'm shouting at him before we're out of his house, trying to make him explain.

'Not here,' he's hissing.

His mum's waiting in the entrance to the kitchen, two cups of tea in her hands. 'Where you two off to?'

'Nowhere!' Joe yells, still dragging me behind.

And already we're out of the house, and this time I'm pushing past him.

'Why were you sneaking about in my room anyway?' he yells after me. 'I would've shown you!'

'But you didn't!'

I'm marching on ahead, towards the park where Joe

and I always used to talk.

'It's not what you think Em, honestly!'

I don't even know what I think. I'm practically running to get to the end of our street and on to the main road, desperate to get somewhere we're alone.

I look in front windows, see people watching telly. Would they close their curtains if they knew Jon Shepherd's daughter was looking in? If they knew the boy behind me had taken photos of Ashlee Parker looking like *that* in Darkwood? The side gate squeaks as I enter the park. When I get to the swings, I turn on Joe.

'I wasn't doing anything!' he says.

But he doesn't look at me. He sits awkwardly in a swing, like a grasshopper folded into a thimble. 'High as you can go?' he says, pushing his feet against the ground to make the swing move. 'Just one game?'

I hold the chains still, won't let him move. Seeing who can swing highest before chickening out seems ridiculous right now — playing a stupid kids' game! I kick the wood-chips viciously, making them fly up. 'When did you take that photo of her? Why?'

He wiggles the swing back and forth, trying to get it out of my grasp, keeps avoiding my gaze. His eyes dart to the climbing frame as if he wants to be on that instead. I push him backwards, hard enough that he has to hold on to the swing chains to stop from tipping off.

'Say something before I go to the police myself,' I demand. 'About you! About how you're hiding something to do with Ashlee Parker! About how you did

266

something with her you never told me about!'

Joe goes red at that.

'Why did you follow her?'

There's this angry feeling inside me, waiting to come out into a scream or a punch that's directed right at Joe.

He opens his mouth, hesitates. 'I . . . I thought I was following you.' His fingers grip on the chains. 'To begin with I did – that's why I took the first photo in the trees. You – *she* – looked like . . . I dunno . . . part of the woods. It was a good shot.'

I let the swing chains go, remembering Joe's other photos too. 'Why would you even follow me? Why do you keep following me?'

Joe stands, shuffles from foot to foot as he towers over me.

'And why didn't you tell me any of this?'

Joe's eyes flick to where a couple of children have come into the park. Immediately he starts walking, giving the roundabout a push as he passes and making it whirl. I get an image of leaning against Joe on that roundabout, sometime before the summer holidays, how his hand had pressed mine as we'd spun. We'd been with Kirsty and Beth and the rest of them, talking about what careers we'd have after school. Kirsty had said Joe fancied me and I'd laughed in her face. Maybe I'd been right to mock it. Maybe it was really Ashlee Parker he'd fancied all this time. Maybe he'd done more than just fancy her.

I jog to catch up with him. 'Where you going?'

'Somewhere private.' He turns left out of the park gates

like we're going towards town. 'Listen, Em,' he says quietly. 'I was taking photos for my project that day, I saw Ashlee, nothing dodgy. I was trying to catch the summer evening light on camera.'

'Ashlee Parker's not a summer evening,' I hiss.

'I know, but I *had* to take that first shot . . . and the second, well . . .'

He stops talking as we pass a group of men, stumbling from town and heading for the pub on the corner. One of them has a *Scream* mask pushed back on his head – a half-hearted attempt at Halloween. As we squeeze past on the pavement, I feel their stares sizzling into me; it's obvious they know who I am, maybe they're even army guys who knew Dad. If stares could physically hurt, there wouldn't be much left of me by now – not with the way this lot's looking. I get a sudden understanding of why Mum wants to move towns and get away from people who stare and hate without knowing the whole of us. Then I think of the photographs on Joe's computer and realise that I don't know the whole of him either. Maybe no one knows the whole of anyone. Even Darkwood's got secrets.

Joe takes the next left on to the footpath that circles around the back of the park. It is more private here, but this path goes past the barracks too and that brings its own kind of memories. When we're halfway along, with the park on one side and the barracks on the other, Joe stops. I watch the wind rattle the fence like it's clawing at it and I think about when Dad and I had stood with our noses pressed against this wire, when Dad was trying to explain what he did inside.

'I train,' he'd said. 'To go away and protect people.'

But what he really should have said was — *To go away and kill people. To kill people who have families and stories. To kill innocent civilians too.*

I shove Joe's shoulder to get his attention. He starts hesitantly, telling me again how he'd thought he was following me that day.

'Then you just disappeared,' he says. 'The next thing I know I'm getting jumped on from behind, hands around my neck and grabbing me.' He stops and finds my eyes. 'It was Ashlee Parker — she leapt on me and took my camera! Right off my neck!'

'Don't be an idiot.'

He leans in. 'I'm serious. She crept up and stole it. Then she just stood there laughing.'

'Bullshit.' That anger inside me swells. Because this doesn't sound like Ashlee Parker. And if Joe really fancied her, why doesn't he just say it? Why is he spinning me lines? 'Tell me the truth, Joe!'

'I *am*!' Joe rubs his knuckles across the side of his face. 'OK, listen,' he says. 'So, Ashlee stood there with my camera, and she said she'd only give it back if I took a photo of her — one photo — that's all.'

I raise my eyebrows.

'So . . . I didn't have a choice, did I? It was my camera — she had it. I had to!'

I don't believe him. 'Why would she want a photo anyway?'

I turn my head and look through the wire that separates us from the barracks, press my fingers against it . . . Dad said he went off to protect people when really he went off to kill. Everyone lies. No one tells the whole truth. There are dark cracks in everything. Even Joe.

'She wanted a good photo,' Joe says quietly. 'I guess for Damon, or, I dunno, . . . I think she was just having fun.'

I glance up at him. 'So why didn't you tell me?'

'I guess . . . I dunno! . . . I didn't want you to . . .' He struggles for words.

I shake my head, not understanding. I watch his neck flush.

'You don't know all of it,' he adds. He squints at something behind me, thinking. 'The photos aren't the worst.'

'So . . .?' I cross my arms.

'So . . .' He sighs. 'After I took that second photo, Ashlee came up close to me — like, *right up* close . . . and . . . well, she kept going on about how I was a good runner, and about how I should play some game with her or . . . or something like that. She was being really nice. Flirting, maybe.'

I'm frowning. This doesn't sound like the Ashlee Parker I knew from school. This sounds like someone made up. Like Joe's fantasy.

'Yeah, exactly,' Joe says, noticing my reaction. 'I was confused too.'

'What else?'

Joe's cheeks turn beetroot. 'Well, *that's* what's strange.'

'Go on.'

'So . . .' He swallows.

'So?'

'So, Ashlee put one hand on my waist and she reached up towards me. She touched my skin, like, right here . . .'

Joe puts his cold fingertips to the side of my neck and I shiver. He strokes me there gently. 'Like that,' he says, softer, thinking. 'I thought she was about to . . . you know . . .'

I jerk away from him. 'What? Kiss you?'

I almost laugh, and Joe sees it. But I can see by how red he goes that this is what he meant. It's ridiculous. Because Ashlee Parker was the prettiest girl in the school and there's no way she'd kiss a boy in the year below her, no way she'd kiss Joe Wilder. And anyway, she had Damon Hilary.

Joe turns away, jaw clenched. 'You think I'm a loser now, right?'

I try to imagine it. Ashlee close enough to Joe that he thought she liked him – that he thought she'd kiss him. I imagine Joe bending his head to Ashlee and being clumsy and unpractised and soft, his breath like Juicy Fruit. It makes me feel weird – uncomfortable – and like I know Joe even less.

'Thing is,' he continues. 'I knew she was just teasing me, knew she wouldn't have really done it . . . but still . . . I still stood there waiting . . . wanting her to . . . hoping.'

He puts his thumb in the side of his mouth and gnaws at the nail, rips bits off. He's still not looking at me.

I remember how close my face was to Damon's in the bunker, and on the bike trail, and how I'd wanted to kiss him. Me wanting to kiss Damon was worse than Joe wanting to kiss Ashlee. Wasn't it? And I'd wanted to keep that secret too.

'And Damon?' I say. 'You didn't care about what he'd think?'

Joe takes a breath. 'Damon was there.'

'What?'

'He might've even been watching the whole thing, I don't know. Either way, he came out of the trees pretty quickly.'

'Well, you were just kissing his . . .'

'No! I wasn't. Ashlee was standing really close, but *nothing happened!* Just that photograph!' This time Joe holds my gaze fiercely.

I'm still thinking about how mixed up this all is, how tangled my emotions are, so I just look at him and wait.

'Damon pushed me against a tree,' he says. 'Thumped me right into it! He said he was going to kill me!' Joe's eyes are boring into mine, urging me to understand. 'And something else weird?' he says. 'Ashlee laughed. She pulled Damon off me, but she was laughing like it was a game. They were both kind of . . . weird, revved up.'

I drop his eye contact. 'Where have you got this story from?'

He shuffles his feet. 'It's not a story.'

But would Damon really be like that? Would Ashlee? And has Joe really gone to the police about it?

'Why are you doing this?' I say.

Joe shakes off this question with an impatient twist of his head. 'How closely did you look at that second photo,

Em?' he says. 'Did you notice anything?'

'Only that it didn't look like Ashlee,' I say fast. 'Only that it looked like she was acting some part!'

Joe squints at the barracks. 'Yeah,' he says. 'But did you see the marks on her skin? They're there, tiny ones, you can see them round the edges of her scarf.'

I stare at him. 'What are you getting at?' There's an uneasy feeling in my stomach.

'On her neck,' he says again. 'I mean, maybe they're love bites or something, but they could be . . .' He's still looking across at the barracks. 'I mean, maybe Damon could've been playing rough with her all this time.'

My eyebrows shoot up.

Joe shrugs. 'He could've been.'

I start shaking my head, which makes Joe move nearer and grab my shoulders. 'It was just a thought! But, well, as soon as I started thinking it, I had to go to the police then, didn't I? I mean, photos like that could be evidence . . . thoughts like this . . .'

'Evidence of . . .?'

'Well . . . evidence of him hurting her . . . doing something . . . and then with Damon being in the woods again last night. It's all adding up . . . it's suspicious!'

My anger flares. 'If you thought that, why didn't you tell the police about it weeks ago? Why didn't you say anything when they arrested Dad? Why didn't you tell me?'

'Why do you think I was at the police station just now, Em?' His anger matches mine, almost. I lean away from it, surprised.

He's got no right to be angry. I'm not the one who's been hiding pictures of Ashlee Parker. I'm not the one keeping secrets.

'You told them everything then?' I say. 'About wanting to kiss Ashlee too? About following her through the woods like a stalker?'

Joe's eyes narrow. I push him, try to shove him and his stories away. I don't know if I'm angry because I believe him, or angry because I don't. I stand on tiptoes and look him in the eyes, as close to as I can. I try to imagine Damon playing rough with Ashlee – I do! – I consider it for about a second before I remember his arm around me in the bunker and how he was trying to make me warm. I think about Ashlee teasing Joe like he's said.

'Ashlee wasn't like that,' I say. 'Neither is Damon. You only have to talk to him to know.'

Joe rolls his eyes.

I'm thinking about my lips so close to Damon's that I could have kissed him – twice now. I'm thinking about how he'd been gentle with me and kind.

'You told the police something wrong.' But my voice is quieter now, less certain.

And I'm also thinking of how angry Damon had been on the Leap, how he'd held out his hand and pointed it at me like a gun. I'm remembering the words he'd used when he'd talked about my dad. I want to look at Joe's photo of Ashlee again – look for the marks, the teasing in her eyes. Could Joe be right about any of it?

Then I remember something else. 'You didn't listen to

what I was trying to tell you earlier,' I say. 'You didn't even look at that sketch I had. The one with Ashlee in it, Dad . . .'

I stumble on the words, feel my cheeks heating up. I can't tell Joe that I've just given that sketch away — to Damon! Joe would be right back at the police station then, he'd be panicking even more.

Joe's face changes as he watches me. He comes towards me. I step back into the fence rather than let him touch me again, though.

'I did look at that sketch,' he says quietly, nodding. 'And I did see Ashlee in it. You're right.' He breathes in and looks at me steadily. 'But your dad didn't draw himself . . . not in that sketch. He drew Damon.'

40

Damon

The sky is bruising grey. I run through the car park and into Darkwood, go on the main path 'til I find where Ashlee's shortcut veers to the left. But I don't take this shortcut. I go right instead, on to the deer path I was on earlier, towards that huge oak where I found Ashlee's collar. There's something pumping through me, making me fast: frustration and confusion and just pure goddamn fear. I get this urge to shout, go hoarse with it. Though I don't, because if the cops are after me, then these woods will be where they look next. I push my fist through bracken, shredding my skin. After the police've been at my flat, maybe they'll go to Mack's house next. And what's Mack going to tell them? About the conversation we just had? That I lied about walking Ashlee to her track? That I made the boys lie too?

Or will he keep trying to protect me? Because this could be what he's doing. This could be why he's being weird. I saw the way his temples pulsed when he spoke to me, how he gripped his skinning knife hard to cover up his shaking fingers. How he was freaking out like me. Is he trying to hide something? It would be just like him not to tell. Telling is against who he is, against all this stuff he believes in: loyalty and courage, soldiers trusting each other . . . all that. Mack don't tell secrets.

But whose secret is he keeping? Mine? What has he seen me do? What does he know?

I go faster, run 'til my lungs are screeching for air. I need to put everything together; I need to do what the internet article said and relive these images. Properly this time – all the way. I know how.

I skid into the oak tree. My eyes go hot just looking at it again, the fact that I didn't just imagine it. I pull Ashlee's collar out of my pocket and hold it in my hand. I remember her lips on my ear, the cold shiver I got each time I'd felt her breath there. I'm remembering my arm around her, then my arm around Emily Shepherd too. And – there – for a second, is something else. I'm thinking about swaying down the high street, and it's late, and my arm's around someone else. Someone is growling at me to keep quiet. Where's this thought come from? I bury my face into the tree's scratchy surface. This isn't the kind of thought I need. This is nothing!

But no other thought comes. So I keep walking down the deer path, towards where that hollow is. I take the joint from my pocket and put it back behind my ear.

At the hollow, I go to the spot I was at before, gather leaves into a pile and lay her collar on top. When I take out Mack's joint I don't let myself question it this time: just light and inhale. I suck 'til I cough, 'til I get those sweet grassy fumes inside me; I need to keep going 'til my mind goes to that hazy spun-out place. Ashlee would've called this Fairyland, this buzzed-out feeling . . . this mix of things real and dream. I don't want to go here again, but this is the last thing I got — my last attempt to remember. It's what the article said: *as many factors as you can . . . put it all together.* Well, I was out of it that night, wasn't I? And I've tried everything else. And there should be no interruptions this time.

Eventually my mind does start to slide someplace. I squint at the pile of leaves and try to picture Ashlee here with me. She was teasing me that night, pressing at me. I try out conversations, things we could've said. She'd wanted something, she'd been asking. She'd told me something too.

I grasp my fingers round her collar, pull it across the leaves. It drag, drag, drags. So I do it again, back the other way, just listening to the sound. I'm remembering that dream in Shepherd's car — that dragging noise — how that noise had made me think about shoes getting caught on rough ground. Made me think about someone being carried — pulled.

I dig my knuckles into the dirt, try to steady my breath. As many things 'til I remember!

So I suck on the joint. And I bend towards Ashlee's collar 'til it blurs in front of me. I bring my lips to the leaves, kiss them. They're rotting and cold. I shiver – badly. Because that's how she'd be now – rotting and cold. In a hole and alone. Her pretty face gone. Her sexy, long legs disintegrating. No more soft skin. No eyes. Just her clothes left. Just bones.

I can't stop shivering. I shout, muffle the sound by pointing my mouth at the earth. I taste mould and mud, dead leaves. Something makes my lips tingle. I take a vicious toke on the joint, breathe it in hard 'til I feel my throat go like sandpaper, 'til the taste of rotting things gets worse. Slimy leaves cling to my cheeks and I push them off rough. Another toke. My vision's fuzzy now. And I want to punch myself. Why don't I remember? Why don't all this just come back clear?

I gather the leaves towards me, as if it's a body I'm hugging, as if it's her. Something crawls on my hand, something else in my hair. I press my forehead against soft, decaying bits of wood. I'm sinking into this forest, rotting too. Keeping my forehead against the leaves, I listen . . . listen . . . and her voice comes back. Distant. I don't know if it's a memory I got now, or if it's her as a ghost. Right here.

I know . . . she's saying. I know what you want.

There's a whispery, chilling feeling around my neck. I see a million damp brown leaves . . . her pink collar . . . my arms clasping it all to me.

Shall I tell you something?

I claw at these words, pull earth towards me.

Damon . . .

Laughter.

There's a beetle on my neck. A thought at the edge of me.

You're not the only one I play with . . .

I breathe in pine needles. Cough. Images fling themselves about in my brain, like a cut-up movie on fast forward: a bundle of pictures that don't make no sense. Sweat on her neck. Hands on my chest and moving up. Ashlee rubbing fairy dust into her gums, like she's brushing her teeth with her finger. Ashlee punching me like Charlie does, short and sharp. Me pointing my fingers like a gun at her head. Mack's hands, shaking.

And she's laughing, laughing . . .

There are other ways to win collars.

You don't always have to play the same game.

You don't always have to play your Game.

Her voice bouncing off tree trunks and echoing round this hollow.

I flop on to my stomach, face against filth, woodlice in my hair.

She'd been talking about the boys.

'Tell me how you play the Game with them,' I'd said. 'How do they win your collar?'

She'd been laughing like she was so clever. Laughing like it was a secret she was spilling.

I press my body into the earth. The images keep coming. I'm seeing her collar fastened tight round Mack's neck. Round Ed's. Even round Charlie's. How many times? Who'd won it the most? I'm on the edge of something, a thought, can almost feel it. I grasp at the leaves. Feel mushrooms in amongst them, slimy cold slugs.

'How did you play the Game with them?' I say it again now, speak it into the earth, as if she can hear me . . . as if she's here.

But there's just the wind round me, moving through branches like a train coming.

I know what makes sense, though – the boys won Ashlee's collar because she couldn't fight like we could, because she was rubbish at the Game. But there'd been a few times I'd seen their collars round her neck too. It wasn't always mine she'd won, not all the time. But Mack would never have let her beat him by fighting. Would any of them? So how did she win?

Do you want to know my Game Plan?

And suddenly she's back, and she's bending close to my ear and she's telling me – she's telling me!

But it's a cold wind rushing through me too, and I'm up against these wet, stinking leaves and I'm still trying to hear.

Shall I tell you a secret?

I reach into the pile of leaves as if they're her, grab a bundle and clasp my fingers round. It's not the collar I'm trying to get at: it's her.

You going to get mad Damon? You going to fight me? . . . You haven't got my collar yet. You still owe me.

Her laughter is echoing round my skull. It's laughter like rain, falling on my neck and spine, sliding everywhere: rain like that night. Rain that started when we should've been screwing. But what were we doing instead? I dig my fingers into dirt, grab fistfuls.

I'm breathing fast.

And I'm thinking about hands on her body, on her neck – and jealousy shoots through me, rushing in my veins like something dangerous. I cough to get the taste gone. Spit.

I should've made Mack tell me why he's been acting so weird. I remember how Charlie's been odd these past few weeks too, and how Ed's been avoiding me. Have they all been keeping secrets? What were the games they all played with her?

I scatter the pile of leaves, throw them anywhere. I want to destroy this place. I want Ed to come along now so I can destroy him too! I remember my hands on his neck and how familiar it'd felt.

How jealous did I get that night?

I shake my head hard and the forest adjusts round me.

I'm *a good person* – that's what Mack said. He said to cling on to it.

But maybe it's hard to know who a person is when they're drunk and out of it on dust – when they're jealous as all hell. Like that, a person could do something so terrible they could block it. Couldn't they?

I feel her laughter shaking my skin. Her neck against

my fingertips. Anger firing me up like a match. I want to punch Mack's face. Punch me!

I suck on the joint. Emily's words are back now too, everything she'd said on the Leap: *there was someone else . . . Dad just found Ashlee that night, he was trying to help.*

And that drag, drag, dragging . . . over and over in my brain.

Someone could leave a body in that small clearing near the bunker and keep stumbling home. Someone could be so out of their head that they don't remember a thing. Someone could hide evidence in a tree.

I want to scream but I suck this joint instead, like I'm possessed, like it's the only thing I got left now, like if I suck for long enough and hard enough I'll get the right answer — the one I want — I'll be the good person Mack says. I won't have done nothing! The trees are turning into shapes above me, shapes like bodies, with arms stretching down and pushing me into the earth. I smell rot.

Could I have carried Ashlee? Could I have found the nearest tree and passed out? Could I have done more than this too?

I gasp in smoke. Mack's words are here, reminding me: *If you even start thinking you've done anything . . . you wouldn't be able to live with it.*

And I wouldn't.

I dig out my phone, try to focus on it enough to turn it on. I need to call Mack — he has to tell me what's true, what he's hiding. My throat goes tight as I think of his shaking hand around the skinning knife. The twitch in his eyes. Ashlee was going to tell me a secret that night. Maybe Mack knew it already. Maybe Mack was part of it. Maybe that's why I got mad.

I'm down to the filter now, but I want every last leaf inside me. I suck right through. My hands are changing shape, merging into the forest, sprouting leaves. I'm becoming part of this wood, this tangle. I get a memory of Emily looking at the tatt on my back, how wide and pretty her eyes had gone then. *It's like it's growing right out of you* – that's what her look had said. I reach to my back and touch where it starts. I don't much feel part of my old man no more, though. Only this wood. Only these rotting leaves. This dying stuff.

I chuck the phone at them, clasp Ashlee's cold, silver heart-shaped dog tag inside my hand instead, wrap her collar round my wrist. I suck at what's left of this joint 'til it burns my fingers, 'til it burns my lips. And my spine is moving like a wave, there's a gulping sound coming out of me. My muscles are heavy; my head a rock carving through the earth. I'm sinking down. Sinking deep. Joining the worms. Joining Ashlee.

41

Emily

'You've been a while,' Mum calls from the kitchen.
I'm slamming the door. I have been a while —
out the whole day. So much has happened. My brain is
rattling and I can't put it all together.

Mum is looking round the doorway at me. 'You all
right?'

I must just be stood here staring. Can she tell I've been
back to the woods, back to the bunker? Can she see my
secrets?

'Why are you so wet?'

I mumble something about being in the park with Joe
and getting caught in the rain. Half-true. But shouldn't I
be telling Mum everything? About the sketch and how I

gave it to Damon? About what Joe just said? I have no idea how to start. There's too much, too many things uncertain.

'Why such a rush?' She's still looking at me.

And I'm still thinking about Joe, still wondering if anything he said could be true.

'Is it trick-or-treaters?' Mum suggests. 'You wanted to avoid Halloween?'

'Something like that.'

The curtains are drawn across the windows of the front room – I think it's Mum who wants to avoid Halloween. This year she's scared of how people might be with us, the tricks they might play. I go through to the kitchen to find her sitting at the table with a mug of half-drunk tea. No wine today.

'Bed early, then? Movie?' she says. 'We don't answer the door?'

I nod. I've turned into a kind of zombie, my brain has so much to think about it's not thinking at all. I stare at what Mum has on the table: a pile of papers about Dad's case, stuff Mum's been meaning to sort through for ages. I'm not expecting this – no wine *and* sorting papers *and* on Halloween. Maybe she's starting to get on with things. Maybe this means something's changed. Is it because of me? Because she thinks I finally believe Dad's manslaughter plea? I can't tell her now that I'm more mixed up than ever.

I can't tell her that Dad doing manslaughter is the thing that makes the least sense of all. I mean, with Ashlee getting to the bunker that night. With the sketch Dad drew. With the things Joe's just said.

'Do you want to see your father before his next hearing?' Mum says. 'He's put in a request form. It might be the last time before he . . . well.' She bends to stroke Florence before she adds, 'But it's your decision.'

I shrug like I don't care, but my heart is pounding and I'm feeling all that stuff again — everything I thought I'd managed to push away. I'm thinking that if Dad wants to see me again then it means he still loves me. And if he still loves me then it means he's a good person. And if he's a good person then it means he didn't do anything bad that night — he didn't kill Ashlee Parker, on purpose or by accident. I shake my head angrily.

Mum turns back to the piece of paper and makes an X through a small box. This gets me panicky all over. I open the fridge and stick my face inside. If Mum knows I'm upset then maybe she'll get upset again too, maybe she'll go back on the booze. I don't want two parents missing in action any more. The artificial fridge light blinds me and something smells off in here, but I wait until I'm sure I can keep the tears inside me. I grab the first thing — milk. As I make Mum a fresh cup of tea I look out at Darkwood and remember being inside there with Damon just this morning, leaning against him in the bunker. I think about what Joe said. That Damon played rough? That Dad drew Damon instead of drawing himself? That Damon could have hurt Ashlee? I drop the teabag twice when I'm trying to get it into the bin. I'm thinking of how Ashlee had looked wild in Joe's photograph, how she'd looked dangerous and beautiful.

When I put the tea in front of Mum, I move the form aside, away from any more marks from her pen. 'Let me think about it,' I say.

Before I go upstairs, I check the deadlock on the front door and peer out at our lane, but there are no kids trick-or-treating. Perhaps Mum and me are worrying about nothing – everyone is too scared to come anywhere near our house now.

I put on warm, dry clothes. Then I sit on my bed, remembering the strung-out look in Damon's eyes this morning. Could Joe be right? The things he's told me don't feel right, but why would Joe make up that stuff? Just because he's angry about a stupid cross-country team? That's ridiculous. I throw my phone on to the bed. I need to get that sketch back. Need to look at Joe's photos again. I thump my head on to my pillow and remind myself of the things that should be facts: Dad has confessed; the police are certain enough to charge him with murder; Dad carried Ashlee Parker out of the woods and into our kitchen; Dad was in a flashback that night; it's not only me who saw Ashlee in the sketch Dad drew.

But who was the wolf?

I walk over to my desk, run my hand over Dad's papers, his shirt, his Swiss army knife. I could use that – I could carve an *A* into the inside of my left arm and make it bleed. Does killer's blood look any different from normal blood? I pick up Dad's combat shirt instead. Holding it makes me think about him returning from service, how I used to think of him as a hero. This is what I need to destroy, these memories. I need to see the facts without the feelings. Look at Dad as a whole.

I lay the shirt out flat on my desk and make myself think of things — bad things — like how Dad turned away when we tried to hug him, how he screamed at Mum, how he kicked Florence once when he was drunk. How — sometimes — even I was frightened of him. How he confessed.

But even now something still nags at the back of my mind . . . won't let me believe Dad is evil. *Can't* let me. That something won't let me believe Damon is bad either.

But who else is there?

What else could have happened that night?

I pick up Dad's knife and I stab it. Straight into the middle of Dad's shirt, near where Dad's heart would be. I rip the knife through the material. I keep hacking until the bits of material in front of me just look like that — an old uniform, not Dad's — until it looks like rags. I don't feel any better from doing it. The words Joe just told me about Damon are still in my head too. Everything is still shot through with holes.

42

Damon

It's murky dark when I wake. Dusk? Past that. I don't know where I am. I get this fear that makes my ribs hurt – something's happened, something bad. I start scrabbling in the dirt, touch cold leaves, my hand tightens around a collar. Am I playing the Game? I rub my fingers across its heart-shaped tag.

Then I remember.

Ashlee.

She's gone.

Dead.

I breathe in hard. A whole heap of other images and thoughts come back at me too. And I'm gasping like I can't get no more air.

This is all my fault.

I need to get out of here – go to the cops. What does it matter if I don't remember it all? If it's all a jumble in my head? What the cops think now ain't true. Can't be.

But I'm too wired. The cops will smell the joint, and how's that going to go down? And the forest is swaying. I'm not sure I can even stand.

I feel around for my phone, shove it deep in my cargos. My vision is shaking, unsure. I need to get out of here before I do anything else stupid. But my legs are weak. I'm trembling like a full-blown druggie, out of control. How long was I out for? How strong was that joint? My brain's fuzzy as fuck! I turn my body in the way that feels right; I let fate decide. One way down this path and I'll go back to town and what I know I've got to face; the other way and I'll keep walking out of here, follow the river to some-place new. I could disappear entirely, become a missing person on a milk carton: *someone last seen*. It's my feet's choice.

Then I freeze. I'm hearing voices. Not anyone's I recognise. I go straight into Game mode, kick leaves and twigs over where I been and head towards the trees. It's like footsteps are everywhere, echoing through this wood. Then I get why: this is like Ashlee said it would be tonight, it's Halloween.

'People will come into Darkwood to look for ghosts,' she'd said.

I hear shouting and laughing coming from somewhere near where the car park must be.

Somehow, I find that deer path I was on before. My steps sound like a rhino's, though — dried leaves, nut husks, bracken, twigs, all this making me loud. I'm stumbling into trunks. I'm seeing people crouching in the dark spaces between trees, laughing and jeering. One of them runs his finger across his neck in a sign like I'm dead. When I look again, they're gone. It's just dark space. Maybe I should go the long way round, get on to the path that'll lead me out near Emily's house instead.

Emily.

I stumble again. Was it only this morning when she'd been with me inside that bunker? She'd been nice to me, *too nice*. Her eyes had been the colour of oceans. I could've drowned. Pulling out my phone again, I think I might call her. But I don't have her number. And anyway, she wouldn't want to hear from me. She thinks I chased Ashlee through these woods. She thinks I chased Ashlee that night. Maybe she thinks I did more than this too. Because she still don't think it's her dad that killed Ashlee, does she?

I tip forwards against a trunk.

Is this what Emily's telling the police right now?

I'm getting that feeling again, that tingling on my neck like I'm being watched, like someone is trailing me. I spin around, squint at the dark. If anyone is here they're still as me. When I hear someone running, fast and close, I slink back into the shadows. This wood is alive, full of the fairies and druids and ghost hunters like Ashlee said it would be tonight. It's freaking me out. And I need to get everything straight before I go to the cops, straight as I can. I need to get these drugs out of my system!

I know where to go. Just for an hour or so. I can stay hidden on animal tracks all the way. No one will see me. Only, I keep feeling it – that tingling at the back of my neck. I try to go faster to outrun it, and the wood spins. I keep turning round to check behind me.

Eventually, I start climbing the Leap. The moon makes the limestone glow, turns branches into bones. Skeletons. I go quick, checking over my shoulder and then above me to where I'm headed. Then, when I'm nearly at the top, that's when I see her.

When I think I do.

She's behind me.

She's weaving between bracken, catching me up, tall and curvy and gorgeous. The tingles on my neck start up again. She's been following me. I blink, try to see her better, but she's gone, disappearing into rocks.

Everywhere I go in this wood, Ashlee won't leave me alone. Maybe even when I head to the police station she'll be there too. Maybe she'll come everywhere now, everywhere 'til I tell the police what I know. Everywhere 'til the truth comes out. But she won't ever let me touch her again; she'll always be out of reach for that.

I blink. This is just the joint.

I pull myself on to the summit. It's quiet and empty and there are no Halloween weirdoes. It's just me. The wind is blasting it. I stay on my belly to crawl to the edge, take a breath and look over.

She's there.

Her face is right in front of me. Her blonde hair whips away from her cheeks, flies back with the wind. Her skin is pale and her eyes a dull brown. I want to touch her. She's floating backwards, across to the part of the Leap with the jagged rocks: Suicide Drop. I follow her around.

No ... Don't leave ... not yet ...

Her voice or mine?

Her eyes spin like whirlpools, drag me closer. Then she blinks again. Gone.

I look over. I want her. Right now I think I'd jump off this summit, straight into the jagged part, if it meant I could collide with her first . . . tumble down with her pressed to me. Feel her for those last few moments, her body up close. One last time. Maybe that — *really* — is the only way out of this. A huge gust of wind grabs at my clothes, wants to take me over. I glance at the rocks below and I think I see her again, but she's further away, just a wisp of light, something fading into black. Is she telling me to let go?

I remember how I was standing up here with Emily Shepherd, how I'd fooled her by jumping on to the ledge beneath. I feel bad about that now — about being so cocky about what I thought I knew. If Emily was here, I'd ask if she could see Ashlee; I might hold on to her instead. Now I grab on to plants and hang over the summit.

I could let go. I could fall head first. It wouldn't be so hard. Maybe it's the easiest way out of this. Then I'd be tumbling into Ashlee, joining her. I'd know the truth —

maybe I would – I'd know what I did that night. I loosen my grip, just a little, feel myself slide. I can still catch myself, can still grab on to things or angle myself on to the ledge below, for a few more seconds I can. But I think about Ashlee lying dead in these woods and I want to hit those rocks with my face. I think of her skin cold and rotting, and I want my skull to crack. I want my brains to spill. My brains never did me no good anyway, never told my stupid drugged-up body when to stop.

And I'm sliding . . . sliding . . . but I don't care. I just want to get close to her, feel her body round me like how she'd promised that night. And I think I'm working out now what Mack's been protecting me from – I think I'm putting together that other image in my head, the one of me swaying down the high street. Because Mack got me out of these woods that night. He must have. Mack got me home. This means Mack knows. He knows what I must've done. This means he's been hiding me from it. This means what I did must be pretty damn bad.

43

Emily

I hear Mum going into her room, but it's too early for bed, even for her. I lie in my own darkening room staring at the ceiling. I thought I'd feel different after chopping up Dad's uniform. But there's still this niggling sliver of doubt. It sits at the back of my head like one of Joe's cracks of light, teasing another world where Dad can still be innocent. It's dangerous to look at too long.

So I think about Damon instead: his lips trembling in the bunker, the pause of his eyes on mine, his tattoo full of stories. I still don't understand why I gave him that sketch. Is he looking at it now? If I knew where he lived I'd go to his house, crawl into his room and steal it from him. I'd take it to Dad – he's the only one who can tell me what it really means. I'll tell Mum to tick *yes* on that form, tell her we have to visit immediately.

I watch the moon creep into the sky. It's full, fat and bright – a proper harvest moon. A hunter's moon too. I go across to the window so I can see it better. But when I get there, I don't look up, I look down. There are people in my lane, walking from the town end towards the gate into Darkwood. Three people – two tall and one shorter – talking with heads bowed together. I press the tips of my fingers under the bottom of my window and pull it up soundlessly, open it a crack. Something uneasy winds into my throat as I see who these boys are.

'We need to find him.' That's the first thing I hear.

It's Mack Jenkins' voice.

I almost tap on the glass to get their attention – almost call down and ask what's going on – but there's something about Mack's face that stops me. It's drawn tight with fear, worry. He's running a hand across his short hair, and his eyes are darting everywhere. I draw back a little. Damon's other mates – Charlie Jones and Ed Wilkes – are either side of him, and they're looking strung out too. Charlie is clenching his hands into fists and then opening them again. Ed is glancing in the direction of Joe's house and scowling.

'He's going to get us all in trouble if the coppers get to him first,' Mack is saying. 'Right now with the way he is, he could do anything . . .'

He stops before the gate and turns to the others. He's talking low and fast. The only other words I catch are *find* him and split up and quick.

Could he be talking about Damon? Could Damon still be in Darkwood? Still where I left him in the bunker this morning? Why else would his mates be looking for him? I think of the dark sketches on its walls, the hangings and guns and death, and I shiver. But if Damon is still there, then it means Dad's sketch of Ashlee as a deer is still there too.

'We got to find him before he does something stupid,' Mack says again, his voice fading as he starts opening the gate. 'You know what he's like . . . fucking phone's even off!'

Each of them looks around before they slip through the gate. Mack goes through last, hesitating for a moment on the other side, looking out of the woods and towards our house. For one second I think he looks right into this window, right into me. He shakes his head once, almost like it's a warning, almost like he knows I'm here, watching. But he can't know this. I'm stood back from the window, deep in the darkness of my room. A second later, he turns around to the other two and they're off again.

'Damon's not himself . . .' I hear him saying, '. . . the last thing Damon needs . . .'

Then they're gone into the woods, even though it's pretty much dark now. Why are they so desperate to find him? What do they think he's done? Or is going to do? I turn from the window, grab my coat and go swiftly down the stairs. If Damon really is still in the bunker, only me and the police, and maybe Joe I guess, can find him there.

Damon's mates will have no luck. Perhaps this is my chance – to get that sketch back and make Damon explain Joe's story, both at the same time. And I'm not scared of him like Joe thinks I should be. I know Damon's not who Joe suspects.

I'm out of the back door and spilling into the lane. I go to the gate and peer up the track into Darkwood. I can still, just about, make out the path. You'd think I'd hear Mack and the others walking down it, though, you'd think they couldn't just melt into these woods. They're boys after all, with heavy boys' footsteps, and they don't know this place like I do.

I hesitate, looking up the path. If Damon is in the bunker he won't have phone reception, he'll be cut off from everything – no wonder his friends are frustrated. I keep myself moving forward by telling myself that I don't have to stay long, that I can just get the sketch and speak a little to Damon. I can slip back into the woods before he even knows where I've gone. I don't even have to go inside the bunker.

It's darker the further into the woods I go, despite the bright moon. I listen for anything, listen with my skin. I shouldn't be in these woods right now, even with a full moon, even if I know this place just by feel. Weren't these always Mum's rules when I was younger – never go into the woods at night and never go into them alone? Now I'm doing both. But the closer I come to Damon, the more I know it's the right thing. I feel that too, in the way my feet step out the path without me even looking down.

There's this strange sort of pull to him. Maybe it's a little like how Joe felt with Ashlee in the woods that day — maybe I shouldn't want this, but I do.

I trip over briars as I hear the roar of a stag. It's not close, but his noise is desperate and deep; he's either protecting a herd or challenging for one. His roar masks the sound of my footsteps, hiding me. I'm careful as I get near the bunker, hovering the other side of the hawthorn hedge and looking across. There's no light coming from inside it, but Damon could have pulled the cover over the entrance like Dad did sometimes. Like Dad, Damon could be sitting quietly in a corner. Again I hear that stag roaring, though further away now. A barn owl shrieks. I make myself think about getting that sketch back, and I slip through the hedge. I go to the bunker entrance, silent and quick. I pull back the lid.

'Damon?' I call down. 'Are you in there?'

44

Damon

I've seen something.

It's something far down the rock face, wedged between the rock and the jagged boulders. I'm trying to look for it again. But I'm scrambling and falling, grabbing at smooth stone. And I'm too late – I'm going over, over the edge of the Leap.

I'm practically headfirst when I hit the ledge below. Somehow I grab at something, hold it, throw myself into the cave. I press myself against stone 'til I'm steady. Breathe.

I look over again. Even in the full moonlight, it's hard to make out. But there's something, far below. I'd only caught a glimpse of it because I was looking at those jagged rocks so long, looking for Ashlee. It sparkles, glints. I rub my hand across my eyes, blink. It's still there. I'm not just imagining it.

First Ashlee's ghost, now this.

45

Emily

There's no answer from inside the bunker. No sound, nothing. How many times have I done this same sort of thing with Dad, searching for him in the dark?

'Damon, are you here?'

I jump down. In the dimness I see the same candle stub still burnt to the same level, the old lamp where I left it. I guess my theory was wrong about Damon being here. It's obvious no one's been here since this morning. That means Dad's sketch isn't here either. I slide down the wall and sit on the cold floor, pull my coat tighter around me. I'm empty now, used up. Damon's got the sketch and he's skipped town with it. He just hasn't told his mates, that's all.

I lean my head against the wall. I could sleep like this, I could dream. Maybe, in another life, I'd be waiting for Damon to come find me here and it wouldn't be for any reason to do with death or pain. In that life Ashlee wouldn't be dead, and my dad wouldn't be in prison. Damon and me would talk for hours, we'd keep the hatch open and look up at the moon and stars. I'd know Damon wasn't bad; I'd know Dad wasn't either.

I dig my hands into my pockets, scrunch my fingers to keep warm. I look at the ribs of the corrugated ceiling, the concrete walls. There's enough moonlight to see the pictures, all those scrawls there, those wolves. They all have the same dark eyes, sometimes with red rims too – the only bit of colour here. These eyes are excited – eyes that want something. In one of the sketches the eyes are rolling back into that wolf's head, just like that wolf is crazy . . . half out of its mind. I can't recognise Dad in these wolves' faces, not one bit, and I'm trying to.

I stand up, get closer. I'm thinking about what Joe said about Damon now too. Can I see Damon in these wolves' faces instead? I'm walking around the bunker, looking at each sketch carefully. I'm half-listening to the wind outside, thinking that it's howling like a wolf too. Then I pause, tilt my head and listen harder.

That's not the wind.

I go extra still, straining to hear, then stand and press my face to the gun slit. This isn't my mind playing tricks; it's something else. I listen harder and . . . yes . . . it's there . . . that howling noise again. It makes me think of the last time I couldn't sleep, when I'd been woken from my dream. It makes me remember standing at the window the night of Ashlee's death. There'd been strange noises in the woods then too. My breath is tight in my throat as I try to hear the howling noise again. One long shiver travels down my spine as I do. This noise is coming from deep inside these woods. I look up at the moon, but it is silent and watching me, waiting too.

46

Damon

I hear them howling. They can't be playing another Game, though, not after last time, not without me. Are they looking for me instead?

One howl, two . . . I wait for the third. A gust of wind blocks my ears. I hunch in tighter to the rock face. It feels like I'm on the run, like I'm playing the Game for real and the boys are hunting me out. But maybe it should be me hunting them out – for not telling me how they played the Game with Ashlee, because Ashlee told me a secret that night that they might've been a part of.

Slowly, slowly, by feel more than sight, I move down the rock face. I'm on the wild, empty side that no one gets to know. Maybe I'm wrong about Mack keeping people's secrets. Maybe he's told Ed and Charlie everything he knows about that night – and maybe now they're coming for me. What do they all think I've done? Are they coming to tell me? Are they coming to tell me to run?

I'm aiming for those rocks that jut out below me like teeth – the boulders – for the crevice I saw in between them, for what I think I saw inside it. The full force of the wind is blasting at me, but I'm glad of it – it's knocked some of that haziness from the joint out at least. I'm glad of the moonlight too. While the wind tries to drag me off, I stay clinging like a limpet, my fingers and toes wedged into tiny cracks. I'm feeling the rough, grainy texture of the limestone, the electricity in my fingers. I sense the empty space of air around and below me. If I slip I'll be heading for that, I'll be free-falling to the bottom. I have to force myself to keep going. Seems this isn't called Suicide Drop for nothing.

It's easier once I've got both feet on a boulder; I lower myself 'til I'm curled between it and the rock face. I don't look at the drop beyond. Sharp wind pierces into my lungs, whirls round me. But there's another sound too, isn't there? Something from the summit? A voice? I don't look up to check, can't risk losing my balance. I wedge myself in tighter to the rock instead. If there is anyone up there, they won't be able to see me here. When I bring my fingers away from the stone they've gone white and stiff, hard to unclench. Very slowly I shuffle sideways across the boulders. I move to the crevice I saw from above. Then I tip forward to the gap and push my arm inside it. The wind is whooshing into my face and making my eyes stream but I keep digging about. I feel moss and pebbles and wet leaves. I force my eyes open against the wind, drop on to my belly, put my face close to see.

It's there!

Just like I'd thought!

Wedged inside this crevice is something pink and sparkly.

It's Ashlee's phone cover. Maybe her phone's there too.

I try to breathe deep, try to stop myself from moving hasty. With shaking fingers, I stretch to grab it. The phone cover's material is sodden through, cold. As I dig about I feel the phone is also here, but it's in several pieces — smashed. I take a hold of what I can and wrench my arm out, pull myself back 'til I'm leant against the rock again. I'm trembling, and not from the cold. I look out to the sky and the dark sea of trees below for one second, two . . .

Ashlee's lips were pink and sparkly that night, the same colour as this phone case, they'd smelt like raspberry.

I take a breath and look at it all in my hand. The phone has split apart. The back of it is detached, the screen a faint cobweb of cracked glass, the battery separate again. How hard was it hurled down here for it to break like this?

I didn't throw it, did I?

I don't remember it.

I stare at these bits in my hand like they can give me some answers. But nothing comes. If I was spinning so much that night that I don't remember getting home — that I don't even remember when I last saw Ashlee — how could I have climbed up here to throw this? I rest my head against the cold rock and try to think. But all I'm getting is some random conversation I had ages ago. I'd been propped up at the bar of the City Arms by Mack's dad – maybe the first time I ever got proper drunk. Mack's dad had held court, telling the whole place about one of his mates:

'He got so drunk once that he chucked his wife off a balcony,' he'd said. 'Seventh floor and all! It was an accident, though, they were arguing, they was just having a holiday! It just got a bit out of control, like!'

I think that's how it went. I remember Mack's dad explaining that when his friend woke next morning and was arrested, he could remember nothing – he even asked where his wife was.

Is that like what's happened to me?

Is there a whole story of terrible things I did that night, that I don't remember? Did Mack see it all? Did he take me home and away?

My throat goes tight. Maybe I should be checking into a mental hospital rather than a police station, maybe Mack was right when he said I was going loony. Maybe Mack saw me going loony that night. Maybe I don't know anything about who I am – what I'm capable of.

I put the phone cover in my pocket with Ashlee's collar, then lay the pieces of her phone out on the rocks. I get an ache thinking about the phone being whole, being held by Ashlee. My hands start shaking again and I almost lose all the bits.

Could Jon Shepherd have thrown it down here instead? I remember Emily telling me that he was scared of heights, but she could've been lying. Couldn't she?

I slot the battery in. I have to wedge the back of the phone in hard to make it stick. I turn it on, expecting nothing, and nothing happens. I bang it against the palm of my hand. Now there's a flicker on the screen: tiny, but there. A spark. I bang it again. And somehow, it works. Somehow this battery still has juice!

Ashlee's home screen comes up. It looks kind of disjointed, and the cracked glass doesn't help, but straight away messages are coming through, hundreds of them it seems, all from me or her friends or her family. They're all asking the same things – where is she, is she safe, what's happened – they get more desperate as they come. It hurts to look – it hurts to hold this tiny part of Ashlee in my hands but not the rest of her. It hurts to know that she never read these words.

I run the back of my hand over my eyes and click on to anything just to make the messages stop. I open up her picture folder, and I feel kind of desperate now. I'm scrolling back to her earlier pictures fast, just wanting to see Ashlee from months ago, wanting to see her alive. I find all the pictures she took and sent me of her in her underwear and pyjamas, but these don't make me feel no better. I want – *need* – to see a picture of her and me. In the photo I finally click open and stare at for ages, Ashlee's got her mouth pressed against my cheek, biting me gently, and I'm staring straight at the camera and grinning like a loon. I got no right to be that happy. It's not fair that the grinning, thoughtless loser in this picture gets to keep hugging her for always.

I move the images on. Now I'm surprised. Because there are loads of films here, not just photos. Which is weird, because I don't remember Ashlee filming anything ever. Even the last two images in this folder are films! And all these films seem to start with an image of something dark and blurred. It's like they're all filmed at night. All filmed some place with trees. And now I'm curious.

I click on the one that's second to last, just because it's shorter. The image starts shaky and dark, and, combined with the cracked screen, I can't make much sense of it. I hold the phone closer and try to work it out. I think I hear wind. Light rain? A rumble of thunder? There's something about this image that's starting to feel familiar, horribly so.

Then the camera flash goes on, illuminating every-thing. The image takes a second to focus. And I see it then. I *see*! My breath leaves me in a rush.

Because in the image is a body slumped on a forest floor.

And I know who it is. Course I do.

47

Emily

I listen in the dark, but that howling sound doesn't come again. My eyes are pressed close to the gun slit watching everything: the way the trees move, how clouds smother the moon then let it shine again, how wind skitters leaves along the ground. Dad did this too once, looked out of here and listened. Did he also listen for this noise? Was it the reason he'd started drawing all those wolves in the first place? I know wind can sound strange moving through trees at night. Depending on the tree it moves, though, wind can make a whole lot of different noises: noises like distant traffic, animals, a fire, a roar, water. Maybe I've just been thinking of that sketch too much, I've got wolves on the brain. Now I'm even hearing them in the wind.

I don't move from this bunker, though. Not yet. Because I'm safe here, in the dark. No one can find me.

As I stay here, listening, I hear other strange sounds in the wood. There are shrieks and laughter like there's a party going on. And when I start to move again there's another noise. It's faint at first, but getting louder. Footsteps? Running? Heavy boots? I feel this strange surge inside me. Has Damon come back here after all? I shrink back into the darkness, watching through the gun slit. I need that sketch he has. Need to talk.

A few moments more and I see a figure moving fast down the small track that runs the other side of this bunker. He stops, looks around, then veers off, heading straight for this clearing. That decides it for me. It's like he's coming straight for me. I move to the entrance hole and pull myself up it, wedge my feet into the sides so I'm half in, half out. I'm about to call out when I see him properly.

He's in this clearing when he sees me too. He stops mid-step. Then his mouth drops into a perfect O of surprise.

It isn't Damon.

'What are you doing here?' he says.

48

Damon

It's me.

This body that's slumped on the forest floor. This one the camera is focusing on. My face is pressed into the dirt and I'm out of it. I'm wearing Dad's combat shirt – the same one I had on that night, the same one I got on again now.

Did Ashlee make a video that night? Did she film me? Like this? Is that what's going on here?

My hand is shaking so much it's hard to keep the phone steady. I jump big as I hear Ashlee's voice and I have to grab at the cliff face behind me and force myself not to look around for her – she's speaking from the phone, on this film.

'Oh Damo,' she's saying. 'You're a bit useless now, honeypie . . .'

Useless.

It's that word again. Is this why I remember it?

The image jolts forwards and back, goes close on my passed-out face. Blurs. When it clears, I see that my mouth is open, my hair is stuck across my cheek. I'm out of it. *Fucking* out of it!

'What are we going to do with you now?' Ashlee's voice is close to the speaker, singsong.

A smudge of water lands on the camera screen. That could be the rain starting. There's wind battering against the speaker too, making it hard to hear everything Ashlee is saying.

'Told you I'd win.' I hear that. 'Guess you won't get my collar tonight after all.'

There's laughter. The camera moves again, goes steady. That's when I see the loser that's me on this screen wake up; my eyes open and I swat out clumsily.

I hear Ashlee laughing louder. 'Knew you'd wake up. Don't want to miss the fun, do you?'

I see my mouth open, and I'm talking to her, trying to. 'You shouldn't have done that.' I sound really pissed off. 'You shouldn't have done that with Mack!'

My throat goes dry as I hear this. What had she just told me? Her secret? Something about the Game she played?

The shot is steady on a close-up of me. I see the frown in my forehead, the anger I got.

'My collar's all yours if you want it,' Ashlee's saying.

'Just take it like I said.'

Then the image shakes all over the place. I get a close-up of leaves. Darkness. Tree trunks. My face again. Hers.

'You'll have to try harder than that,' she's saying.

Am I fighting her? Is that why the image is jolty? What's going on?

'Can't believe you'd do that!' It's my voice again. 'Why would you even . . .'

She says something that I don't hear. Only the words *Try it . . . Don't get mad about it . . . Playing . . .* and *. . . Game.* She's laughing or crying, I can't tell which. Then the image freezes on dark branches. There's no more sound. No more movement. Just her laughter ringing in my ears. Just this sick feeling in my guts. Because I'm starting to remember now, ain't I? I'm starting to think I know what she told me that night – starting to think I can remember her secret. It's coming back. I nearly drop the phone into the dark air, my feet have to dig into the boulder to stay firm. Yes – it's in my head now – this secret. This secret she kept with Mack. I clench my free hand into a fist and slam it into the rock face.

'I don't want you to be my girlfriend no more.' That's what I'd told her that night. 'I don't even know you!'

There's an empty feeling all through me. That night, had I tried to break up with her? The ache of it gets me hard. She'd been mad about it – I know that.

I close my eyes to feel cold, sharp air against my

eyelids. There's one more film on this phone. It's the very last thumbnail image in her photo folder. It has to be from that night too — it has to be the last thing she ever filmed. I click to open it. Because I can't stop now. I got to know how this ends.

49

Emily

Mack lets out a breath of air. He's standing in the middle of the clearing, watching me. I see his pupils big in the moonlight.

'What are you doing here?' he growls again. He's staring at how I'm half in the ground, half out, trying to understand it.

'My dad's bunker,' I say, explaining. And it feels strange to say these words out loud, to him – strange to say them now.

I can't say how I was hoping to find Damon, though, or how I need to get that sketch back. Something stops me. Mack's looking all around the clearing then back at me, back at the bunker.

'It's well hidden,' he says.

I nod.

He digs in a pocket to take out a torch, flicks it on, blinds me with it as he tries to shine it down the entrance hole. 'Is Damon in there?'

'Why would he be?'

Mack gives me a strange look. But why did he ask this? Has Damon been talking about me to Mack? Has Damon told Mack everything? Even about being here this morning?

When Mack comes closer, his boots make sucking sounds in the mud. It's almost as if he's going to barrel straight into me, push me backwards into the bunker with him falling on top. I lean away, wedging my shoe tips into the sides of the entrance.

'Why you looking for him?' I say.

And again, Mack gives me that look.

Up close I see that Mack's eyes are squinting with tiredness, are kind of red. He's moving in small, quick movements. This isn't the cool and collected Mack Jenkins from school – not the tough boy everyone knows him as. He starts craning around me to see inside the bunker. I don't want to let him in but I think he's going to come down anyway.

'There are no steps,' I say. 'Wait!'

I find myself moving down into the bunker, start feeling for the lamp. Mack must know what's going on with Damon, maybe he even knows what Damon's done with the sketch. Maybe I could talk to him. Ask him. Maybe he's got answers.

Mack jumps inside before I've got the lamp properly lit, I hear the smack of his boots hitting the floor. He flicks the torch on again. In its brightness, the bunker disappears; all I can see is Mack's face, huge and panicking. I keep my eyes on him as I light that candle, plus two others I find in the drawers. I place them all along the gun slit ledge. If anyone else comes close to us now, they'll see this. Maybe they'll find this bunker. Suddenly it seems important that someone else can find me out here. That Damon could. Or Joe.

Not that Joe would come looking for me now, after the things I've just said to him. I feel for my phone, then realise I never picked it up from my bed. I angle myself so I'm closer to the exit.

'What's going on, anyway?' I say. 'Why is everyone so desperate to find Damon? Where's he gone?'

Another flick. The torch turns with Mack and I get blinded again. 'Don't you know?'

Mack's tone of voice is nasty. It's not just the torchlight that's too much for down here, it's him. Mack's too big, stooping as he walks, buzzing and on edge. It was a mistake letting him come down here.

'Ever since Damon started talking to you,' Mack says, 'you've made him think everything's his fault.'

Up close, I smell booze and sweat on him, I see a streak of mud on his neck. He seems even more jumpy than Damon was.

'I know Damon feels guilty . . .' I start, hesitantly, '. . . about what happened.'

Another flick and the torch is off. In the candlelight Mack's face is shadowy and strange, his features distorted. 'You should've kept away from him! I told him!' There's a warning in his voice.

I watch a bead of sweat trickle from his cropped hair.

'You're the one who started this,' he murmurs, '. . . who keeps telling him he needs to go to the police!'

I try to back away, but the wall is too close. 'I never said that!'

'What are you trying to make him do anyway?'

I can see that Mack is scared. He's also moved between the exit hole and me. Suddenly I don't like the thought of being trapped down here with him. I exhale, calmly as I can. Mack's eyes are moving around the bunker, looking at the pictures, in the corners, on the floor. I can tell he's freaking out, taking all this in.

'How do I know you're not trying to set me up too?' he continues. He moves towards me with his arms out, starts grabbing at me.

I step away. 'I'm not trying to do anything!'

'You are! You're trying to make Damon believe he did it.' His eyes narrow. 'You're trying to make him think he killed his own girlfriend!'

My breath catches. 'What?'

He glares at me. 'He didn't, you know.'

I stay silent, frozen.

'You'll do anything to get your dad off,' Mack keeps on. 'You're desperate! That's why you're here now, isn't it? You're waiting for him. You're waiting to get the info you need to run off to the police.'

My mind's racing. I think again of Joe's words from earlier — how convinced he'd been of Damon being involved that night. And now, Mack bringing it up like this?

'But Damon didn't . . .' I start, and then I wonder something else. 'Is that why you think he's disappeared? Because he . . .?'

Mack comes towards me fast, grabbing my coat. 'Damon couldn't hurt anything,' he says. 'He's not like that. It's just what *you're* making him believe!'

He watches me, looking for some sort of reaction. I don't think he finds it.

'Stop trying to hang this on him!' Mack shouts.

Mack's too insistent, too panicked. He's making me nervous too. And now stuff is nagging at my brain, a whole pile of it — images. The mark on Damon's face this morning. Joe's story about him being angry and rough with Ashlee. His expression when I showed him Dad's sketch. And then, there's how Mack is acting now.

Other thoughts are piling up too. There's that howling noise I've heard, there's Damon being in Darkwood the other night, there's the way Damon has just disappeared.

I try to think this through. Try not to react like Mack is. But I have no idea what to believe any more. Has Damon been keeping secrets this whole time? Deep, dark secrets? Is he not who I'd thought at all?

'You were there that night,' I say quietly, trying to hold Mack's gaze. 'What happened, really? You must know, out of anyone . . . How did Ashlee . . .?'

Mack raises a finger, points it at me. 'You know what happened! It's like everyone says! Ashlee was drunk. Your dad killed her because he's evil! Damon. Didn't. Do. Anything!'

He says these last words slowly and deliberately, like each word's a bullet. I'm not sure he believes his words, though, it's more like he's trying to force me to. More like he's panicking. He hulks over me, his finger close to my cheek.

'You started this,' he says again. 'You changed everything. And you're never going to believe it was your dad, are you? Whatever evidence there is. You're always going to keep going after Damon!'

He pulls away to look out of the gun slit. I notice the pulse in his temple, beating fast.

'I know what you're doing,' he adds quietly. 'You're playing on the guilt Damon's got, you're poisoning him!'

'No!'

'You're trying to scare him into saying something untrue. You're trying to frame him . . . frame us . . .'

'I'm not!'

He reaches out, grabs my coat again, his fingers searching through it almost like he's checking for wires.

'You'd ruin Damon's life just to get your dad released?' he's saying. 'Even when your dad admitted it? Even when you know your dad *wants* to be in prison?'

I pull away from him sharply. 'I don't know that. No one does.'

'They won't believe you, you know,' he says. 'At the end

of the day, your dad's the one in prison, not Damo. They're not going to start all that investigation stuff again now.'

I'm still trying to shrug his fingers off me.

'Maybe we should find Damon,' I say. 'Maybe we need to calm down and get out of this bunker!'

'I've looked for him!' Mack's arm flings sideways, narrowly missing one of the candles. 'Has he gone to the police already? Have you told him to?'

'I wouldn't do that!'

I'm about to tell Mack that I don't think Damon hurt Ashlee that night, I'm about to try to make him see that I'm serious about this – but my mouth jams up. I'm thinking of Joe's determined face, the fear in Damon's eyes this morning, and that sketch. *That sketch!* I'm trying to remember how that wolf looked in it.

'It can't be,' I say. 'It just . . .' But I can't say it. Because I don't know who anyone is any more, what anyone is capable of. I look to the wolves on the ceiling instead, back to Mack. He's as still as a rock, watching me. His dark eyes look glazed and on fire at the same time, a hundred questions blazing out.

'It wasn't Damon!' Mack shouts. 'It was your dad that did everything!'

I stare at the wolf above me. I'm seeing things, I must be – because now I recognise this wolf's expression. Right now, I recognise its eyes. I dig my fingernails into the palms of my hands, hard – feel that I'm still here, see that this wolf is still there too. I'm not imagining this.

No wonder Damon was so freaked out this morning

when he came inside here. No wonder he kept looking at the pictures on these walls, over and over. No wonder he wanted to keep that sketch. He knew it too.

How could I not realise all this before? For certain?

It was what Dad was best at — finding the animal in people, drawing them like that. Suddenly these wolf eyes become glaringly obvious, its expression is clear. And I know who Dad was drawing. Absolutely. Of course I do.

50

Damon

I turn and climb fast, my hands scrabbling to keep a grip. The air is catching in my throat, but I can't fall. Not with this phone in my pocket – not with that final film on it. I push on 'til my fingertips find the ledge where the tiny cave is; I scrape the side of my cheek as I pull myself up and on to it. I roll on to my back and look at the moon, though all I'm seeing is that film.

I see hands.

Her neck.

I push my fists against the rock 'til my knuckles graze. There's a freezing wind on my cheeks.

Ashlee falling.

The moon is shining on my brain, like the lights in that

interview room. But my brain's clear now, clearer.

Her words.

Laughter.

Shakily, I drag myself to my feet. And breathe . . . and breathe . . .

I head for the deer track down. I'm tripping and stumbling as I'm running, but I don't fall. I skid into a tree, knocking air from my lungs.

I'm trying to listen for any more howling, but the wind shoots up, freezes me, grabs my old man's combat shirt and whips it against me. I see a star above, winking like it knows every terrible secret . . . like it knows what I've just seen. I wipe blood off my cheeks, keep moving.

51

Emily

On the ceiling behind Mack's left ear is a sketch of a wolf. It's snarling, blood dripping from its teeth. There's another one beside my shoulder. I'm surrounded.

How could I have ever thought that the wolf in these pictures was Dad? Dad is slighter and short. His eyes are pale and watery and his expression hesitant. He's more like a bird, something fragile. There's nothing of the wolf in him.

Mack is shouting something at me, something about Damon. Does Mack know? Did he see these pictures as soon as he got down here and work it all out? I'm dizzy and need to leave. But Mack is standing in my way.

I push at him. 'Let me through!'

Mack shakes his head. 'Damon's my mate, my brother . . .'

I push him harder. I'm not going to stay here, not with him, not with those pictures.

'You're not going to the police!' he shouts.

And there's another sound. Above us, on the forest floor, coming closer. Footsteps. For the second time tonight. I feel Mack's fingers go stiff where he's been grabbing my arm. We wait.

When I look up at the bunker hole, Damon is there. He's peering in, squinting at both of us then looking at the candles. Did he see the light and follow it? Hear us? He looks so confused.

'Mack?' he says.

But he's looking at me. Wide eyes. There's blood or dirt or something on his face, his hair's stuck up everywhere. His chest is heaving like flanks.

Mack lets go of me. 'I've been looking for you, Damo! All bloody evening!'

Only then does Damon drop my gaze and stare at Mack instead. I press myself to the wall. I have to get out of here, but there's two of them now to get around. Damon is crouching over the entrance, he's jumping down into here! I step away from them both and want to melt through these walls, want to dig myself up to the surface, make a tunnel. I can see it so clearly now . . . the long taut body, the focused expression, the long nose and muscly shoulders and *those eyes*. Those exact same dark and fiery and exhausted eyes! Those eyes are here in this bunker, right now, with me.

I have to leave.

But Damon is coming towards me like he's about to say something. Mack grabs his shoulder fast.

'She thinks it's you, Damo,' Mack says. 'If you don't stop her, she'll go to the police.'

This makes Damon snap around to him. I breathe out slowly, inch along the wall.

'Good!' Damon's voice is loud.

He thrusts his shoulders into Mack's chest and pushes him back, makes him stumble. Mack's got his hands up, but he's not shoving him away.

'Mate!' I hear him say. 'What are you on about?'

'I saw the film, Mack!'

I stop moving, listen.

'You been keeping secrets!'

I'm almost under the entrance hole when I see Damon grab Mack by the throat with one hand and reach into his pocket with the other. He takes out a phone, waves it in Mack's face.

Mack's body goes slack as he sees it. 'Where'd you get that?'

'You know where!' Again Damon pushes Mack, so hard I hear something crack on the bricks.

Mack gasps for breath. 'I didn't . . . I didn't do anything!'

I look from Mack's eyes to Damon's. Mack's hands are flailing towards the gun slit as Damon's grip tightens on his neck. I'm under the entrance hole now. I just need to jump up so my hands can find the ledge, wedge my feet into the sides, climb up, and I'm gone.

'Tell me what's going on!' Damon's yelling. 'What did you do, Mack? What happened that night?'

I don't jump for the ledge. Instead I turn back and see Damon still waving that phone about. I see that it's beaten about and covered in dirt.

'I didn't do anything!' Mack roars, finally throwing Damon off him. 'I didn't!'

He's furious, red-faced, and he's looking at me now.

'You should stop her!' he says. 'Seriously!'

His dark, glinting eyes reflect the candlelight. I don't move. Not yet. I'm still wondering about that phone.

'She'll go to the police,' Mack repeats. 'She'll tell them everything about us . . . the Game, Ashlee . . .'

His lips are curled back as he speaks. I see the wolf in him so clearly that I almost gasp. That makes me reach up, makes me grab the edge of the entrance hole.

'Stop!' Mack yells, and he lunges.

But Damon's after him, pulling Mack back. He holds the phone out of Mack's way and he looks right at me.

'Let her go to the police,' he says.

There's a challenge in Damon's eyes, like there was when we were on the Leap together last week, like when he held his hand like a gun.

Mack uses that moment to grab Damon, to get him in a headlock. I bring my feet up until my toes are against the wall, start to climb. But Damon is still looking at me, and that look is desperate, pleading. That's when Mack knocks the phone out of his hand. It skitters across the concrete, comes to rest just underneath me. And I don't think. I just drop back down into the bunker and I reach for it.

52

Damon

I'm going to kill him.

And I have to, don't I? After what I saw . . . after what he did. But he's shouting something. About how we're brothers, how we look after each other, how we don't tell no secrets. He's saying it wasn't his fault.

'We got each other's backs!' he yells. 'Always! I didn't do nothing!'

He's not going to have a chance to tell nothing more. Because I'm stopping his voice, stopping his air. Stopping him. I hear Emily's footsteps above, racing away.

I press my hands round his neck. 'How hard do I push?' I ask him.

His eyes go wide.

'Yeah,' I say. 'I saw it all *mate.*' I say the last word like I'm mocking him. 'I saw those films you made.'

And I'm thinking of Ashlee falling down. About how Mack laughed.

'What were you playing at?' I shout.

I need answers. Need to hurt him. I don't know which I need most.

'She wanted it,' he's saying. 'I swear!'

'Why would she want that . . . ?'

Words catch in my throat. I'm thinking something else — *remembering.* Ashlee had placed my hands on her that night. I'd felt her neck between my fingers, her pulse. I remember her daring me.

I twist away and Mack slams me to the side of the head.

'Get a grip!' he shouts. 'It was Shepherd, OK — him! You know this! I would never have hurt Ashlee . . . not intentionally, not . . .'

His voice is shaky, unable to finish.

I'm stumbling across the bunker, seeing flashes of light from where Mack's just punched me.

'You don't know shit!' Mack's saying. 'You don't know what I did with Ashlee, what it meant.'

My stomach clenches. Mack and Ashlee kept secrets. Ashlee did things with Mack she didn't do with me. Mack's just admitted it.

I glare at him nasty. 'You chased Ashlee! You chased her and then you . . .'

'No,' Mack says. 'You don't understand!'

Something's coming together, though. It's so big and

terrible, it hits me like a tsunami. I don't want to face it, because I know that soon as I do, there's no going back. There's nothing! It's just the getting flattened, the drowning. The blackness and emptiness of knowing that . . .

'You killed her!' I scream. 'It was you! You!'

I feel my jaw and my throat tense. There's streaks of pain shooting through me. But I grab Mack and push him so hard he makes a thudding noise against the bunker wall.

'You!' I shout. 'You wrapped your fingers around her. You squeezed.'

And he made me believe it was Shepherd, all this time! I think of Emily running hard to the police station – I want her to get there faster.

I push Mack again. His arm splays out towards the candles, scatters them – I see sparks of light in the air. I hear the lamp smash. But I can't stop. Not until I know why. Not until I hurt him as much as he hurt her.

'What were you doing?'

He's moving his head sideways, much as I'll let him, he can hardly get words out. 'A different game,' he gasps.

I've got my fingers round his neck, and I'm squeezing 'til I see red lines through his eyeballs, 'til his look goes kind of vacant. Did he see that in Ashlee's eyes too, that night? Did he keep going anyway? I'm shaking so much I don't know how hard I'm pressing. But I'm seeing his big dirty hands all over her, and I'm hearing his wide mouth laughing as she fell . . . and I don't want to listen to his excuses. Don't even want to look at him. I just want to squeeze, do it hard.

'I saw it all!' I yell again.

I just want him hurt. And I still have Ashlee's collar in my pocket. I could wrap this around Mack's neck and draw it up tighter than I ever done before, 'til he coughs and gasps. And maybe that would be right.

'Not brothers any more,' I say.

53

Emily

I'm running – stumbling – heading for the track to my house. When I get there I'll keep going, all the way to the police. I hold the phone tightly in my hand. I can still hear them shouting in the bunker behind me, fighting. Damon is yelling and yelling. If this phone even works, I should stop and use it to call the police. The ambulance too. Because, from these sounds I can hear back there, it's like Damon and Mack are going to kill each other. I hear a huge shout, then a smash like the lamp's gone over. I'm breathing hard when I slow up and lean against a tree. I'm not sure I can leave, not with all that.

I look at how scratched and dirty this phone is, wonder where Damon found it. What did he see on it to make him so mad?

My hands are shaking, but I've got to do it. I can't leave until I know. So I start pressing at the phone, my fingers fumbling. There are so many films here, though. Which one was Damon meaning when he was shouting at Mack? I click on the last one, press to make it play. The film starts dark and jolty, I can make out trees. A camera flash goes on and it turns the branches white and brittle. There's black sky. I can't tell much else. But there are voices, somewhere off-screen. Laughter. Rain? Definitely wind – I hear that battering, whooshing sound against the speakers.

What's going on?

Then I hear it – Ashlee's voice. She's speaking in a high-pitched and singsong way; she's on this film.

'Seven seconds!' she's saying. Least that's what I think she says. 'Let's go, baby!'

There's another voice in the background too, I can only just make it out. A boy's? It's low and murmuring. A high-pitched laugh makes me jump – Ashlee's. It's as if she's here, right next to me in this wood, she sounds that close.

'Damon's passed out again,' she says. 'He didn't want to play anyway . . .'

What's she on about?

The image blurs as the phone moves again. I breathe in hard. Now it's Ashlee's face on the screen – it's real and close and so alive, her eyes are shining like an animal's. This time she's speaking directly to the camera.

'Fairyland!' she's saying. 'There's only one person left to take me.' She leans so close to the camera that all I can see is her lips, perfect and plump. 'You,' she whispers.

It's like she's talking directly to me, that's how it feels. I press my head against the tree trunk and look up at branches, I send my breath up to the leaves in puffs. In this film Ashlee is wearing green – the same shade as she was wearing the night she died. There's something around her neck. My stomach twists. Something horrible is on this film and I'm about to watch it. I'm about to see what made Damon mad enough to get so angry with Mack. I don't know if I want to. But I have to know the truth. And this was filmed that night. Wasn't it? It *has* to have been. So I wrench my eyes back. Because this is important, it's the missing piece. It could be.

On the screen, Ashlee's mouth pulls back into a smile. I watch her mouth words at the person behind the camera.

'Take me,' she says. 'Dare you!'

The image jolts. I see trees flash past, blurred bodies: two of them.

'I can't hold this *and* do it too!'

That voice is different. Louder. Excited. I know that voice.

Mack's.

He was the one filming this. He was there with Ashlee.

There's a dull thudding sound like something being kicked. Then the camera goes black, like it's being held against clothing.

'He's not coming round any time soon.' Mack's voice, muffled.

'Useless!' That's Ashlee. 'Serves Damon right for . . .'

And I don't catch that bit, but she's laughing and laughing. The camera moves again. 'Come on, do you want my collar or not? Game's not over yet.'

I hear footsteps. The camera moving in a rhythm, pointing down towards the ground. They're walking. I see dirt and leaves and fallen twigs. My mouth is full of something foul-tasting, water I can't swallow. I don't want to keep watching this — don't want to see what's coming next. But I won't turn it off.

'Hold the phone in your mouth, Mack!' Ashlee's voice, loud. 'When you do it . . . I want to see my face when I—'

And they've stopped now.

'How?'

'Bite the case in your teeth — you know how!'

'Fine!'

I hear wind whooshing, a loud rumble — thunder? Then the image goes close up on Ashlee's face, on her neck too.

'Are we making a deal?' she says.

Her fingers are unbuckling whatever it is that's fastened around her neck, the thing I'd caught a glimpse of before. It's some sort of collar I think, like something you'd put on a dog. It's pink. There's a mumbling sound — Mack saying something, trying to, but maybe the camera is in his mouth now like Ashlee suggested.

The image jolts again and I see two hands — Mack's? They stretch into the shot and wrap around Ashlee's neck. Just like that. She doesn't stop him. She even smiles a little.

'Fairyland,' she says, nodding.

I breathe deep, force myself to keep my eyes on this. I don't understand it. Why is Ashlee letting him do this? Why isn't she struggling? Trying to get away? I want to shout at her – warn her – I want to jump into this film and grab Mack's hands. I want this to stop! Because it looks like Mack is squeezing her neck, and he's doing it harder. And harder. Ashlee's breathing is changing, getting more laboured and rattly, like there's fluid stuck in her throat. Her face is flushing red, her eyes going distant.

'Stop,' I whisper. 'Please.'

Mack is squeezing so hard that Ashlee's eyes roll back. But still, Mack keeps his hands there. Keeps squeezing. I want to scream. Want to do something! But what can I do now? Ashlee's eyes flicker. Shut. I'm gripping the phone so hard I'm scared it's going to break. And still Mack keeps going. Ashlee starts to fall. Her head tips forwards towards the camera and the image jerks. It goes black. My lungs go tight. I wait.

What's happened?

Then the image is moving again, pointing at trees and clothes, there's that rustling sound of things touching the speaker. And then . . . Ashlee's face. Her eyes are closed, and her head is lying back on the forest floor. I stare. Is she dead? Is this how it happened? Did Mack just do it, like that? So calmly? Like it was just a game? Why didn't she struggle?

The image goes black again, fast, like Mack's dropped the phone.

'You did it!' I hear him saying, over and over. 'How was it, baby?' The image stays on black. 'Ash?' I hear. 'Ashlee?'

There are more rustling sounds against the speaker.

Still black.

'C'mon, Ash, you coming round?'

I can hear him shaking her – I think this is what those noises must be – I can hear him starting to sound more desperate too as he calls her name. There's the sound of the wind. Rain. Mack's breathing, loud.

Then even those noises stop. I tap the screen, try to make the film keep going. But it's finished. The end. I shut my eyes up tight, make myself breathe.

I should be racing for the police station, should be doing anything other than just sitting here. But I think I'm starting to understand something. Already my fingers are moving to open up the next film back, and I'm starting to watch it. And I'm listening out for the noises in the bunker behind me.

54

Damon

Someone is shouting at me. Grabbing my arm. 'You have to stop!'

Emily? She's back? She's pulling me. And there's a different noise too, like crackling. A heat.

'Stop!'

I let her wrench me away.

Mack's cowering on the floor. His eyes are shutting like he's going unconscious. I did that? But he's moving – just – I think he is. My face feels sticky, hot. I put my hand up to it and find something dark. Red. Blood? It's everywhere. Where from? Emily tries to turn me.

'We have to get out!'

She's dragging me – trying to – but I won't let her pull

me away from him, not entirely, because I ain't finished yet . . . I can't have. He's still got some movement in him.

'Fire!' Emily yells. 'There's flames!'

I see it then, behind her: flames where the lamp has fallen over. They've caught on the pile of wood in the corner, they're moving up Shepherd's chest of drawers. It's not a big fire, not yet, but it might not take long.

'Come on!'

I let her drag me. And somehow I make my hands into a step so I can get Emily out of the entrance hole first. Because even when I don't know what's going on, I know she's done something for me . . . stopped something. I know it's not fair for her to get trapped here too. But as I'm coming up after her, she's leaning down and she's still shouting at me.

'Mack! Get Mack! You can't leave him!'

I look back and he's still there, still half-unconscious. It won't be long before the fire is right beside him, smothering him, making him choke. I want to let it. I want to let him suffer for what he did to Ashlee . . . for being a liar and not a brother at all. But I can't, can I? Even now I can't do that. And Emily is screaming something else.

'It was an accident! A game! You can't leave him!'

And I don't know whether she means about the fire starting, or Ashlee's death, or all of this mess. But I'm remembering what Ashlee wanted me to do to her that night.

'Try it,' she'd said. 'A new sort of Game.'

Could Emily be right?

So, I return to him. Somehow I pull him up and get him half-draped across my shoulders; blood from his nose smears across my neck, stains my old man's combat shirt. He comes to a little, starts using his legs. He's murmuring at me, I can't make any sense of it, I think he's trying to explain.

I push him towards Emily through the bunker entrance and she's dragging him outside. But the fire's bigger now, and I'm starting to cough, and it's all I can do to struggle up after him. I lie on the forest floor with smoke circling from below.

'We have to close it.' Emily's crawling away from Mack and pulling at the bunker lid. She's got her mouth pressed against her shoulder, trying not to breathe in.

I feel too weak to lift anything else, but somehow we do it together and shut the lid with a thud. We shut the smoke inside. Then I'm going back to Mack because I'm making sure he doesn't run and I don't know whether I want to hurt him some more or do something else. But he's not going anywhere. His eyes are red and sore-looking and wet. Wet? I ain't ever seen Mack cry, not in all the time I've known him. But now he presses his head into the forest floor, away from me, and I see his spine curl and shake. I lay my hand against it, more to keep him here than anything, more so he doesn't run. He reaches up and grabs my arm, just below where my elbow is, grips me tight.

'Sorry,' he's murmuring, over and over, 'I never meant

to . . . neither of us did . . . it was just a . . . we were just trying to get . . .' His words don't make no sense, but something in me understands them. Whatever he did with Ashlee was something that went wrong, that went too far.

'You've got to believe me, mate,' he whimpers.

He's begging and murmuring and coughing and apologising and gripping hard at my arm. I lean my head close to hear.

'Brothers,' he's saying, '. . . still brothers. Never meant to . . . not hurt . . . not Ashlee . . .'

And I think my eyes might be wet too.

55

Emily

There are lights, sweeping the forest floor, flickering in the trees. And I'm scared, because I don't know what they are or why they're here – because it could be Mack's friends coming to back him up, or weirdoes because it's Halloween. Maybe I should make a run for it, take the evidence and go. I could leave Damon with Mack now – the fight's out of him. I'm breathing hard, panting like an animal. I'm looking around at the paths and willing my legs to stand. But they're not listening to me. None of me is moving.

The lights are getting closer. Torchlight? For a second it's like I'm in Joe's game and these are the cracks of light he talks about – the cracks in the dark, the exits to other worlds. But I can hear people calling, I can hear someone shouting my name. Am I just imagining this?

Damon and Mack are crouching over each other, Mack's coughing and talking fast. I can't understand anything he's saying. And there is someone coming into this clearing. There are a whole load of people.

'Listen!' I shout it at Damon and Mack.

When Damon turns, I see blood on him. Is it Mack's, or his? I feel sick. Scared enough to shake.

Torchlight is sweeping everywhere now. And there are all these different voices, men I think, deep sounds. But someone gangly and tall is leading them all. I'd know his loping figure even in this darkness.

Joe moves quickly towards me, waving a torch. 'Emily? You all right?'

He doesn't even see the other two, not straight away. He bends down as he gets close and wraps his arms around me. And this time I let him hug me. I bury my face into his bony shoulder and I'm apologising about before, and he's saying something the same.

'This way!' he shouts back to the people and the flickering lights. 'She's here!'

From inside Joe's hug, I see the other people emerge into the clearing – police in high-vis jackets. Torches and movement and voices. Joe's brought them all.

'When your mum called I knew you'd be here!' Joe says. 'At the bunker.'

His eyes widen as he sees the smoke seeping up through the gun slit. He touches my face.

'You've got blood on you,' he says.

I point at Mack. I try to explain how it's his blood from when I helped get him out of the bunker, and Joe tries to pull me away fast.

'What the hell are you doing?' His eyes are going from the smoking bunker, to them, to me.

I try to explain what I can. I say that it was Mack who killed Ashlee; that he didn't mean to.

'They were playing a game,' I say. 'It went wrong.' I hold up the phone and tell him about the evidence.

I'm trying to tell him more, but I can't get the words. I'm just gabbling. Saying nothing. Gasping for air. I'm aware of Damon coughing, and of two police officers coming across. I hear Damon starting to explain, start to say the same things I'm trying to tell Joe.

'It wasn't Dad,' I whisper, finally. 'Not Damon either.'

I gasp in cold forest air. As I look back at Damon and Mack, I see other people stumbling out from the trees behind them, like they've been drawn to these lights too: Charlie and Ed are standing on the edge of the clearing, staring at everything. They look at Mack and Damon, and then over to where Joe and I are crouched, they're looking at the smoking bunker. I see someone in a high vis jacket stop them before they move off again.

Then, finally, I see a police officer coming towards me, carrying a plastic cup.

'We should move out of the smoke,' Joe says, grabbing my arm.

I let him lead me. I reach out and grab Damon's other

arm, try to get him to move too. We all sit on the edge of
the clearing, leaning against trees.

I keep breathing deeply.

56

Damon

I slump forward on the interview table, my chin on my hands. It suddenly seems important to talk – to say it all. And I'm trying to keep my eyes focused on the two detectives, but I can't hardly put words together. Maybe the joint's finally worn off and I've got a weed hangover. Or maybe I used the last bit of energy I had getting Mack out of that bunker. For whatever reason, I'm hazy as fuck. Exhausted. But I'm trying . . .

This is important.

I know.

There's a camera up high in the corner of this room and it's pointing direct at me, winking red lights now and then. Maybe Mum's arrived. They said they were calling her and that she'd watch from another room.

I force my eyes back to these detectives, the same ones as last time – the hard-faced DC West and the woman, DC Kalu. They're still staring at me quietly. It's like they're watching an animal in a zoo, checking its behaviour. I stare right back. I've got nothing to hide this time, and they should know it. Again, the woman sits a little away from the table, half in shadow: I'm pretty sure she's the one in charge.

Even with all this, though, it doesn't feel like how it was the last time I was here. For one thing, there's no legal rep beside me. For another, I don't want to lie. I rub my eyes, hard, as if that could make me wake up a little, and I explain how things started. I even say about the games I used to play with my old man when I was a kid. I say how Mack and me started to muck about in the woods after my old man died – how we started his games again but made them harder: how it was training at first.

'We did it to get our minds off things,' I say. 'Plus we was training to get into the army.'

I say how Ashlee had heard about the Game and wanted to play it too. But I'm getting hit by a whole load of memories and thoughts as I talk.

'I think Ashlee must've played the Game differently, though,' I say slowly. '. . . with all of us. Different rules. Different rules with each . . .'

Something's coming together in my mind.

I'm thinking about how Ed's brother is a dealer, and how Ed could get drugs. I'm thinking about that packet of fairy dust he'd had during that last Game. Is it possible that Ashlee got the fairy dust from him that night? And all the weed and other stuff she'd used?

'I been thinking that maybe Ashlee swapped her collar for things she wanted,' I say. 'That this was her real Game Plan.'

Maybe it makes sense – a collar for drugs, a collar to play a secret game with Mack. But what about Charlie? I'm frowning and the detectives are watching. Maybe it's possible that she just wanted to fight him? Maybe she just wanted the adrenalin like the rest of us did? And maybe Charlie was the only one of us who'd fight a girl, who didn't hold back. I'm remembering his words from Biology. Hadn't he said as much then?

DC Kalu brings her chair forward. She leans towards me and looks at me very serious. 'Did you know about Mack and Ashlee before, Damon?'

I twist my face away, because those words hurt. Those words say I was the shittest boyfriend in the world. DC Kalu stays still, watching.

'Did you know what game they were playing?'

My throat's gone tight and painful. I shake my head.

DC West coughs once. 'Not your game, was it?'

He looks across at his partner, who gives him a nod, takes a breath.

'Sometimes kids choke each other,' he says. 'They do it to get themselves high – apparently the lack of oxygen gives them a cheap thrill. Some of them call it seven seconds, knockout game, gasp, pass-out game . . . any of these sound familiar? What your girlfriend called it, maybe?'

'Fairyland,' I say. 'She said that. Sometimes.'

DC West nods. 'Could be.' He exchanges a look with DC Kalu. 'These kids think it's safe. I mean, it's just a game, right?' He turns back and I smell onions on his breath. 'But, Damon,' he says, 'too often things go too far.'

He continues, explaining how other teenagers have died from playing this game, how some have got brain damage.

'Depriving yourself of oxygen is about the most stupid thing you can do,' DC West says.

And I can't stop thinking about Ashlee now. How she was obsessed with going to Fairyland, with getting out of it and escaping. *Disappearing.* How she was always looking to get high. I'm remembering what Mack used to say when we fought each other — *Living on the edge, mate!* — he'd got off on that stuff too. Did he think this game with Ashlee was training somehow? Was playing it another way of testing himself? Being tough?

DC West is laying out pictures of people either passed out or dead, plus close-ups of bruised necks and red eyes. He's asking if I ever saw Ashlee look like any of this.

'The bruises, yeah,' I say. 'But we all have bruises — from playing our own Game — the one I explained to you.'

DC Kalu keeps talking, saying how people can play Ashlee's game alone too, how sometimes they choke themselves with their own scarves until they pass out. I think about how Ashlee wore scarves. How long had she been doing this, chasing this stupid rush? How long had I not noticed?

Then DC West lays out two more pictures. These ones are actually of Ashlee. In one she's up close to the lens, looking beautiful and sexy, in the other she's a blurred figure in the woods.

'Who took these?' I say. 'Where'd you get them?'

But I'm already getting a feeling about that. That day in the woods – Joe Wilder – the reason why I dropped him from the cross-country team. DC West points out the tiny marks you can see on Ashlee's neck in that close-up. And I'm annoyed at Wilder all over again.

'Why didn't he just say something?' I say. 'Why hide something like this?'

I press my chin on to my hands and I tell them about that night – her last night. I tell them the stuff I've been remembering – about how Ashlee had grabbed my hands and put them on her neck, about how she'd urged me to press . . . about how I'd been too drunk and out of it to realise she wasn't playing my Game no more, but hers instead.

'She was trying to show me what she did with Mack,' I say, '. . . trying to get me to play it too. She was asking me to. Only I was too . . . I dunno . . . I didn't get it!'

But it's why I got mad – because Ashlee tried to choke me when I was spinning on drugs. Because she'd wanted me to do it to her. And when she'd told me about the game with Mack? That's when I'd tried to break up with her. She'd pressed more dust to my teeth and I'd passed out all over again. Maybe she'd thought I'd forget the next day, I dunno. But all these bits of memory, I guess they make sense now. But why Mack and Ashlee did something so stupid in the first place? *That* don't make any kind of sense.

'The choking game,' DC West tells me, getting my attention back. He sucks air through his teeth. 'It's like Russian roulette: either a few seconds of buzz, or death.'

I think about Ashlee's description of what Fairyland was like: *tingles and lightness and slipping down into another place.* But killing yourself just so you can get a rush? It seems the dumbest thing of all. Perhaps the booze and drugs and fighting wasn't enough for her – getting off with me wasn't enough of what she was looking for, neither.

I think of Mack talking quietly to me in that police car, less than an hour ago now.

'Shepherd must've been there the whole time,' he'd said. 'In that bunker – he must've heard me shouting . . . panicking . . . and when I couldn't wake Ash up . . . he must've heard that too.'

He'd told me about how he'd been going to call for help but had found Shepherd standing behind him instead – all spaced out and in a flashback and calling him *soldier* – how he'd arrived out of nowhere like a ghost.

'I was hallucinating,' Mack told me. 'That's what I'd thought at first.'

And then the thunder had cracked. And the rain had come. And he'd run. Guess that makes him a coward, running like that; guess it makes him a lot of things.

He'd sunk down against the police car window, relieved, as he'd told me. Mack will be in another inter- view room now, saying all those words again.

And that dragging sound? The one that kept going in my brain, over and over? That was Mack too, coming back for me after running from Shepherd. He'd pulled me through mud and leaves with my arm across his shoulder, he'd dragged me through the rain. Just like a soldier would do. He'd taken me from the hollow and down that deer track. And when we'd got to that huge oak tree, he'd pushed me against it, told me to wait. He'd shoved Ashlee's collar into my hand, panicking.

'Keep it safe.'

I'd done what he'd said. Now I can remember turning that collar over, feeling the soft wool of its inside – I remember my head had spun too much to hold it tight. I'd put that collar in the safest spot I'd known: the middle of an oak tree.

It's why it'd all felt so damn familiar. That tree. That hole. It's how I knew it was there.

Mack had told me in the police car about how, when he'd gone back, he hadn't been able to find Ashlee in that clearing – how no one was anywhere no more. Not even Shepherd.

'I was freaking out, man,' he'd explained. 'I thought I might've imagined the whole thing.'

That's when he'd got rid of the phone, chucking it down the one place the living never go: Suicide Drop. He'd been half mad, I think. And then he'd come back for me.

So, that memory of stumbling down the high street with Mack was right after all. He'd thought he was looking out for me, getting me home. He was panicked out of his brain.

'If I'd known they were playing that,' I tell DC West. 'I would've stopped it.'

I hope I would've.

But I'd wanted to hurt Mack just a few hours ago too, and I would've done it. It might've taken just one squeeze more, a little more anger, just for Emily Shepherd not to have been there. I cough, my throat on fire. It's like I've got my own burning bunker trapped inside me.

But I tell the cops everything. Finally. I let it out, don't even worry about what happens next. Then I'm sinking down, my head against the table. It's like Emily's hand is still on my arm, like it was when we were in the waiting room earlier, and I'm glad to feel it: that warmth. I shut my eyes, keep sinking, into some other dark place that doesn't feel so bad. I don't need to worry about waking up, not this time. For the first time in months, I let myself go . . . just sleep. And I don't dream.

NOW

57

Saturday. November.

Damon

I'm running my fingers over Ashlee's collar. The police took the photos they needed of it and I've cleaned it up. It's buckled and ready. I go to where she died, on the edge of the clearing round Shepherd's bunker, and I lay it there. I don't look left, don't want to see the mess of that bunker — don't want to think about how I'd wanted to hurt Mack there either. Shepherd's drawings were burnt off in that fire — that's what the police said — I don't want to check. I watch a beetle marching slowly forward. Then I dig about in my pocket, find my own collar. I lay that on the ground too so Ashlee's collar is circled inside.

'You won, Ash,' I whisper.

But she lost too: lost everything. And somehow I don't think she's in Fairyland right now, neither. I bite down hard on my lip as I think about all that again, taste blood. Mack should be here, doing this with me. I thought about asking Charlie and Ed, but they're not speaking to me all that much right now – too weirded out by everything; they still can't believe what Mack did, what Ashlee wanted. Or maybe they feel guilty for their part in it all. They've been in the police station pretty constantly, but they won't visit Mack in custody. Though Ed, at least, will probably end up there soon enough anyway, maybe his brother too – seems the cops are coming down hard on their drug possession.

I sit on the cold winter ground and stare at those two collars. I hear birds singing, even now on a freezing mid-November day, even when there are puddles iced over and only a few berries left on branches. If Emily was here, she'd be able to tell me what those birds are, give me some fact that makes them special. Hearing these birds makes me think of the first day I saw Emily in Darkwood, that very same day I'd heard that my old man had died. That was the first day I'd fought Mack in here too. Sometimes I wonder whether I should've stayed with Emily that day, whether anything would've been different if I'd watched the birds instead of running off with Mack . . . taken that other path.

I dig my teeth into my lip again. I should be thinking about Ashlee right now, not Emily, that's what I came here for. But I'm thinking of all sorts of things, everything inside me blurring into one mess of noise. Strangely, I'm thinking of my old man most of all. How it's about a year since he died. How he would've been ashamed over the Game I started in these woods. I grab a stick and draw his tree tattoo – and mine – into the dirt; I do it just from memory. I'm remembering Emily's face when she'd looked at my tattoo in the bunker – she'd thought I was a mystery then, someone with stories. I want her to look at me like that again.

When I'm done, I rub my hand over it all, smudge the tree into the earth again, smash it up like that bomb smashed Dad. I guess whoever built and buried that IED out there in the desert will never know how far that blast travelled. But all things ripple out, cause shrapnel. Maybe if I'd never started the Game, Ashlee would never have died. Or maybe Ashlee would've got to Fairyland some other way. I don't know. But I'm still responsible, still could've stopped it . . . If I'd just seen what Ashlee was doing all those nights . . . *realised*.

Maybe.

I hear a noise behind me, a light cough. I turn. Emily. Found me. How long has she been there?

I get up silently, leaving the collars circled into each other. I don't even bother to wipe the water from my eyes as I walk to her, because she's seen it all anyway, hasn't she? She knows who I am, the all of me. *Somehow* she's still here. I wrap my arm around her shoulder. I want to keep her safe and exactly like she is – this girl who sees the whole of things, who, even now, isn't scared of these woods . . . who's not scared of me . . . who, even now, is helping.

I try to turn us away from this place, but she resists.

'Squirrels,' she explains, pointing.

I follow her gaze and see them. Two of them, darting in and out of Shepherd's bunker. I'm looking at it again before I even realise. 'Hiding food?'

She nods. 'For winter.'

I don't look for long. The bunker's too blackened and ruined, too dark.

'Come on,' I say.

But Emily stays, looking, listening. 'There are deer here too,' she whispers. 'They've been watching us.'

I see them when I look in the spaces between the trees. I see sunlight falling through bare winter branches and on to their backs.

'You've got eyes like an owl,' I say, smiling a little.

I squeeze Emily's shoulder tighter, rest my cheek against the top of her head. And the deer are gone, leaping quicker than a heartbeat and jumping deeper into the woods.

58

Emily

I store the image of the deer in my mind like a photograph. I'll tell Joe. It's something he could talk about in his project – those sunlit deer backs – those cracks of light even there.

Damon and I walk back together in silence. In the lane he pauses. 'You'll be all right today?'

I nod. He hugs me. It's a soft sort of hug, hesitating. I know he wants to kiss me. I see it in his eyes, in the way they haven't left me since I found him in the clearing. There's something grateful that's winding through his body now, entwined like his tattoo. I watch his copper eyes, get lost there a while. I can't do it yet. I reach down and take his hand instead, thread my fingers through his, just like I'd imagined doing so many times before. I bring our hands up to my mouth and brush my lips across the backs of his knuckles. He tastes like the woods, like dirt and trees. It's not a real kiss, not yet.

'Good luck,' he says.

Then he's walking back towards town and to his own home, his shoulders slumped. He's got his own journey to make today.

As I walk, I text Joe to say about the deer. He texts me back fast, invites me around to his place later: *Got a whole bunch of films. And Mina's coming too. Tell me about the deer then!*

Mina. It gives me a smile when I think of her and Joe hanging out so much now. Maybe it wasn't only me who Mina was trying to be friends with after all.

I'll be there, I message back.

Then I look at the message Kirsty sent me. Since the truth's come out about Mack and Ashlee she's been trying to be friendly, even invited me to hang out with them all in the park again. It's just because she feels guilty, and maybe one day I'll go and say hi; probably I won't.

Mum is waiting at the kitchen table, reading Dad's letter all over again. Dad knows everything now; Mum's still not sure he believes it, though. That's partly why we're going today: to see him in his new place, to see what he believes, to see what he wants to do now too. What he wants from us. Even though I've read Dad's letter a heap of times, I wrap my arm around Mum and look over her shoulder and read it again.

It's quiet here — I read — *Not so bad.*

Mum's got a theory. She thinks Dad knew all along that he didn't kill Ashlee. She thinks Dad confessed because going to prison was another way out: an exit from the life he couldn't cope with. She thinks he might have killed himself otherwise, like some of the pictures on the bunker walls seemed to suggest. But I don't know about that. Someone would have to be in a very deep, dark place to knowingly take the blame for a death.

Damon and I have talked about this. We think the pictures Dad drew were warnings: Dad was trying to get the fears out of his head and make them known. He drew Mack and the rest of the boys as wolves chasing Ashlee because he was scared of what might happen in that Game. He drew ways of killing himself because he was scared of that too.

Dr Daniells, Dad's psychiatrist, says that Dad was in a flashback so severe there's every chance he had no idea what was really going on that night. Dr Daniells says that during Dad's flashback – when he'd heard the thunder and lightning, when he'd heard the movement and noise from the boys' game – he might easily have thought it was soldiers. He might have thought he was back in combat, back in the place he'd been trying to avoid for so long. When he'd heard Mack yelling to Ashlee that she'd done it, he might have thought Mack was the same soldier who'd told him he'd killed a civilian. Dad had read those psych reports over and over – he knew what he was capable of, what they'd warned him he could do again. Maybe he'd believed it.

I linger on Dad's words at the end of the letter: *I'm looking forward to seeing you again.* I hope he means it.

I help Mum get things together for the trip. The weather forecast says it's going to snow so we're packing a thermos of coffee and blankets. I help her carry it all to the car – *Dad's* car. The air is cold enough to slice into me. Mum doesn't talk, maybe she's nervous. She'd thought Dad was one kind of person for a long while, and then the opposite for another long while, and now it's all changed again. As Mum loads everything into the car, I pick the rest of the 'abandoned car' notice from the windscreen.

Before I get in, I take one last look at Darkwood: its tangle of briars, the sunlight weaving through it all and turning leaves golden, all that light and shade, all those things hidden and seen. I see a flash of a robin's chest lighting up like a ruby.

'There's magic in those trees,' Dad had told me once.

And he's right: there is magic and light all woven through them in a patchwork, there's darkness and secrets too. But there are no wolves, no more dark games. It's just a wood again, sparkling in morning frost.

In the car, Mum glances over at me. 'You ready?'

I nod.

We're almost halfway when the snow starts. It begins lightly, falling like stray thoughts. It's gentle and delicate, like how I know I'll need to be with Dad now. We're driving without the radio, the only noise the low *drr* of the motorway tarmac as it races by beneath us, just the swish of the wiper as it sweeps away flakes. I press my palm to the window.

Dad knows.

I'm not sure what the plan is for him now, but I don't think he'll be coming home: not straight away. When Dad's charges were dropped he agreed voluntarily to go into a psychiatric hospital, and now he's waiting for assessment. I press my forehead to the window glass. Perhaps sadness and anger and violence aren't only in Dad. I'd seen that stuff in Ashlee and Mack too, even Damon, even Mum, even me. It's in us all, tangled in our own dark forests, wrapped with the secrets we keep.

Mum looks across, probably wondering why I'm so quiet. 'Nearly there.'

She's got the blue top on that Dad gave her years ago. It's too big for her now, but the colour's still nice on her. Her fingers are tight around the steering wheel, her nails bitten back so much I see blood. She doesn't smell of booze.

Dad will be in some sort of family meeting room when we see him. He won't have handcuffs and there'll be no sheets of Perspex between us. We'll be able to hug him. Perhaps we could coax him to return to us, slowly and gently, with water and love and sunlight: like how we used to coax snowdrops up through hard winter ground. Then, out of nowhere, I remember it — Dad's hug, the strength it had, the smell of his combat shirt pressed against my face, the rumble of his laugh. I remember him crouching beside me, patting the earth.

'Snowdrops come from a deep, dark place,' he'd said.

'They're made tough enough to push through snow.'

I'd rested my head against Dad's chest until I could hear – and feel – his heartbeat.

Now I look out of the window at the motorway verge. No snowdrops here yet, not for weeks. They'll come, though.

'How long will we stay?' I ask Mum.

She flicks the indicator, goes into the slip lane to come off the motorway. 'As long as he wants. Long as *we* want. The hospital's not as strict as the prison.'

I reach across, find one of her hands on the steering wheel, and we drive like that together. After a while the road narrows and there are fields either side. I think about Damon and the journey he's making today, how he'll stay with his brother in the city for a few days . . . how, from there, he'll visit Mack in the youth offenders' institute. They've charged Mack with murder, like Dad was; Damon said they had to. But already there's been talk of that charge changing. The papers are reporting that what happened that night was a horrible accident, something gone too far. The police will probably take everything into consideration, look at Ashlee's films, realise who she was too.

With my free hand I type Damon a message, wish him the same he said to me this morning: *Good luck.* I tuck my phone into my inside coat pocket so I'll feel it against my chest if a message comes back.

And there it is – finally – the psychiatric hospital where Dad has been taken. It's huge and grey and rises like a mistake among all these fields. I look up at the windows. Can Dad see us already?

The snow must have started falling here earlier, there's already a layer on the ground as I step from the car, it crunches under my trainers. I feel cool light flakes on my cheeks, my hair. I don't pull my hood up.

'Ready?' Mum asks.

We walk towards the hospital. I want to scoop up snow and press it into Dad's hands – show him how sunlight falls on ice and makes diamonds in it. I want to walk with him in Darkwood again too. I want him back. I'm looking at Mum and she's smiling, just a little. And we move quicker now, until we're half-sliding across the car park, the sun bright in our faces.

'Race you,' I say.

We're coming, Dad, I'm thinking, *we're almost there.*

Just before the entrance I pick up a handful of snow and hold it. As it starts to melt, I see the tiniest leaf left behind. It's light green – almost yellow – perfectly miniature and beautiful. The smallest piece of art there is – frozen, yet warming in my hands. And I take it for Dad, a small crack of light in this dark.

ACKNOWLEDGEMENTS

This book has been a long time coming, consequently a whole bunch of wonderful souls are due thanks for helping me get it here. Without three people, in particular, this book would not have happened: Catherine Atkins, my friend, unofficial editor and general beam of light; Andy D, my writing partner and part-time muse; and Linda Davis, this book's patient agent and my inspiring and kind friend.

Mum, Dad, and Barb — thank you for your ever-loving patience always, and for reading so much so often. Derek Niemann, for your always considerate and positive writing advice. Julia Green, for inspiration and your 'sunbeam effect'. Cam McCulloch, Hannah Alexander, Dan Burrows, Kristen Wheeler, Maya Farrugia, Hemanthi Wijewardene and Penny Lawson — thank you for reading and offering advice. Special thanks to Sarah Benwell for quick reading in a slow spot. Roma Arnott — for long rides through the countryside talking about killing and violence. And Nicola Barr, who came into my life like a flash of brilliant lightning.

Thank you to all who helped with the technical research. In particular, Nick Tucker, Francis Jones, Andy Smith, Dr Harvey Wickham, Paul Wells, Matt Bone, and magical Johanna David. Thank you to Pat Johns and Colin Titcombe for helping me discover bunkers in the woods. Thank you to everyone on Facebook who helped with random research questions, and to the helpful soldiers on the MOD live chat site. AJM, thanks for the debrief. Thank you to Cercopan, a wonderful charity doing amazing work in Nigeria, who were so helpful when this book was originally set in Africa!

Thank you to my publishers, Chicken House and Scholastic, for all their assistance, faith and support. Thank you to the readers of Stolen and Flyaway who have been so patient in waiting for this one.

A special thank you to Simon Read and his band Quiet Marauder for providing the soundtrack to this book. You can check them out here – www.quietmarauder.co.uk

Last but not least, thank you to Topaz the wonderhorse, and Ella and Ollie the superdogs, for company during those long walks through the woods.

A NOTE FROM THE AUTHOR

I thought I knew my writing process: I find a setting I want to explore and from there come the characters, theme and ending. Previously, nearly everything I've written has arrived as an idea almost perfectly formed. *The Killing Woods* was different. Much like the activity of walking through dark, unfamiliar woodland, this book has been 'felt out' as I went along. All I knew at the beginning was that I wanted to write about a wood, and I wanted the story to be dark – the rest has been tentatively discovered, by torchlight, often hiding behind my hands and crawling forward on my knees. Writing this novel has made me realise that there are many ways to approach creativity – in a conscious way, but also in a subconscious way. It has also made me think about how darkness can be a source of inspiration and, often, a necessary part of creativity. Dark places aren't just deep, endless pits of despair – they can be times of discovery and creation, and they are often unavoidable. In a curious way, it is the darkness that illuminates the candle.

The characters in this novel discover more whole versions of themselves through acknowledging their hidden, 'darker', sides. Writing this novel has made me realise that the creative process, as well as the process of life itself, can be acknowledged in a more 'whole' way too – as a time of, and drawing from, darkness as well as light; a time to rely on the subconscious as well as the conscious.

If you have felt disturbed by anything in this book, or have been travelling through a dark place that you're not sure you want to travel through alone, look for the beams of light, the 'helpers' – your friends, the people you could talk to, the helplines and professional help, and read some Jung. Most of all, don't forget the beauty out there in the world, the sunbeams threading the forest that return each morning.

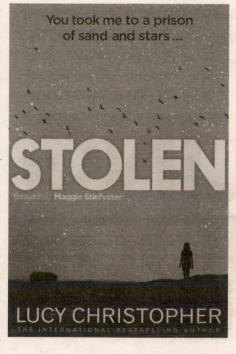